SHERLOCK HOLMES
AND THE
POWER PRINCIPLE

The Early Casebook of Sherlock Holmes

Book Nine

Linda Stratmann

SAPERE
BOOKS

SHERLOCK HOLMES
AND THE
POWER PRINCIPLE

Published by Sapere Books.

24 Trafalgar Road, Ilkley, LS29 8HH
United Kingdom

saperebooks.com

ISBN: 978-0-85495-708-8

From
Memoirs of a Medical Man
by A. Stamford FRCS

1924

CHAPTER ONE

Sherlock Holmes has very few firm friends. The reasons for this are not hard to discover. His manner is generally cold, aloof and unapproachable. He regards his intellect as superior to that of most men, and the fact that he is correct in this will hardly cause others to warm to him. I am sure that somewhere beneath the granite exterior beats a sympathetic heart, but it is rare to see any suggestion of its existence. My friendship with him is, I believe, based on loyalty and mutual trust, two of the qualities he most valued, the third being courage, to which I have never laid claim. When in 1881 I introduced Holmes to Dr John Watson, a retired army surgeon with battlefield experience, whose surgical dresser I had been at St Bartholomew's Hospital, I had a good idea that here was a man who would stand solidly by Holmes's side through all the travails the world could throw at them.

My association with Holmes has brought me many challenges, and when I consider the dangers I have fallen into as a result of our adventures I can only marvel that I have escaped with a whole skin. The summer of 1878 posed a new challenge, and I was not sure how to address it. Having passed my final examinations, I had been formally offered the post of junior surgeon at Barts. The position came with a room and meals at the hospital. With the allowance I received from my parents, and any small fees I was able to earn assisting at lectures, I would be able — by carefully managing my expenditure — to afford additional courses in ophthalmology, and even accumulate some savings. My hope was that one day

I would be able to purchase a medical practice, but I knew this might take many years to achieve.

There were drawbacks to my position, of course. The new accommodation was small and humble and might have to be shared. I could be called upon in an emergency at any hour of the day or night. I would also be obliged to give up my current lodgings, which Holmes had been in the habit of commandeering for use as his private office. His own rooms in Montague Street were abominably cluttered, the air dense with tobacco smoke, and quite unsuitable for receiving visitors. In anticipation of embarking on the career of detective, he was busy seeking new cases to pursue, absorbing information and acquiring skills at an alarming rate, and his self-confidence knew no bounds. In the face of this fearsome energy, I needed to break it to him that he would no longer be able to appropriate my time and my home without warning. While I waited to take up my post, I pondered on this situation and said nothing to Holmes on the subject.

My ruminations were interrupted by a fresh summons from Holmes. He had received a message from a solicitor of our acquaintance, Mr Ineson, for whom he had pursued an investigation last autumn. Holmes's meticulous and perceptive methods had made a favourable impression, and it now appeared that Ineson had another commission for him. Even if it should prove to be a commonplace task, offering no stimulation to the intellect, it was another step on Holmes's journey towards his goal, and he was eager to accept.

*

As one enters the offices of Ineson and Randall, Solicitors, the scent of old wood, old leather and old money must immediately inspire the visitor with confidence in the quality of services provided. It far exceeded in style and value any location that I was ever to call my home. There was a plaque in the foyer listing previous incumbents, showing that the present senior partner, Mr Ralph Ineson, was the third such in a line commenced by his grandfather. Randalls had come and gone over the years, their daughters conveniently marrying Inesons, and the old name was now merely a distant echo.

Mr Ineson's formal brusque manner was not perhaps the most inviting. A small, trim gentleman in his middle years, he sat behind a desk whose vastness commanded an already impressively furnished office, the keenness of his gaze suggesting that nothing hidden could ever escape him. I can, however, attest on personal experience that if one is ever arrested on suspicion of involvement in a burglary, his arrival at the police station to act on your behalf would be greeted with immense relief. Fortunately, he did not refer to my previous predicament, but as we took our seats, opened the meeting by congratulating me on the result of my final examinations. He added, with a touch of pride he made no effort to conceal, that his eldest son had recently met with similar success, and would soon be admitted to a junior position in the practice.

'I have asked you here, gentlemen,' he began, 'because you are not merely investigators but men of science, which is a rare and possibly unique combination. The task in hand will require both of those skills.'

I saw Holmes tilt an eyebrow and knew that his interest had been engaged.

'I was recently contacted by a valued client, a Mrs Beauregard,' Ineson continued. 'She is the widow of a financier and has long been active in the support of charities. Since the death of her husband four years ago, she has devoted most of her considerable energies and generous sums of money to the welfare of the needy. She is a leading light of the Essex and Hertfordshire Ladies' Philanthropic Society, which raises funds for hospitals, orphanages and the deserving poor. She recently approached me for advice concerning releasing a substantial portion of her personal funds, which are considerable, in order to invest in a new company, which is in the process of being set up — Baumann Motors Ltd.'

Ineson picked up a document from a neat pile of papers that lay before him. It was a letter, penned in flowing script, which he regarded without enthusiasm.

'She explained that the managing director, Dr Baumann a Swiss gentleman, was developing a marvellous invention which would be of incomparable benefit to society. He has been building an engine on advanced scientific principles using methods which he has pioneered. This engine would enable the operator to produce enormous volumes of power from a simple combination of cold water and air. She has already seen it demonstrated and intends to view another such exhibition at which Dr Baumann promises significant advances in its efficiency.'

'This sounds like the Keely motor,' said Holmes, with a frown of suspicion.

'Keely?' I queried.

'John Keely. He is an American who has made very similar claims in recent years. Although he has attracted a number of investors to his scheme, he has yet to produce a motor which he will submit to the examination of experts. The scientific journals have reviewed his theories and have declared the entire enterprise to be a humbug. Which must explain why he has so far failed to obtain a patent.'

'Mrs Beauregard says that Dr Baumann is aware of Keely's claims,' Ineson replied, 'and has made it clear that he does not wish to be compared to him. He says Keely's idea has not been properly developed, and his is far superior.'

'These demonstrations of Dr Baumann have not been announced to the public,' said Holmes. 'Is Mrs Beauregard a friend of his?'

'No, she learned of him from one of her philanthropic friends, a Mrs Young. Her husband owns the premises where the motor is being developed. Apparently, Dr Baumann is avoiding public announcements while the motor is still undergoing trials. He fears that the press will dismiss his efforts out of hand and deter investors. He has therefore been approaching acquaintances and men of business in person, and the news has travelled by word of mouth.'

'And Dr Baumann claims to produce power at little or no cost?' I asked.

'He does. The main cost to the purchaser is the price of the machine,' said Ineson. 'The Baumann motor promises to change the world of industry and transport as we know it, make manufactured goods cheaper, trains run without the need for coal, and so forth.'

'And throw large numbers of men out of their daily work,' I said.

'One cannot halt progress, only deal with its results,' said Ineson, drily. 'But my concern, as I am sure you will appreciate, is that this new enterprise, like the Keely motor, is highly speculative. It may collapse as unworkable, and the investors will have paid a high price for shares which have become worthless overnight. Whether this is a well-intentioned but fallacious adventure, or something more sinister, remains to be seen.'

It was obvious, even in the thoughtful silence that followed, that we three shared the same concerns.

'I gather that Baumann's machine has not yet been patented,' said Holmes.

'As yet, no. The intention as far as I was able to discover from Mrs Beauregard was to perfect it to the inventor's satisfaction, and then secure a patent. It would then be marketed all over the world. This perfection will be expensive to achieve but if successful, the shares would be extremely valuable. Naturally the scheme is attracting attention amongst men who are not concerned with any benefit to society. They are hoping for a substantial return on their investment. The business of these men is to take risks, knowing that some will fail, and others pay out handsomely. It is the private investor, like Mrs Beauregard, who place all their hopes in a single venture, who may suffer.'

'So the purpose of her proposed investment is to supply funds for the development of an unproven machine?' I asked.

'It is. I have advised Mrs Beauregard not to be precipitate. I told her that before she parts with a penny, I will have the matter looked into so I can assess the potential of the investment. It may be that she would be better advised to place her funds elsewhere or simply leave them safe where they are.'

'How would you like us to act for you?' asked Holmes.

Ineson passed us a document. 'This is the date and location of the next demonstration, at which Dr Baumann will be available to answer questions. Mrs Beauregard and another of her friends, a Mrs Murray whose husband is a landowner of some importance in Hertfordshire, will be there. If you would also attend, I would like to receive your report.'

'We shall certainly carry out your wishes,' said Holmes.

'Since I have already advised Mrs Beauregard of my intention to send an observer, you may say that I have sent you. I will notify Mr Young to expect your arrival.'

'In the meantime,' said Holmes, 'I will undertake a further study of the literature of the principles of production of power. I will be fully prepared. I suggest, however, that we employ a small subterfuge. We should allow Dr Baumann to think that we are your junior employees in which case he will not consider that we have any scientific understanding. He may be more forthcoming in his pronouncements.'

'I agree,' said Ineson, with a nod of approval.

Holmes studied the document. 'Young's Toolmakers, Abbey Mill, Waltham Abbey,' he said.

'Yes, Mr Young is a successful manufacturer of tools and cutlery. He hails from Canada where he has a factory and wishes to expand his business to other countries. About three years ago, he purchased an old watermill in Essex, and has thoroughly renovated and modernised it, supplementing the waterpower with steam. The county has been attracting many similar industries in recent years, ever since the railways reached the towns. Naturally he is very interested in the possibilities offered by Dr Baumann's motor and was happy to provide some of the space at his disposal for the work.'

'So he is already, in a sense, invested,' said Holmes. 'Dr Baumann appears to be adept at gaining support. This motor should be subjected to a close expert examination before too much money is spent.'

'On the subject of money,' said Ineson, 'I appreciate that you have not yet entered into the profession of detective, however our practice would not wish to engage your time without payment. I will arrange for a fee and any expenses to be paid.'

I wondered if Holmes would, as he had done in the past, utter a dignified refusal, on the grounds that he was not a professional detective. I was interested to see him accept without protest. He was starting to place a value on his services.

CHAPTER TWO

The morning train soon left London and its rows of grey houses behind and afforded more colourful views of farmland, market gardens, villages bright with summer flowers and commercial waterways. In the warm sunshine much of what we saw looked very inviting. The countryside attracts many town dwellers as visitors with its promise of refreshment and repose. It also offers scenes of wholesome rural industry in far pleasanter locations than crowded cities with their grease and grime, malodorous dust heaps and ugly factories fouling the atmosphere with smoke.

We alighted at Waltham Cross station, just half a mile to the west of the banks of the River Lea, part of which formed a busy canal route. It lay a mile from Waltham Abbey, a historic market town with some notable features of interest, which curiously did not include a railway station of its own. Our map showed that Mr Young's watermill was a mile or so north of Waltham Cross along country roads. Fortunately, there were traps available for hire, and the drivers knew the way to the mill, so we engaged one. The road brought us alongside the bank of the river and then proceeded beside one of the streams which served it. Before long, we passed over an old stone bridge, after which the roadway made a sweeping turn to bring us directly in front of the mill.

A long well-made brick building three storeys in height, it sprawled along the bank of the stream, as if it was confidently entitled to take up as much space as it pleased. A placard, painted in rustic style, proclaimed the name to be Abbey Mill.

We descended from the trap, which made a quick turn about with practised ease and headed back to the bridge.

The waterwheel itself was out of our view at the rear, although we could hear it rotating. The sounds of industry were like a small orchestra with the washing of waters, creaking of wood, and a rhythmic percussion like the beat of a drum. From the mill's interior came the unmistakable resonant thud and hiss of a steam engine, the rumble of machinery, and faint whine of grinding tools. A small chimney puffed little pale clouds into the sky. Two men were unloading sacks from a wagon stocked with coal and carrying them through a side door to be emptied, the tumbling loads emitting flurries of dust.

There were two doors on the front of the building, one of which, to our left, was large and stoutly built with an industrial appearance. The other was smaller and neater with a bell pull for visitors. There was a brightly painted sign: *J M Young and Co, (England) manufacturer of fine tools, knives and scissors, and best cutlery.*

I was especially interested in viewing the waterwheel, having never had such an opportunity before, and Holmes indulged my curiosity. We walked around the side of the building nearest to the heavier door. The wheel was much larger than I had anticipated, at least twelve feet in diameter. It turned about a large central iron cog, set on a drive shaft which travelled through the factory wall to deliver the wheel's power. A long wooden chute travelled alongside the outer back wall, bearing fast-moving waters which I assumed must have been directed there from some point further up the stream, and deposited the cascade onto the wheel from above. The two parallel sides of the wheel were connected by a series of struts carrying hinged containers, which filled with the water, its weight and the energy causing the whole to rotate. On reaching the lower part of the wheel, the containers tilted and tipped their contents into a narrow watercourse which ran downstream below, then righted themselves and were carried up empty to be filled once more. It was a simple but beautifully elegant arrangement.

It was almost time for the demonstration. At the small entrance door, the bell pull summoned a smart young man bearing a notebook and pencil, who took our names, checked them on a list, and ushered us to a waiting area. The factory sounds were more intrusive once we were indoors but remained tolerable. There was comfortable seating, and the walls were washed with paint and decorated with engravings of the countryside and the watermill in earlier times. Here we were introduced to two ladies, Mrs Beauregard and Mrs Murray, who had also come to witness the Baumann motor. The smart young man said he would notify Mr Young of our arrival and left us to converse.

Mrs Beauregard was a lady of about fifty, rather tall, and well formed. She wore a half-mourning gown in violet silk with a crisp white lace collar and a hat which set off her face and hair rather well. She was not a great beauty but clearly a woman who prided herself on her appearance and was prepared to take some trouble over it.

Mrs Murray was younger and slighter, her graceful form flattered by a pale green gown in the fashionable Princess of Wales style. Her manner was reserved, almost subservient to her companion, whom I thought she regarded with awe.

'You must be the young men from Mr Ineson's office,' said Mrs Beauregard in a richly toned voice. I sensed that the attribution 'young men' was not, as she expressed it, a compliment, and she assumed that her wealth and position in life gave her dominance over us.

'We are indeed,' said Holmes, deferentially.

I watched with interest his masquerade as an innocent requiring instruction. It was part of his growing catalogue of disguises, and required a mildness of both expression and voice, which usually drew out the information he sought without arousing suspicion.

'We are very interested and not a little excited to see what Dr Baumann has to show us,' he continued.

'Ah, he is such an extraordinary man!' exclaimed Mrs Beauregard. 'He is Swiss, I believe, and has studied abroad for many years before developing his marvellous motor.'

'I had not heard of him before now,' said Holmes.

'That is because his experiments had to be conducted in strict secrecy,' said Mrs Beauregard. 'There are jealous men who would stop at nothing to steal the work of others. What you will see today will prove to you that his motor does everything he says it can do. But he will not reveal the precise details of the principle. Not before he has his patent.'

'I do hope it is safe,' said Mrs Murray, anxiously. 'One hears such terrible things.'

'Do not concern yourself, my dear,' said Mrs Beauregard, soothingly, much as one would have spoken to a child. 'I have seen it perform before and during the demonstration the power is very carefully controlled.'

'Then I suppose we cannot expect him to offer us even a suggestion as to how it works,' said Holmes, regretfully. 'I think it must be a very great advance in science.'

'It is,' said Mrs Beauregard. 'I do not profess to understand it all, of course, but my eyes have shown me the evidence.' She paused, then leaned forward as if about to impart a great confidence. 'Have you heard of the etheric force?' she asked, her manner suggesting that she expected us to know nothing of it.

Mrs Murray uttered a little sigh as if she had heard of it far too often of late.

Holmes and I looked at each other with expressions of great mystification. 'I am not sure I have,' said Holmes. 'My education in that area is somewhat limited. Would you be kind enough to explain?'

Mrs Beauregard, having firmly established her superiority, gave us sympathetic but knowing looks. 'It is the life force of the universe,' she said. 'Invisible to the human eye, but no less powerful for that. It exists both between and through all things. Too long have men of science addressed themselves only to forces which they can see or measure. Electricity, magnetism. But these things are only a part of the universal force. The effect of the force, which is the true provider of all that we perceive and feel, has never been measured or made available for our use. Or at least, not until now. Dr Baumann's work has opened a new portal to the world. He cannot imprison the force, of course, no mortal can do that, but he can harness its vapour, if you like. How he does that took him many years to achieve. It is the secret all men would like to have.'

'And you have seen it in operation yourself?' asked Holmes.

'I have indeed!'

'How marvellous!' I exclaimed with all the youthful wonder I could summon.

She smiled. 'And I will tell you something now which is the best of all. I have not dared tell Mr Ineson for I am sure that he would laugh at me. I have felt the force myself.'

'How did it manifest itself?' asked Holmes.

'Dr Baumann told me that there were some rare individuals who are sensitives to a very high degree. He has learned to recognise them and thought that I was such a being. He tried an experiment to determine this. We sat together in a room, facing each other.'

'A darkened room,' whispered Mrs Murray.

Mrs Beauregard flashed a severe look at her companion. 'Well naturally for the experiment it had to be dark. Dr Baumann took my hands in his and looked deep into my eyes and told me that he saw there the glow of the force. And as he said those words, I felt it, the vibrational tremor of the force passing through me, as if I could feel my very soul.' She exhaled a blissful sigh. 'Of course, I cannot imagine that a man like Mr Ineson would understand it. But then ladies are more receptive than gentlemen. That is a known fact,' she added, setting her mouth firmly in an aspect of unquestionable certainty.

Before we were able to respond, two more arrivals joined us and we were introduced to a Professor Novak and the Reverend Doctor Woodley.

The clergyman was a robust-looking gentleman of about fifty-five with a harmonious smile and direct manner. As he looked about him, I felt that here was a man who would appear comfortable whatever his surroundings. He exuded an air of confidence in the Divine as powerful as Mrs Beauregard's belief in the etheric force. I confess that at first I thought it strange that a minister of religion should be interested in Baumann's motor. How wrong I was.

Professor Novak was a rather rotund gentleman of about sixty, his hair amounting to little more than a pale fluff about a bald pate, his face adorned with thick-lensed spectacles. My study of ophthalmology suggested to me that his eyes must rely very substantially on those lenses and he would be in some difficulty without them. He spoke with an accent I could not place but was happy to introduce himself.

'I am a visitor from Prague,' he said. 'I have for many years been studying the role of the odic force in nature.'

'Is that the etheric force by another name?' asked Holmes.

'That is to be determined,' said Novak, 'but I think it is. The principle of a powerful force in the aether pervading not only all things both living and mineral, but the space between them, has long been proposed by leading men of science, such as Isaac Newton. Is the name Reichenbach familiar to you, Mr Holmes?'

'No, not at all.'

'Baron Carl von Reichenbach, a great pioneer of science, now sadly deceased, wrote extensively of what he termed the odic force. But he was more than a mere theorist, he conducted numerous studies on human subjects, in which he was able to satisfy himself of the existence of this force. His reward, as it often is with advanced visionaries, was to be attacked by other men sometimes in the most insulting terms.' He shook his head, sadly. 'Was it not the great Goethe who said, *"Wir sind gewohnt dass die Menschen verhöhnen was sie nicht verstehen?"*'

I knew that Holmes read Goethe in the original German and marvelled at the restraint with which he pretended not to understand the quote.

'In essence,' Novak explained, 'Goethe says that men mock what they cannot understand.'

'And then they are the first to say they always understood, when the object of their mockery is proven right,' said Mrs Beauregard.

'Indeed so,' said Professor Novak. 'For several years I have been trying to replicate the Baron's experiments, in which he proved beyond doubt the existence of the odic force, but thus far have not met with success. I was hoping to go to America to see the Keely motor demonstrated, but some excited whispers in scientific circles led me here. I have seen a number of Dr Baumann's demonstrations and each time the power generated is greater. I hope at last to see the Baron vindicated.'

At that moment, I recalled seeing a mention of the odic force in a newspaper. It was not in some scholarly article, but in one of those advertisements one sees from time to time, offering a cure for a wide array of common complaints, both internal and external, physical and nervous. It seemed to involve purchasing something magnetic and placing it on the affected part. Had it been a cure for all ills I was sure that all practitioners of medicine would have welcomed it, but so far none had done so. Naturally I said nothing.

'The force is proof of God!' said Reverend Woodley, rather loudly, as if from a pulpit. 'God moves through and sustains everything in nature. It is the wonder of physical science as we presently understand it, which reveals to us the flow of spiritual energy and opens our eyes to God.'

'Indubitably,' said Professor Novak mildly, 'but I should mention that the Baron in his wisdom has issued words of warning. When we seek to use the powers of the force for the good of mankind we must beware. Just as spirit mediums may unintentionally conjure bad spirits along with the good, so the force has both a light and a dark side, and great care must be taken to ensure our safety. I am concerned that Mr Keely may not be expert enough in that endeavour.'

'What is his expertise?' asked Holmes.

'Ah, well that may be the reason for his recent failures,' said Novak. 'And perhaps we ought to be grateful for that. As far as I have been able to discover he is not and never has been a theoretical or practical scientist. He has no qualifications in that area. He is a simple mechanic and uses those skills to build motors to demonstrate his claims to have discovered a means of liberating energy at no cost. I am far from being convinced. Dr Baumann, on the other hand, is a Doctor of Philosophy, his research extending to and often uniting such disciplines as chemistry, electricity, heat, light and magnetism.'

At this moment we were joined by three more gentlemen who arrived together, not from outside, but from the interior office.

One of the gentlemen, an affable-looking fellow in his forties, took the lead at once and with a friendly smile introduced himself in a noticeably transatlantic accent. 'Welcome to Abbey Mill everyone. I am John Mackenzie Young, and these are my good friends in business, Mr Green and Mr Jamison. I know you are all very interested to proceed with the demonstration, so please follow me.'

Our host led us along a corridor of unpainted brick, which led away from the factory, the sounds of manufacture fading as we went. On our way we passed a number of doors which we were told led to storerooms for finished products, tools and materials, as well as a luncheon room for the men.

'You are American, Mr Young?' asked Reverend Woodley.

Young must have been asked this question many times, but he smiled indulgently. 'I am from Canada,' he said.

'Oh, and what attracted you to this part of the world?'

'Well, I have business interests in Canada and America, but I want to expand into other countries. Preferably where we share a language. And what brought me here was water — the power of water, God's given power for man to use.'

'Ah,' said Woodley, approvingly.

'I made a trip, and it was suggested to me that I view the watermills of the River Lea. Further south the mills are tidal, but here the river needs a little help from weirs and reservoirs. And I found this place. It hadn't been used in a long while and was in need of renovation. But the building is good and big and sound, with land to build on if we need it. There are big city factories whose owners would envy us the space we have here. I found a local man — Jenkins — who was employed by the previous owner. He knew the machinery and how to get it working again, and the price was too good to quibble over. And when my wife saw Waltham Abbey she quite fell in love with it, so we have rented an old corn merchant's house there for the duration.'

There was one last door at the end of the corridor, where we paused.

'In my business,' said Young, his hand resting almost reverently on the rough painted door, as if he could sense the promise within, 'we need more power than the wheel alone can provide, and that is supplied by steam — which is just water in another form. But that is what interested me in Dr Baumann's motor. He has shown that he can conjure more power from plain water than has ever been thought possible.'

Young knocked on the door. 'Dr Baumann,' he said, 'I bring your visitors.'

We waited for a voice within to grant permission and entered.

The room opened out into a space lit by lanterns, several of which hung from the ceiling. Additional light seeped in through a large window at the far end, filtered by layers of net curtains. A desk stood below the window piled with papers and journals. A deep shelf affixed by iron brackets to the rear wall and supported by stout wooden posts was covered in notebooks and a collection of tools, and scattered with pencils. I saw a small handheld blowtorch and a glass jug which appeared to be full of water. The space underneath was cluttered with large jars and canisters.

In the centre of the room, draped in a cloth, was something about two feet wide, five feet in height, and as much in length.

The man who stood before us was an imposing presence, and it was apparent that he had the power in his address to make the heart of even the stoniest matron flutter. I would not say he was exceptionally tall or handsome, but he had the carriage, posture and confidence to make onlookers believe he was both. The words with which he greeted Mr Young and his visitors as we were introduced one by one were important announcements, and his eyes seemed to address each of us personally. He made a special point of saying how delighted he was to see those who had visited him before, those being Professor Novak and Mrs Beauregard, who he felt certain would see how well the motor had advanced since their last viewing.

It was hard to assess Dr Baumann's age because of the luxuriant dark brown beard that covered his cheeks and chin and flowing waves of hair of the same hue, but the tell-tale wrinkles about his eyes placed him at about forty. He had doffed his coat, revealing a waistcoat and loose shirt with cuffs folded back, baring his forearms like a magician demonstrating that he had nothing to hide. He spoke with an accent from the heart of Europe, conjuring images of castles and snowy mountains, although his command of English was very accomplished.

Lurking in the back of the room was another man, whom Baumann introduced as his mechanical genius, Mr Gorrie, his valued assistant who made science come to life. Gorrie said nothing. He was a small, wiry man of about fifty, whose bowed legs gave him an odd lurching gait. His furrowed face was topped by wisps of unkempt grey hair. His working clothes hung loosely on his thin frame, the shirt unbuttoned at the throat, over which he wore a leather apron much marked and stained, with a deep pocket at the front, stuffed with tools.

There was nowhere to sit, so we guests stood looking about us and waiting for enlightenment.

Mr Green and Mr Jamison, both in their twenties and the image of ambitious businessmen, looked very similar in both posture and grooming, but stood at a determined distance apart. I could not tell if they were associates, rivals, or merely two relatives who did not like each other very much.

Mrs Murray was regarding the arrangements with increasing concern. I thought she was trying to judge what was in most danger of exploding. Her glance darted about the room, occasionally rested on the object cloaked from our sight, and then quickly looked away. She seemed unable to look at Dr Baumann, but kept very close to Mrs Beauregard and clutched a small, beaded reticule as if it might do duty as a shield.

On the wall above the shelf was affixed a large framed drawing made on heavy paper, which illustrated what must be the ultimate aim of the endeavour, for it depicted an extraordinary machine. The size of the machine was easily apparent as it towered over the man who was portrayed operating it, though the picture was careful not to reveal precisely what he was doing. The apparatus consisted of several enormous metal containers, a series of globes and onion- and pear-shaped vessels, which were endowed with rotating wheels, pistons and stopcocks, all apparently connected with each other by an array of pipes and cables.

Since I am not an engineer, I could not imagine what such a machine might be capable of. The apparatus of chemistry with its glass vessels might seem complicated at first sight, but once one is familiar with its structure, and the principles by which it is bound, it educates the onlooker. One can easily see where heat must be applied to its contents, and trace the flow of liquids, the course of vapours and gases, the site of condensation, and places where the touch of a match would produce combustion. The illustration of the motor, however hard I studied it, provided me with no such logic.

Holmes, too, studied the drawing, but I also saw that his interest masked other movements of his eyes, his gaze passing over the items on the shelf and underneath it.

'This, ladies and gentlemen,' said Baumann, gesturing to the cloaked device, 'is just a small prototype of the motor which you see illustrated in this drawing in its ultimate form. Humble as it is, it is effective enough to show you the principle involved, and you may conclude from that what a full-sized motor will be able to achieve. The energy it produces is such that the vessels and pipes of the completed motor will need to be constructed of the strongest possible materials to withstand the forces within. You may say that such a device will be costly to construct, and it will be, but it will generate power from a simple mixture of air and water. It requires no heat, no fuel of any kind. The supply to factories, mines and railways, will be so abundant that the cost of the motor will be paid for in just a few months. A perfected machine only twice the size of this prototype will easily power a small factory.'

He removed the cloth with a dramatic flourish. If it had not been for the image of the larger machine, I think that we onlookers would have had serious doubts as to his claims. A confirmed sceptic would have greeted the sight with open derision. The apparatus sat upon a long table endowed with six sturdy legs and consisted of a number of connected items. There was a metal canister, shaped like a large thick-necked bottle, with a screw top and a flexible tube coming from the neck which ended in a mouthpiece. A pipe emerged from its side and plunged into the base of a mysterious contraption beside it. This curious device had a heavy base several inches in depth of smooth shining metal, which gave no external clues as to its purpose. It supported a thick column to the top of which was attached a vertical disc of pierced and etched brass. This in turn was connected by a rod with a series of gears and wheels to a small beam engine. I appreciate that my description hardly does justice to what I saw, but I do not think that hours of sketching, had I been permitted, could have rendered the machine in any way that would enlighten someone who saw the resulting picture.

There were some moments of quiet contemplation. We waited, but nothing occurred. The machinery was quite still. The only sound came from outside the building, the running of water along the wooden chute, on its way to drive the mill wheel; nature, for the moment, outdoing science.

At last, Mr Jamison coughed and said, 'Dr Baumann, it seems to me that you are following in the footsteps of the American inventor, Mr Keely, whose motor attracted a great deal of interest at first but has thus far failed to produce results. Recent scientific publications have declared it to be a delusion, or worse, and Mr Keely has been unable to impress his critics. What do you have to say about that?'

Baumann smiled. 'That name comes up very frequently. I have never met Mr Keely or seen his work, but I have been told that he is no scientist but a mechanic who proposed a theory and built a machine in an attempt to prove it. To my mind, both kinds of expertise must be united in harmony to achieve a result, which is what we have done here.'

'I concur,' said Professor Novak. 'Keely may have been inspired by the work of Baron von Reichenbach, which has the most exceptional merit, but I feel he simply does not fully understand the principles involved to develop them into a working motor. Dr Baumann's prototype may seem to the novice to be very simple, but do not judge it for its appearance. It can do things out of all proportion to its size.'

'Well, let us see what it does,' said Green.

'Certainly,' said Baumann. 'Mr Green, might I invite you to take a look inside the vessel?'

'Very well,' said Green with a shrug.

Baumann unscrewed the cap of the large container, and Green peered inside suspiciously, and sniffed at the contents.

'It is empty,' he said, 'I can't smell any kind of fuel.'

'Thank you,' said Baumann. He brought the glass jug over to the apparatus. 'Mr Jamison? Might I ask you to come forward and examine the contents of this pitcher? Please be assured, it is nothing but pure water.'

Jamison hesitated, and Baumann smiled, took a small dipper from the tool bench, with which he scooped up a sample of water and drank it.

Jamison stepped forward, cautiously smelt the liquid, then dipped his finger into the jug, and rubbed a fingertip and thumb together, smelt them, then ventured a taste with the tip of his tongue. At last, he nodded. 'Plain water,' he said.

'Thank you,' said Baumann. 'Reverend Woodley, would you be so kind as to pour the water into the drum? This quantity will suffice for the demonstration.'

Woodley obliged, and Baumann returned the empty jug to the shelf.

'And now,' said Baumann, 'the only other requirement is air, which must be delivered under pressure. The pressure for this purpose is no more than might be achieved with human lungs or a bellows.' He took a small bellows from the shelf and approached the apparatus, but then stopped and paused with a smile. 'But we have here in our midst a lady whose sensitivity to the force has already been demonstrated. Mrs Beauregard, would you favour us with your breath into this machine?'

'Oh,' said Mrs Beauregard, visibly flattered, 'what must I do?'

Baumann returned the bellows to the shelf, then, with an obsequious bow, took the lady by the hand and drew her towards the apparatus. There he showed her the nozzle on the end of the tube connected to the canister. 'If you would be kind enough? One deep breath is all that is needed.' He produced a snow-white handkerchief from his pocket and ostentatiously used it to brush away any hint of dust from the nozzle. 'You just put your lips around it and blow.'

'Well, that seems simple enough,' said Mrs Beauregard.

There were eyebrows raised amongst the gentlemen and Mrs Murray, whose cheeks had acquired a rosy hue which had not been there before, bent her head, as if she was unable to watch the process.

Mrs Beauregard stepped forward, clasped her hand about the tube, took a deep breath, fastened her lips about the nozzle and blew.

'I am most grateful to you,' said Baumann, and he took the tube from her hand, produced a little cap from his pocket, and applied it to the nozzle. 'And now we have everything we require.'

'Is that all?' asked Jamison.

'It is.'

'Do you not heat it? I see only candles here, but they might do.'

'No. It only remains to wait for a few moments while the water and the air, both of which are charged with the force which has yet to be liberated, combine their particles. Please observe the beam balance which has yet to receive the force and produce power.'

The balance remained still and a small dial showed that no power was currently being generated.

Baumann indicated a stopcock on the pipe leading from the canister into the mystery apparatus. 'But the air and water, even though their molecules rub against each other, cannot yet release their power. That is the purpose of this device —' he indicated the curious apparatus with the brass wheel — 'the amplifimoderator. When I open the stopcock the air, which is now imbued with the force having been combined with the water, will pass into it. It is my own invention, about which I can tell you almost nothing since it has yet to be patented. But expressed simply, it will act upon the particles and capture the force within them, which will be expanded and released as power. The result will be visible.' He turned to the mechanic. 'Mr Gorrie, you may now activate the motor.'

Gorrie scuttled forward and pressed a lever on one side of the beam balance. He then opened the stopcock, and after a short pause, there was a slight creaking, whispering sound. The brass wheel on the amplifimoderator began to turn, the rod and its gears rotated, and the beam engine began to move. A meter revealed the frequency of its action and the amount of power generated. Mr Gorrie took a notebook from his pocket and proceeded to note down the readings.

We stared at the meter, as Baumann read off the figures. 'Mr Holmes,' he said, 'you look dubious. Please come forward and touch the canister. You will be assured that there is no power being supplied to the apparatus. All the power is that which it generates itself. Please do not touch anything else as it is very sensitive equipment.'

Holmes stepped forward to the table and placed one hand against the curve of the metal drum. 'It is quite cold,' he said.

'Exactly,' said Baumann.

Professor Novak came up to look at the readings and declared himself impressed. 'You have been making great strides in its efficiency since I last saw a demonstration,' he said.

Gorrie grunted and showed him a page from the notebook.

'Ah yes, last week's figures confirm it,' said Novak, with an emphatic nod. 'A far stronger output than before. My associates in Prague have been working on something similar for some time but are far from achieving success. You are years ahead of them, Baumann. How long before you are ready to apply for a patent?'

'Before I make the application, I wish to ensure that the motor is quite perfect and free from any possible hindrances,' said Baumann. 'Some of the parts may have to be replaced with better and stronger materials. I would say three or four months — six at the most.'

Mr Gorrie, whose services would be called upon to carry out the work, glanced up sharply at this statement. He did not look pleased.

Holmes was about to take a closer look at the mystery device when Baumann smiled and whisked the cloth over the apparatus. 'The demonstration is over,' he said.

Holmes merely bowed and stepped back.

Reverend Woodley, brimming with excitement, approached Dr Baumann and wrung him by the hand. 'I thank you, sir, from the bottom of my heart!' he exclaimed. 'You are doing God's work! The power and beneficence of the Almighty has been made visible!'

'Thank you, sir,' said Baumann.

'There are several gentlemen of my acquaintance who would be very interested in your motor. Respectable men of business. I shall make sure to tell them to come here and see it for themselves. Mr Hodgkins, who is a furniture-maker, Mr Ross, a brewer, and Mr Feather, builder and surveyor. Why, the world of industry will be changed forever by your invention!'

'May I offer you a glass of something, gentlemen?' said Young. 'Let us leave Dr Baumann to his work; there is still much to do.'

It was a talkative throng as we joined Mr Young in his office and sampled some rather fine Canadian whisky. I was curious about the interest shown by Mr Green and Mr Jamison, and during the conversation discovered that Green was a junior partner in a finance company owned by his father, and Jamison was a director of a family firm which made agricultural equipment.

There was an air of optimism in the company as toasts were drunk to the Baumann motor. A second glass all round sealed its future.

'Concerning Mrs Beauregard,' I began hesitantly, as Holmes and I returned to London. We had the train compartment to ourselves, so our conversation could not be overheard. I had thought it best to say nothing in the hearing of the driver who had conveyed us to the station.

Holmes made no immediate reply but gave me a look of concern. The intricacies of the minds of women were a subject he never really mastered and we were both innocents in the ways of courtship. I think he regarded women almost as a separate species, which he could only view from a distance, trying by observation to understand their ways of thinking in order to interpret their actions. Some men regard women's minds as directed along simple, predictable, pathways. Others see only caprice and unpredictability. Holmes did neither; that was his difficulty.

I was not about to say anything of a vulgar nature, but I recalled a comment made by my mother regarding a friend of hers. 'My mother once told me that a widow who is missing the company of her deceased husband is particularly vulnerable to the addresses of fortune hunters.'

'Your mother's observations can be extremely perceptive,' said Holmes.

'I am also reminded somewhat of my cousin Lily,' I said. 'She is a dear girl, and I am sure she will settle down one day, but when she admires a young gentleman, she always thinks he can do no wrong. Despite the disparity in age, I think Mrs Beauregard may be of the same mind as regards Dr Baumann.'

'I fear so,' said Holmes. 'Dr Baumann's actions — the holding hands and gazing into the lady's eyes — while appearing to be a test of her sensitivity to the force was also a deliberate ploy to engage her affections. He knew precisely the effect it would have, and he was entirely successful. He has drawn her into his fold and elevated her self-belief, which was already strong, to a pitch from which she cannot permit herself to retreat.'

'And has thereby encouraged her to invest in his motor scheme,' I said. 'Have you formed an opinion of that? It is rather hard to do so, considering he will not provide any information.'

'The apparatus is almost laughably primitive,' said Holmes. 'It appears to have been welded together from general supplies and a decorative feature. I am sure I saw parts of a desk lamp in there somewhere.'

'But it appears to do what he claims.'

'Does it?' said Holmes. 'We are given no explanation of the principle and are not permitted a close examination of the motor. Even Mr Young who owns the mill has to knock for admission to Dr Baumann's domain. Short of burglary I cannot seek the answers I require.'

'You're not suggesting —'

'I am not ruling it out. But I shall tell Mr Ineson that it is too early to be certain and therefore far too early to invest. First, however, I have some investigations to conduct.'

'Into motors?' I asked.

'Into Dr Baumann,' said Holmes.

CHAPTER THREE

The next day we appeared before Mr Ineson once more, and Holmes handed him a written report of our visit.

'My conclusion,' said Holmes, 'is that Dr Baumann is engaged in a highly speculative project based upon a scientific principle which has yet to receive approval from experts in the field. The motor itself is at a very early stage of development. It appeared to have been assembled from a variety of ill-assorted parts, joined together by pipework. The mechanic, Mr Gorrie, has not been afforded any great wealth of materials, or equipment. It did seem to generate power, sufficient to operate a miniature beam engine, and there was as far as I could see no source of power in the workshop. But I was not permitted to make what I consider to be an essential close examination. Baumann says he has secrets to protect. Of that I have no doubt. Baumann may prove the experts wrong in time, of course. I cannot dismiss that idea entirely. However, when Baumann promised a patentable device in six months or less, Mr Gorrie appeared not to share his optimism.'

'What would be your advice to potential investors?' asked Ineson, with an expression of amusement.

'If someone wishes to invest a small sum in the hopes that it will grow into a very large sum, that is their business as long as they do so with their eyes open and with money they can afford to lose if Dr Baumann does not succeed.'

'And my client?' asked Ineson. 'I fear she is not contemplating risking a small sum.'

'I would strongly advise Mrs Beauregard that at present she should not invest large sums of money in this venture. I suggest that she should wait until the new motor has been built, is proven to work and granted a patent before she even contemplates subscribing for shares in the company. But much depends on what her intentions are. If she thinks of her investment as a charitable donation, for which she expects no financial return, then so be it. It is her money, and she may do with it as she pleases.'

'Do you think she believes in the principle of this motor?' asked Ineson.

'I think she accepts what Dr Baumann has to say about it,' said Holmes. 'I have delved a little further into the literature, and note that quite recently the American, Edison, claimed to have found proof of what he has dubbed the 'etheric force' which confers the ability to send messages at a distance without wires or cables. He does not however claim that it will generate power at no cost. Advances in science are being made, and who can predict what will emerge next? I cannot, and neither can Mrs Beauregard.'

'If I might comment,' I said, 'I think she admires Dr Baumann. He has attempted with some success to engage her affections. Therefore, her opinions and actions will be influenced by her feelings.'

'If that is the case then I sincerely hope that the motor does work, or the lady may be doomed, and no-one will be able to save her from herself,' said Ineson. 'I acted for her late husband for many years, and I am sure he would never have involved himself in such a venture. I am only hoping she does not marry the fellow.'

'Have you been able to discover anything about Dr Baumann?' I asked.

'No, it appears that Baumann is not an uncommon surname in Switzerland. And he has revealed very little about himself. In fact, it is a subject on which he is noticeably reticent.'

'He may be a widower,' said Holmes. 'There is a mark on his ring finger suggesting that he once wore a wedding band there.'

This fact did not improve our mood.

'Since meeting Dr Baumann I have spent some time in the museum library searching for any publications he might have authored,' said Holmes. 'He has said that his secret is not yet to be given to the world, but I would have expected to find earlier studies which would reveal his field of work and suggest how he might have arrived at this principle. I found nothing. He does not appear to be attached to any school or university.'

There was nothing more we could say, but all three of us agreed to continue to observe the situation. Mr Ineson wrote a cheque for our services and expenses. I was reluctant to accept anything other than a reimbursement of my travel costs for what was for me not a professional exploit but assisting a friend. We did however dine rather well that night.

A week later Holmes showed me a letter he had received from Mr Ineson.

Mr Holmes,

I regret to inform you that matters regarding Dr Baumann and his machine have continued along the expected path. Mrs Beauregard has, as I feared, not listened to my advice. A limited company, Baumann Motors has been formed. The directors are Dr Baumann and Mr Young. The solicitors and accountants concerned are reputable London firms who handle Mr Young's affairs in this country. Several interested gentlemen and Mrs Beauregard have subscribed for shares, and a considerable sum of money has been raised to further the construction of an improved motor.

Dr Baumann continues to promise to be able to patent the device in no more than six months. The only small crack in this ambitious edifice is the mechanic, Mr Gorrie, who has recently expressed disquiet with the progress of the work. He thinks that six months is optimistic. Personally, I am more inclined to believe him than Baumann. If you could visit Abbey Mill once more and discover anything further, I would be much obliged,

R. Ineson

It was no hardship to repair once more to the Essex and Hertfordshire countryside, with its charming villages and busy watermills, on a sunny summer's day. Of course, I did this in company with Sherlock Holmes while on a mission, but surely, I said to myself, as we alighted once more at Waltham Cross station, this was a simple task, posing no danger to life or limb, to discover the truth behind what Mr Ineson thought was a risky investment for his client. There would be more than enough time during our trip to enjoy fresh air and peace at the generous expense of solicitors Ineson and Randall.

'Is Mr Young expecting us?' I asked.

'I have not alerted him,' said Holmes.

'Nor I.'

'Good. I often find that people are more forthcoming if taken by surprise.'

We took a cab to the mill and rang the visitors' bell. The smart young man came to the door. 'Oh, gentlemen, I wasn't expecting you,' he exclaimed, looking in his notebook. 'Do you have an appointment to see Mr Young?'

'We do not, Mr —?'

'Norris. I am Mr Young's secretary.'

'We have come at the request of Mr Ineson.'

'I see,' said Norris, hesitantly. 'Is this concerning the motor?'

'It is. Might we have a word with Mr Gorrie?'

'He — er — is not available at present.'

'Then we will have to wait until he is. Might we come in?'

'Oh, yes, of course. Kindly wait and I will let Mr Young know that you are here.'

We took our seats in the little waiting area while Norris went to see Young.

'"Not available",' said Holmes. 'An interesting choice of words.'

Norris soon returned. 'Mr Young will see you now,' he said.

Mr Young greeted us politely but without enthusiasm. He was not the smiling man we had seen before. He was at his desk, and before him was a pile of documents, which appeared to be invoices and bank papers. He reminded me of a card player who was considering an unpromising hand and trying unsuccessfully to arrange his cards in the most favourable way.

'What brings you here, gentlemen?' he asked as we were seated, barely concealing the fact that he hoped our business with him would be brief.

'A request from Mr Ineson,' said Holmes. 'He understands that Mr Gorrie does not share Dr Baumann's optimism about how soon the motor can be perfected. Perhaps we might have a word with Mr Gorrie, if he is not too busy?'

'I am afraid that won't be possible today,' said Young. 'He has gone to acquire materials.'

'I see. Might we speak to Dr Baumann?'

'He is busy in the workshop. He does not wish to be disturbed.' Young smiled weakly. 'I am sorry if you have had a wasted journey. Now, if you don't mind —' he gestured at the papers on his desk.

Holmes remained seated. 'Then I must speak to you,' he said. 'When we attended the demonstration and Dr Baumann promised a patentable motor in six months or less, I noticed that Mr Gorrie did not appear altogether happy with that statement. Mr Ineson has since been told that Gorrie has openly expressed his concerns. On behalf of his client, Mrs Beauregard, he has asked us to discover further details. A great deal of money is at stake.'

'Yes,' said Young. 'Mrs Beauregard was here the other day, on business. She saw Gorrie shuffling about mumbling to himself, as he so often does, and asked me what the matter with him was. I said that he had mentioned that the motor might take longer than six months to be ready. Personally, I thought that Gorrie was simply unhappy about the hours of work he was being asked to do, but that could be addressed. Mrs Beauregard said that she had perfect faith that Dr Baumann would remove Mr Gorrie's concerns and was happy to go ahead and subscribe for shares.'

'Is there anything else you can tell me?'

'No, I — no.'

'Perhaps Dr Baumann can tell me more. I will wait to speak to him.'

Mr Young fell silent for a moment. 'I don't think he can tell you more,' he said.

Still Holmes remained seated. 'Mr Young,' he said, 'I am employed by Mr Ineson to gather facts on matters regarded as highly sensitive, where the utmost confidentiality is required. He has the most impeccable reputation in his profession, and he trusts me and Mr Stamford to carry out his wishes to his standards. I cannot return to him and provide him with a story which I feel is — let us say — incomplete. Kindly be open with me.'

It is often a relief to tell the truth, however difficult it might be. Although Mr Young still appeared uncomfortable, his furrowed brow had relaxed. I sensed that there was a realisation that Sherlock Holmes was a man who could be trusted absolutely.

We waited. Young took a deep breath.

'About three days ago Gorrie asked me for a private interview. He had looked thunderous ever since Dr Baumann promised the directors a motor in a few months, so I had a good idea what he was about to say. But he was blunt enough. He said that he had done his best while working under the direction of Dr Baumann, making everything to his specifications. In fact, he hinted that being a mechanic and not a theoretical scientist he knew better in some areas than Dr Baumann did what would work and had made adjustments accordingly. Dr Baumann never noticed or objected; he was happy with what Gorrie had done. The demonstrations produced results, but this had made him too confident. A prototype is one thing, but a full-sized patentable motor which can be shown to power heavy industry is quite another. The task would take not months but years. In fact, the possibility existed that it would never succeed. The parts had not yet been made which could withstand the power generated.'

At this moment, Young's voice broke, and he took a handkerchief from his pocket and pressed it to his forehead. It was some moments before he could continue. 'I tried to offer him encouragement. I pointed out that the motor was attracting more visitors and investors, so funds were becoming available for stronger materials. I showed him a list of the gentlemen who were due to visit in the near future, and who I felt sure would acquire shares. I said if the work was too arduous, we could engage an assistant. None of this seemed to satisfy him or make him change his mind.'

'I assume if he does not continue the work then those visits will be cancelled.'

'I fear so.'

'What advice did you give him?' asked Holmes.

'I was unable to comment on the mechanism, of course. And the principle behind it has never been revealed to me. But I felt that just as Dr Baumann is optimistic about the prospects, so Gorrie might simply be of the opposite disposition. I suggested that he go and speak to Dr Baumann about his concerns and if they put their heads together, they might arrive at a resolution.'

'And did he do so?'

'No. According to Dr Baumann, Gorrie never discussed anything that was troubling him.'

'And what is the current position? I assume Mr Gorrie has not gone to acquire materials.'

'I don't know where he is,' Young admitted. 'This morning, I arrived at the mill as usual, together with my secretary, Norris, and Dr Baumann. Soon afterwards Dr Baumann came to me saying that Gorrie was not at work. Thinking that Gorrie might be unwell, he had gone to the cottage where Gorrie is staying. Gorrie wasn't there. All his things were gone, his travelling bag, his clothes, everything.'

'Had he left a note? Told anyone of his intentions?'

Young shook his head. 'No. Dr Baumann is very upset. He fears that Gorrie has gone to sell his secrets to another man. It is a major setback and will inevitably increase costs. Delays always do.'

Holmes was writing in his notebook. 'When did you last see Mr Gorrie?'

'Yesterday. He was here working on the machine when I went home at six o'clock. Dr Baumann and Norris travelled back to town with me as usual. We have asked the men if anyone had seen him today, but it seems he has not been seen at all since last night.'

'How many men do you have working here?' asked Holmes.

'Other than Norris, there are ten in the grinding room, as well as the storekeeper and a general labourer. Mr Jenkins looks after the wheel and keeps the water channels clear.'

'And who occupies the cottages?'

'Gorrie has one to himself; that was at Dr Baumann's request. He wanted his business to be kept private. Jenkins and his sister have another. Eight men share the other four. The workmen who have wives and families live in Waltham Abbey. They come up by wagon on Mondays and usually share the end cottage during the week. They have had to make do in the other cottages since Gorrie took it.'

'Where does Dr Baumann stay?'

'He is a guest of my family.'

'Who apart from yourself knew where Gorrie was staying?'

'I think everyone who works here must have done. No-one else I can think of.'

'Can you suggest where Gorrie might have gone?'

'As far as we know he has no family or friends in this vicinity. I am hoping that he is cooling his heels in a tavern not far from here and will soon find he has no option but to come back. I am sure Dr Baumann would have him back, as that would enable him to continue the work without interruption, but under very strict control.'

'Have you looked to see if Gorrie took anything he ought not to have taken before he left?' asked Holmes. 'When an employee leaves suddenly his first thought is often to help himself to the wages.'

Young paled at the thought. 'I never considered that,' he said. After quickly checking his desk drawers, he turned to a small safe in one corner of the office, which he opened and peered inside. He gave a small sigh of relief. 'No, all is as it should be. Only Norris and I can open the safe, but then, I suppose Gorrie might have found a way to do so.'

'I would like to examine the cottage where Gorrie was living,' said Holmes.

Young shrugged. 'By all means.'

'What effects did he bring with him?'

'Very little. He carried everything in a carpetbag, or in his pockets.'

Young was careful to lock his office door before we left the mill and walked up to the row of cottages. They were of the style which gave two rooms on the ground floor and two bedrooms above. All had plain curtains at the windows.

'Are the cottages kept locked?' asked Holmes.

'No. Old country ways, I believe. And nothing worth stealing. This is the one where Gorrie stayed.'

Young pushed open the door of the last cottage in the row, and we went inside. Although there was no lock on the front door, we saw that a bolt had recently been attached to the inside of the door, presumably by Gorrie. There was a fireplace, which did for cooking and drying clothes as well. The only furniture was a small dresser with the usual cups, dishes and cutlery, a table and two chairs. A rug lay on the stone flagged floor. Holmes pulled the rug back to look underneath and examined the flagstones.

'What are you searching for?' asked Young.

'Anything hidden, recently disturbed or unusual,' said Holmes. He replaced the rug.

The fire in the grate was merely cold cinders. Some cooking pots appeared unused. On the table was the remains of a meal which had been composed of bread, meat and beer.

The only lighting available was candles, for which flat stoneware holders and matches were supplied. There was also a rather ancient-looking lantern without a candle in it. Holmes examined the lantern, studying the splashes of candle grease within, and opening and closing the gate which was loose at the hinges and did not fasten as well as it should. He took it to a window and let the natural sunlight fall upon the interior. 'Hmm,' was his only comment. He produced an envelope from his pocket and scraped some residue from the interior of the lantern into it with a penknife, then he set it aside.

'Anything of interest?' queried Young.

'Possibly,' said Holmes.

The smaller room at the rear of the cottage had a bare stone floor, and a sink large enough to wash anything one might want to wash, including an adult the size of Mr Gorrie had he chosen to do so. The usual offices were down a short pathway at the back. Holmes went outside to inspect the path, a neglected patch of weeds, and the outhouse. Young and I watched him work, but it was clear when he had finished that he had discovered nothing of note.

'Is there a well?' asked Holmes.

'No,' said Young, 'they draw water from the millstream, it's fresh and clean, better than London water. And there are rainwater butts.'

'Where do they obtain provisions?'

'A wagon comes up from town most days.'

'Did Gorrie sleep upstairs?'

'I assume so.'

We returned indoors where Holmes mounted the stairs, and we followed. I recalled the last time I had seen him search a premises. On that occasion the corpse of a murdered man was lying on the floor. The police had been present and limited what Holmes was permitted to disturb. Now he had a house under his control, and he was making the most of it. One of the two small upper rooms looked unused. The bedstead was not made up, and there was a pile of linen lying ready. The other room was where Gorrie had slept. The bed was made up, with its utensil underneath, and there was a side table, a bowl and jug for water, and a small chest for clothes. Holmes made a meticulous search of everything. I noticed Young watching him with close attention. It must have been dawning upon him that my friend had done this before. Perhaps he thought Holmes was regularly sent by Mr Ineson to search the homes of deceased or disappeared clients.

There was a candle in a holder and some matches beside the bed. Holmes asked if there was any other lighting and Young said he thought not.

Holmes consulted a pocket almanac. 'Sunset would have been just after seven,' he said. 'If Mr Gorrie left shortly after six o clock it would still have been light.'

'I wouldn't have minded if he had asked to share the carriage,' said Young, 'there was room. But he said nothing. Perhaps he didn't want anyone to know he had gone until he was too far away to be found.'

Holmes stripped the sheets off the bed, and shook them out, then looked under the pillow and inside the pillowcase. There was a key under the pillow. 'Is this the workshop key?' asked Holmes.

'It is,' said Young. 'I'm glad he didn't take that with him. Let me have it, I'll put it in the safe.'

With noticeable reluctance Holmes handed Young the key.

Holmes pulled the mattress off the bed. Underneath, resting on the bedsprings, was a small packet wrapped in oilcloth.

'Is this Gorrie's?' asked Holmes.

'I don't know,' said Young, 'I have never seen it before.'

Holmes carefully folded back the wrappings. The contents were modest enough. A worn leather wallet with banknotes, some English and some American. There was a card on which was written the name Edward Gorrie and an address in New York. 'Placed here for safekeeping,' said Holmes. 'He is American?'

'I think he is primarily of Scottish extraction judging by his accent,' said Young. 'He may well have migrated there of course.'

'But if, as we have been led to believe, Mr Gorrie packed all his possessions into his carpetbag and left the mill of his own accord, it is curious that he left this packet of money behind,' said Holmes.

'Perhaps he was in a hurry and he forgot,' suggested Young. 'In which case,' he added hopefully, 'he will be back soon enough to collect it.'

Holmes made a note of the New York address, then handed the packet to Young. 'Kindly place that in your safe. I would like to take a look in the other cottages. And all the outhouses.'

'Yes, of course,' said Young, a little bemused by the request but content to comply. 'Gorrie might have decided to go back to America,' he said. 'He might have family at that address. Perhaps they know something. I have an office in New York. If he doesn't return soon, I'll send a cablegram, ask them to look into it.'

The other cottages were mostly unoccupied, as the men who stayed there were at work. Holmes's searches were, as always, meticulous, taking in all possibilities, in particular looking for recently disturbed flagstones and turned earth. Mr Young watched with growing concern as he came to understand what Holmes might be looking for.

Jenkins was not in his cottage, but Young told us to expect his elderly sister to be there and hoped she would not be upset. He knocked at the door. 'Good day, Miss Jenkins. It's Mr Young. Might I come in?'

A thin voice piped assent, and we entered. The room was well provided with simple but sturdy home-made furniture. In one corner was a single bed, where I guessed Miss Jenkins slept in the warm. We found her sitting by the fire, gnarled hands clutching a hot drink, wrapped securely against a chill only she could feel.

Young greeted her in as cheerful a manner as possible, and she made no objection to us looking about. 'I just want to show these gentlemen what fine cottages we have here,' he said. 'Are you keeping well?'

'Well enough, Mr Young, sir,' she said, drawing the edges of her shawl more tightly across her chest.

Holmes was no less thorough, but he was able to give Miss Jenkins the impression that he was a surveyor of buildings rather than someone searching for a body. His examination of the cottage complete, he looked outside to find in addition to the usual outhouse, a small well-tended garden plot and a toolshed. The shed was stocked with the necessities of both gardening and Jenkins's trade, as well as pots of paint, brushes, lumber, and offcuts of wood destined for some future use. Once Holmes had completed his searches, he declared himself satisfied that Gorrie was not in or near any of the cottages.

'I intend to make some further enquiries concerning Mr Gorrie,' said Holmes. 'Where is Dr Baumann?'

'In his workshop.'

'Then I will start with him.'

'He has locked himself in and does not wish to be disturbed.'

Holmes gave Young an enquiring stare.

'He really has, I promise.'

'I see. Well, he has to emerge some time, so let me know when he does, and tell him I wish to speak to him.'

'Very well.' Young paused. 'Er — Mr Holmes —'

'Yes?'

'If you should happen to encounter any of the other investors or directors, it would be best not to mention this yet. About Gorrie going away. I wouldn't want to alarm them. Gorrie may reappear and no harm done,' he added with a weak smile.

'Of course,' said Holmes. 'I would like to speak to Mr Jenkins, now. I assume he knows that Mr Gorrie has gone?'

'Yes, I asked him about Gorrie when I looked this morning. He has gone to check the wheel for weed. He should be back here soon.'

'Very well. We will keep Miss Jenkins company until he arrives.' Young prepared to return to his office, promising to inform us if he received any news.

'If we hear nothing soon, would you agree to my making enquiries in town?' asked Holmes. 'I will make sure not to alarm anyone or reveal any secrets.'

Young sighed. 'As long as you are discreet. While Gorrie remains at large, we cannot be sure of the progress of the motor.'

As Holmes and I waited to see Jenkins, I said, 'I am no engineer, but I did not see anything in Dr Baumann's apparatus which would pose any difficulty to a good mechanic. Surely they can find another man soon?'

'I agree. But Dr Baumann's concern is sharing his secrets with others. And who knows what happens inside those vessels? There is something strange about this affair and the key to the mystery lies in the workings of the Baumann motor.'

CHAPTER FOUR

Jenkins returned from his morning labours to make either a late breakfast or an early luncheon. He was a weathered man, his sun-darkened skin bony and tough as a cord, and any possible age between seventy and ninety. He put a large corner of bread on the table and made up a mug of dark tea, making sure to see that his sister was comfortable before he sat down. We declined his offer of refreshment. He seemed friendly enough and happy to talk to us when we asked about Gorrie.

'I last seen Gorrie last night. He didn't say anything to me, but I could see he wasn't best pleased about something. What it was, I couldn't say.'

'What time was that?'

'It was some time after Mr Young and Mr Norris and Dr Baumann had gone. Gorrie was coming out of the workshop. I saw him lock the door. He and Dr Baumann were very careful about that. Didn't want people coming in and stealing their secrets, did they? Then I went to have my dinner.'

'Can you estimate the time?'

'I didn't look at a clock, but when I went to have dinner, it was still light. Half past six or a bit later maybe.'

'When he left the workshop, was he carrying anything? Materials? Documents? A bag or box that might have held something of value?'

'Nothing that I could see. He locked the door, put the key in his pocket and walked away.'

'How was he dressed?'

'Same as usual. I seen him going back and forth when he was about his work, and he was never any different.'

'Did you hear or see him return to his cottage?'

'No, but then his is not next to mine. His is the one furthest from the mill. I never saw him go out again, but then if I was having my dinner and seeing to Maggie, I might not have looked out front. Now Mr Phillips, he's the foreman in the grinding room, he said Gorrie was still in his cottage a bit after sunset because he saw a light in there, just a candle, moving about.'

Holmes wrote in his notebook. 'It would be useful to know which way he went,' he mused. 'How long have you lived here, Mr Jenkins? I expect you know the area well.'

'Oh, nigh on forty year, back when it was a corn mill. I know this place better'n any man here. When it stopped grinding corn, the owner asked me to stay on and keep an eye on it, stop it going into ruin, so he would get the best price for it.'

'The water that drives the wheel, does that come from the stream or the river?' I asked.

Jenkins gave me that smile that country folk sometimes give to city people who need the simplest things explained to them. 'I'll show you,' he said, pushing his plate away and taking us to the cottage door. 'Up there,' he said, pointing in the direction away from the little bridge and the road we had arrived by, 'is a weir across the stream, and a sluice gate, which is one of the things I take care of. If the gate is open, which it usually is, the water goes into another channel, what we call the head race, which comes down this way and is taken into the penstock.'

'The penstock?' asked Holmes. 'Is that the wooden chute that brings the water to the wheel?'

'That it is. Then the water comes down from the wheel into the tail race, that's the channel which carries it back into the stream.'

'Can you control the speed of flow?' I asked.

'I can, by raising and lowering the gate. I check on it twice a day, to make sure it is a clear flow. Don't want branches and dead fowl in the water. There's a screen to collect all that, and if anything is trapped there, I clear it away. If we need to make repairs to the wheel, it has to be stopped. There's a lever in the grinding room but I always close the gate as well, so all the water goes over the weir.'

'What about fish?' I asked. 'Are there any in the stream? Don't they get trapped?'

'Anything that swims that comes through the sluice gate can go back to the stream through the overspill channel, what we call the fish pass.'

'How far is the weir from the mill?' asked Holmes.

'Just a few minutes' walk, for young legs,' said Jenkins. 'A bit longer for me nowadays.'

'If someone was to walk from here to Waltham Abbey or Waltham Cross, what would be the best way to go?'

'You'd take the downstream path; you wouldn't go up to the weir, it's a longer walk to the nearest bridge over the Lea. Downstream way is the road where wagons and carriages go, across the bridge between here and town. That must have been the way you came here.'

'And Mr Gorrie would have known that was the right road to take if he wanted to go back to town?'

'I am sure he would. But if he had made a mistake and gone the wrong way, he would have known as soon as he reached the weir. There's an old signpost pointing downstream to the town and upstream to Cheshunt. So if he saw that he would have turned back. Or he might have walked on if he wanted to go up to Cheshunt instead.'

'Does anyone who works at the mill live in Cheshunt?'

'No, sir.'

'He didn't take his lantern,' I said. 'If he left after sunset, he might not have been able to see his way. Are there lights on the road after dark?'

'No, we carry our own. Last night there was moonlight enough just after sunset to see your way if you happen to know the path,' said Jenkins, 'though him being a stranger here it wouldn't have been that easy.'

'Thank you, Mr Jenkins,' said Holmes. 'If you happen to discover anything more about Mr Gorrie's whereabouts, do please let us know.'

'I'll do that, sir,' said Jenkins.

'I think our next course of action is to speak to Dr Baumann as soon as he is available,' said Holmes as we returned to the mill offices. 'If that provides no enlightenment, we will return to Waltham Abbey to make our initial enquiries. Mr Young, Mr Norris, Dr Baumann and some of the workmen all travel between there and the mill. Gorrie may have had enough resources in his pockets not to require his packet of banknotes. He might have departed by train or stayed at a tavern or with someone he knows. Perhaps he sent messages by post or telegram. We have no evidence of a connection north of the mill, but if we find nothing, we will have to extend our searches in that direction. I expect we will have to take rooms in town tonight. But even if Gorrie should suddenly reappear, that does not to my mind end the matter and I will question him very closely. Perhaps he did not tell Mr Young the whole story. I would be very interested to discover precisely what was causing him such disquiet.'

Mr Young was in his office and remained bereft of news. Baumann had still to reappear. We reported what Jenkins had told us.

'When I return home tonight Dr Baumann will accompany me, as he usually dines with us,' said Young. 'If you are free this evening you could join us for dinner. I have also invited Professor Novak. I had mentioned Gorrie's concerns to him some days ago, in case Gorrie wished to consult him, but it appears he did not. Should Professor Novak offer to speak to Gorrie I will be obliged to tell him something. I could say that our mechanic is away seeking information or machine parts for his work. I mean, that might be the case, we don't know.'

'Professor Novak might be more helpful if you told him the truth,' said Holmes. 'Is he a director or investor in Baumann Motors?'

'No, not as yet. He is certainly taking a close interest in the project but is exercising caution at present.' Young looked thoughtful. 'I think, yes, you are right, Mr Holmes. On reflection, I had better advise him of the true situation, that Gorrie has gone away without notice. The professor is an astute man, and I am sure he will be discreet. He may have some useful insights, and I would welcome his advice.'

At that moment we heard approaching footsteps. The office door opened and Dr Baumann appeared. He was surprised to see Holmes and me, and looked at us as if he expected Young to dismiss us, in preference for his company, but Young did not.

'Come in, Dr Baumann,' said Young. 'Mr Holmes and Mr Stamford have come at the behest of Mr Ineson and have determined to make every effort to see where Gorrie has gone. Have you received no communication from him? Did he say anything of where he might have wished to go?'

'Nothing,' said Baumann despondently. He came in and sat down.

'We will make some enquiries for you in town,' said Holmes. 'If anyone has seen him, they might remember him — his unusual gait, and the carpetbag. Can either of you describe the carpetbag to me?'

'Well, I suppose one is much like another,' said Young, vaguely. 'I think I only saw it once, when he arrived.'

'Was it large, such as gentlemen take on their travels?' Holmes continued. 'New, or worn with use? Can you recall the colour, the pattern?'

'I am sure it was large,' said Young. 'A man's bag.'

Baumann nodded agreement. 'And not new. As to colour —' he shrugged. 'Brown and red like a lot of carpets. Some sort of pattern. That's all I know.'

'Would you oblige me by permitting me to examine the motor you have been developing?' asked Holmes. 'I have so many questions.'

Baumann smiled sadly. 'Ah, how many men have asked just that. But it is not yet ready. And the design is as yet unprotected by a patent. I cannot make exceptions.'

'When Mr Gorrie left, did he take anything with him from your workshop that might cause you disquiet? Papers, drawings, components? Do you suspect him of intending to try and sell your secret to others?'

'I have looked very carefully, and I can find no evidence that he removed anything at all from the workshop. But of course, he knows more than any other man about my motor. He has his notebooks which he carries with him at all times. And I think some plans are only in his memory. If I hear of something similar being built by another man, that would be very upsetting.'

'How did you meet Mr Gorrie?' asked Holmes.

'When I came to England, I visited factories and workshops trying to interest them in my motor,' said Baumann. 'I think Gorrie must have been employed by one of them, and he came to me privately saying he would like to come and work for me. He had excellent credentials and experience, and after seeing what he could do I decided to employ him. His work was of the highest quality. Even when funds were short, which they were at first, he performed miracles from the most basic materials. And he has never betrayed my trust. But I ought to make this clear, he knows only what I have chosen to tell him. He knows the parts, but not the principle.'

'And he constructed everything?'

'He did. The prototype you saw may appear to be very simple, as there is nothing remarkable about the vessels, but the details of the amplifimoderator are very precise and any slight deviation from my measurements would mean failure. As you have seen, it works. A few more adjustments and tests are all that are required and I can make the application for the patent. But I need Mr Gorrie to assist me.'

'If we hear nothing soon, I shall make sure Jenkins and Phillips know that if they or any of the workmen here should see Gorrie in the vicinity, I am to be informed at once, but no-one else must be told,' said Young. 'I shall offer a reward to the man who comes to tell me. Of course I am very concerned, but I do not wish to spread alarm unnecessarily amongst the investors.'

'Is your foreman Mr Phillips available?' asked Holmes. 'I would like to ask him a few questions. He may recall what time he saw Gorrie in his cottage last night.'

'I'll have him sent for,' said Young, and Baumann, hoping he was no longer required, slipped away.

Norris was dispatched to fetch Phillips from the grinding house. He was a stocky fellow in his thirties, with a confident look about him.

'Mr Phillips, I understand you saw signs that Mr Gorrie was in his cottage yesterday evening?' asked Holmes.

'Yes,' said Phillips, 'his is next to the one where I stay. I was a bit late at the factory as there was a machine needed some seeing to, just a bit of cleaning, but once I had done that I went back to my cottage.'

'What time do you usually finish work?'

'This season, before seven o'clock.'

'And how late were you yesterday?'

'Maybe an extra half hour. The sun was going down and I had to get a lantern to finish what I was doing.'

'Did you happen to see Mr Gorrie?'

'No, but he must have been indoors as there was a light. I saw it through the curtains.'

'Was the candle in a holder, or a lantern?' asked Holmes.

'From the way the flame moved, it was just a candle. He must have been walking about carrying it because it went back and forth.'

'And this was after seven o clock?'

'I'm not sure about the time, but the sun was down by then. It must have been well after seven.'

'If he had gone out after sunset, do you think he could have seen his way even if he had no light with him?' asked Holmes. 'I ask because Mr Gorrie did not take the lantern from the cottage with him. It's still there with no candle in it.'

'I don't know about that,' said Phillips. 'A man who knew the path could have travelled by moonlight if the sky was clear. But when I went indoors there was already cloud coming in.'

'Did you see or hear him go out?' asked Holmes.

'No, and we've talked about it amongst ourselves and none of us saw him go.'

Holmes thanked Phillips, who returned to his work.

Young's manservant, Saunders, brought up the carriage to convey him home and Holmes and I were able to join them. Holmes asked for us to be left at Waltham Cross railway station as he intended to commence enquiries about Gorrie there. He reassured Mr Young that he would adhere to his promise to carry out the task with appropriate delicacy. We agreed to be at Young's home in Sun Street for dinner at eight o'clock.

'Do you think Mr Gorrie left by train?' I asked.

'I think I should start by ruling that out as a possibility,' said Holmes.

It took very little time to establish that no-one of Gorrie's description had been seen at the station recently and neither had anyone left a carpetbag there to be called for.

There was a comfortable-looking old inn close by, the Queen Eleanor, where we made further enquiries, and established that Gorrie had not been seen there. We then proceeded to the post office where we confirmed that no one of Gorrie's description had sent a letter or telegram.

'If Gorrie was trying to avoid either Mr Young or Dr Baumann, or both, which is possible if he was unhappy with the motor, then it is unlikely that he would have spent much time in the vicinity of Sun Street,' said Holmes. 'Which is where we are now bound.'

Sun Street is the most delightful little thoroughfare where every kind of household purchase may be made, all of good quality at fair prices. A lady did not have to go far to grace her table with fine food and wine. There were tailors, dressmakers, shoemakers, and drapers, all within a short stroll, and even the smallest and simplest of shops had taken the trouble to be pleasing to the eye.

We secured rooms for the night at the New Inn on Sun Street, which promised comfortable accommodation and a good breakfast, and was conveniently close to both the police station and the house rented by Mr Young, both of which were on our itinerary for the evening.

Holmes speedily wrote a report to advise Mr Ineson of the current situation, saying that we proposed to remain in Waltham Abbey at the New Inn to continue enquiries. He despatched a messenger boy to post the letter.

Waltham Abbey police station was both handsome and capacious. It had been opened only two years previously and was thought to be one of the finest buildings in town. Apart from the usual cells one might expect, there was generous accommodation both for married officers and their families, and single constables, with kitchens and bathrooms a hotel might envy. Stabling for two horses was provided separately nearby.

We approached the front desk, which was manned by a sergeant, a solid and competent-looking officer of about thirty-five. 'How may I help you, gentlemen?' he asked.

Holmes produced his card. 'We have been sent here by Mr Ineson of Ineson and Randall, solicitors, of London, to attend the demonstrations of the Baumann motor taking place at Abbey Mill, on behalf on one of his clients. When visiting today we were told that Mr Gorrie, who is the mechanic employed by Baumann Motors, has taken a short period of leave. He departed at some time after six o'clock yesterday evening. While working at Abbey Mill, he was staying in one of the workmen's cottages, which he has vacated, taking his luggage with him. We are anxious to speak to him, as he left behind him a packet of banknotes. He may not yet have noticed it is not in his bag and when he does, he might fear that he has lost it or been robbed. If he should come here making enquiries about it, please could you reassure him that the mill owner, Mr Young, has it in safe keeping for him and would be pleased to return it to him?'

'Certainly, sir. Might I have a description of Mr Gorrie?'

'He is about fifty years of age, a little bow-legged and walks accordingly. He is probably carrying a large carpetbag which I am told is red and brown in colour. He speaks quietly with a Scottish accent. If anyone of that description is seen in town, he should be alerted. I have already enquired at Waltham Cross railway station, but he has not been seen there or left his bag. It is just possible he might have travelled the other way, to Cheshunt.'

'Thank you, sir. I have not seen anyone of that description but will report to Inspector Tubb who will ask our men to look out for him. And we can ask the Cheshunt police if they have seen him.' He made a note of the details. 'Do you know where he might have gone?'

'I am afraid not,' said Holmes.

'You have no address for him? Or his friends or relatives?'

'His papers included only one address, in New York.' Holmes supplied the address which the sergeant noted down.

'Do you have any reason to believe he might have come to harm?'

'Only that he appears to have been travelling during the hours of darkness and is not familiar with the area. It is possible, I suppose, that he might have lost his way, or met with an accident. But I hope that he will be found safe, as I have questions to ask him on behalf of Mr Ineson. If you do find him, kindly inform me. I can be reached at the New Inn.'

Our business done, it was time to make the short walk to Mr Young's home, to see what we might discover there.

'Do you think Gorrie has come to harm?' I asked.

'If this was London I should not rest until he had been found,' said Holmes.

'And in Waltham Abbey?'

'He is engaged in something questionable and seems to have run away. I shall not treat his disappearance lightly.'

CHAPTER FIVE

Mr Young's house was a good-sized property of the kind that prosperous men built in the previous century to display their respectable prosperity to the world. The front was of washed red brick, and above the doors and lintels was a row of wood carvings, well preserved, with symbols of the trade of corn milling.

We were admitted by a maidservant, who showed us to a charmingly rustic drawing room made comfortable with patterned rugs and beautifully upholstered seating. Mr Young rose to greet us, and his expression told us at once that his earlier mood was unchanged.

'I have received no message as yet,' said Young. 'Do you have any news?'

'Mr Gorrie has not been seen at the railway station, the post office, or the Queen Eleanor Inn,' said Holmes. 'I have been careful not to declare him as missing. I have asked only if he has called at those places, and he has not. I advised the police that he might make enquiries at the station thinking that he has lost his packet of money. They are looking out for him both here and at Cheshunt, and if seen, they will tell him to return to the mill where you have it safe for him.'

'Ah, yes, good thinking,' said Young, approvingly. 'I hope this can be resolved soon. I am particularly concerned as there is a meeting of directors and shareholders to be held at the mill tomorrow afternoon. If Gorrie hasn't appeared by then I am not sure what I should tell them. And I must say something soon as Dr Baumann refuses to hold any further demonstrations without Gorrie. They will be extremely unhappy with unexpected delays, especially after his promise of success in six months.'

'Will you enlighten Professor Novak?'

'I have already done so. He arrived a few minutes ago. He is in the office talking to Dr Baumann. They will join us shortly.'

'Am I correct that thus far only we, Dr Baumann, Mr Norris, Professor Novak, and the workmen employed at the mill know that Gorrie has departed without notice?' asked Holmes.

'I have told Mrs Young.'

Holmes was unable to conceal some displeasure at this news.

Young smiled. 'I know what you are thinking, Mr Holmes, ladies and their gossip, but I can assure you that my dear wife is a sensible lady who has been afforded a far better education than most men. She is my most trusted helpmeet. She assures me that she will not reveal our concerns to anyone but will make sure to keep a careful look out for Gorrie when she is out shopping.'

Once Professor Novak and Dr Baumann joined us, Mr Young moved the subject of conversation away from Gorrie. Mrs Young came, with a smile of welcome, to advise us that dinner would be served shortly. She was a comfortable-looking lady the same age as her husband, with an unruffled demeanour which suggested that she was capable of withstanding setbacks and dealing with them efficiently. I understood Mr Young's confidence in his wife. A man who had to face the vagaries of business life should place infinite value on such a companion.

In the dining room, surrounded by paintings of the Essex countryside, we took our places at a long oak table set with silverware. A manservant poured wine, and the maid brought in some soup and bread rolls. 'How long have you gentlemen been working for Mr Ineson?' asked Mr Young.

'A matter of months,' said Holmes. 'We engage in general duties, and travel on his behalf to carry out work outside London when Mr Ineson must remain at his office.'

'And Mrs Beauregard is a client of his, I understand?' asked Baumann.

'A valued client,' said Holmes. 'Mr Ineson, who formerly acted for her late husband, undertakes to look after her interests and advise her.'

'And he has sent you here to represent him? To report on the viability of the Baumann motor?' queried Professor Novak. He made a thoughtful pause. 'Are you qualified in any branch of science?'

'I am not,' said Holmes, modestly, and this was quite true, since despite all his studies, he had taken no examinations. He did not, of course, mention his intense and innovative work in the libraries, laboratories and dissection rooms of St Bartholomew's Medical College and the reading room of the British Museum collections during the last three years. 'I am to report only on what I see, the evidence being placed before potential investors, who may not themselves be men of science. What I have seen so far has however aroused my curiosity. I have endeavoured to learn something of the principles of chemistry, magnetism and electricity, and so forth. All are very large fields of study, and I was daunted to discover how many important texts are in the German language and still await translation.'

'I regret I do not speak German, either,' I said. 'I have no advanced knowledge of chemistry.' I could have added 'beyond what is required for qualification as a surgeon,' but I did not.

Professor Novak smiled and nodded knowingly. 'Yes, a knowledge of German is a requirement for the study of many of the sciences, especially chemistry.'

'I was able to locate an English translation of the works of Baron von Reichenbach, whom you recommended to me, Professor,' Holmes continued, 'which I confess I found quite perplexing. He ventured into areas which have aroused considerable controversy.'

'Oh indeed,' said Novak, 'and the arguments continue to this day. I, and others of my opinion, continue to maintain his reputation. He will be vindicated in time, I am sure of it.'

'I noticed that it was his German counterparts who levelled the most savage criticisms of his work, which of course he has refuted. I found some of their publications and have tried in vain to understand them with the aid of a German dictionary, but I can scarcely comprehend that educated men should stoop to such terms. Perhaps, Dr Baumann, you could satisfy me of my correctness or error in that respect.' Holmes took his notebook from his pocket and leafed through the pages. 'I had to write this down, and I am not at all sure that I am pronouncing these words correctly. Please excuse my ignorance of your language. Words such as *Betrug*, *Hochstapler*, *Lüge Komplize* — am I understanding them properly? And what is *Nervenkrankheit*? I am not at all sure what that might be.'

Baumann seemed startled by this question. He pushed a piece of buttered bread into his mouth and chewed on it, while he considered his response.

Professor Novak smiled at Holmes's clumsy attempts to pronounce German. 'I am sorry to say that Baron von Reichenbach's critics did not moderate their expressions in their ill-mannered assault upon his reputation,' he said. 'They attacked him without troubling to study his methods in any detail. *Nervenkrankheit* refers to nervous diseases, as some of his sensitives, who were the subjects of his experiments, were women afflicted with conditions such as hysteria. He is therefore accused of relying extensively on their observations of phenomena which he himself, not being a sensitive, was unable to see. But he also worked with healthy men, so that cannot be a consideration. The worst accusations, which in my opinion verge on the libellous, refer to — and here those words which have puzzled you can be explained — deceit, imposture and lies, on the part of his subjects, in which it is alleged he may have been their dupe or even, dare I say it, complicit.'

'That is outrageous,' said Holmes, as Baumann swallowed his bread with a loud gulp. 'Thank you for your enlightenment, Professor.'

Novak smiled appreciatively, and with a shake of his head, muttered a few words which I was unable to make out as he had turned his head away from me.

'I think,' said Mr Young, 'that for the sake of our guests we should speak English, unless of course they happen to speak French?' He uttered a phrase in which, so my recent studies in French told me, he declared it to be the most beautiful and elegant of languages. I was tempted to respond in French but held my tongue as Holmes and I were feigning ignorance.

Baumann frowned and grunted. 'I am in England, so I speak only English here,' he said.

There was general agreement around the table that henceforward we would all speak only in English.

'I wish to educate myself to better understand scientific principles,' said Holmes. 'Dr Baumann, do you have any suitable publications in the English language? If so, I would be most interested to read them.'

'None as yet, I am afraid,' said Baumann. 'I have a volume in preparation, but the work will not meet the eyes of the public for at least another year.'

'I await it with interest,' said Holmes. 'And you, Professor Novak?'

Novak smiled modestly. 'I published a volume on the principles of chemistry, some twenty years ago. It is greatly outdated now, I fear. You will not find it in your English libraries.'

The soup bowls were cleared away and we were regaled with roast mutton and vegetables.

We ate quietly while the spectre of Mr Gorrie hovered about the room like Banquo's ghost.

'I take it that nothing has been heard from Gorrie?' asked Baumann at last.

'Did he not leave you a note saying where he was going?' asked Young. 'Perhaps he did, and it was lost.'

'No, nothing.'

'Perhaps he had gone to fetch materials,' said Novak.

'You may be right,' said Young. 'I suppose, given the nature of his work, he must be finding it hard to obtain precisely what he requires. And he never struck me as a talkative man.'

'He was not,' said Baumann.

'But you must know what suppliers he visited? What materials he needed?' asked Mrs Young. 'Let me know, and if there are suitable places in town, we can send our man Saunders to ask for him.'

'I left all of that to him,' said Baumann. 'He knew what he required.'

'Perhaps he needed to go to London for his supplies,' suggested Novak. 'Or even further afield.'

'Well, let us hope we hear from him soon,' said Young.

'I assume, Dr Baumann,' said Holmes, 'that you, like Mr Young and Mr Norris, last saw Mr Gorrie last night at six o'clock, just before you returned here?'

'Yes, that is so.'

'Jenkins has told me that he saw Gorrie leaving the workshop a little later, but did not see him again after that,' said Holmes. 'Did you all dine here yesterday evening?'

'I was not in Waltham Abbey last night,' said Novak. 'I dined at my hotel in London and spent the evening working on a paper.'

Young nodded thoughtfully. 'We took Norris to his lodgings as usual, then I returned here. I was in my study until eight o'clock, when we dined. Dr Baumann, you had a meeting with some potential investors last night. You didn't dine with us then.'

'Yes, I was meeting with some gentlemen,' confirmed Baumann.

'New investors?' said Holmes. 'That is good news for the company. Are they men of business or private wealth?'

'Perhaps I know them,' said Young. 'What are their names?'

Baumann gave a strained smile. 'They prefer to remain anonymous until the papers have been signed,' he said. 'Nothing has been approved as yet. I promised to give them a demonstration once a few improvements have been made to the motor. Of course, that will be delayed now.'

'Not too long, I hope,' said Young.

'What improvements do you have planned?' asked Holmes.

'I believe that the amplifimoderator can be made to operate at double its present efficiency,' said Baumann.

'That is very encouraging,' said Young.

'I do not think we have seen the full potential of the device,' said Novak.

'But suppose Mr Gorrie does not return?' said Mrs Young softly.

'What do you mean?' said Young.

'We hope he will, of course, but you ought to be prepared in case he does not,' she continued. 'You yourself told me he was behaving in a curious manner. Muttering and grumbling to himself. Something dissatisfied him. Do you know what it was?'

'Perhaps it was the hard work that would be required of him to meet the promise to the investors of a finished motor in six months,' said Young. 'I did offer to hire an assistant.'

'Had he had a disagreement with anyone?' asked Mrs Young.

'Not as far as I am aware,' said her husband. 'He was a man of few words.'

'If he was unhappy, he might have gone to look for another position,' said Mrs Young. 'Dr Baumann, did he tell you that he needed to acquire materials?'

'Er — no — but he was very much a law unto himself. He did his work, and that was all.'

Young turned to Professor Novak. 'Professor, what do you advise? We cannot wait much longer.'

'I agree,' said Novak. 'There must be mechanics of great skill who work for colleges and universities, constructing apparatus, and would be more than qualified to take his place.'

'I am not sure,' said Baumann. 'Let me consider it. Let it rest for a few more days. Gorrie may think better of his actions and return after all.'

There was a reflective pause about the table. The conversation that followed was mainly devoted to the excellence of the roast mutton, and the cook's expertise in matters of gravy.

Once the dinner was concluded with a custard pudding and followed by some idle conversation over a glass of whisky, we decided to make our departure. Young's manservant drove Professor Novak to the station for his London train. Holmes took the opportunity to ask for a private conference with our host before we left. I did not witness this, but I saw afterwards that Young was not heartened by my friend's words.

Once we were on our way to our lodgings, I asked, 'What did you say to Mr Young?'

'I advised him not to spend one penny more on the Baumann motor until my enquiries are completed.'

'Will he take your advice, do you think?'

'He is a man of business some twenty years my senior, so I doubt it, but I had to say something. I could not remain silent.'

'Did you happen to hear the words Professor Novak spoke so quietly? I couldn't make them out.'

'I did. He spoke in German. He said, "the young men know so little". But he was not addressing Dr Baumann. He spoke to Mrs Young, who appeared to understand him perfectly.'

'I thought Dr Baumann looked very uncomfortable during much of the conversation.'

'With good reason,' said Holmes. 'As Professor Novak said, a knowledge of German is essential for the study of many of the sciences, chemistry in particular. Dr Baumann claims to be Swiss, where they speak both German and French, and to have a doctorate in the sciences including chemistry, yet he speaks neither German nor, I suspect, French. My conclusion is that he is not Swiss, not a chemist, and most probably has not been awarded a doctorate. I would not be surprised to learn that his name is not Baumann. He is, however, very adept at convincing people of the unshakeable truth of ventures which they passionately wish to believe in. Men of science such as

Professor Novak, who devote themselves to the search for truth, are especially vulnerable. Ladies in love are even more so.'

'We can't accuse him of imposture without proof,' I said.

'Indeed. It is more than ever important that we find Mr Gorrie, who may be the key to this whole affair.'

'You mean he might have suspected that Baumann is a fraud and that is why he left? But the machine works — we saw it.'

'And Mr Maskelyne's automaton works too,' said Holmes. 'It appears to be driven by magic or the power of the spirits, but it is neither. And for a few shillings we are entertained.'

'There is a great deal of money staked on the motor's success,' I said.

'Precisely,' said Holmes. His nostrils flared. 'I scent a crime, Stamford, serious crime, and perhaps more than one.' He rubbed his hands together. 'And now to prove it!'

At the New Inn Holmes retired to the lounge bar with his pipe for the remainder of the evening. There was no word from the police.

The following morning, we awoke early and made a hearty country breakfast. A telegram from Mr Ineson was delivered, authorising us to remain in Waltham Abbey at his partnership's expense, and make enquiries. 'I would have stayed here even if he had asked us to withdraw from the field,' said Holmes. 'There is much to do.'

We called at Sun Street where the Youngs and Baumann were just finishing their coffee, to learn that there was still no news of Gorrie. Mr Young asked if we intended to return to the mill, in which case we might travel with him, but Holmes declined, saying he had other courses of action to pursue.

'And what do you plan to do next?' I asked, as we proceeded on our way.

'We return to the mill,' said Holmes.

'Oh — but —'

'I refused a carriage ride? Naturally I did. The men who travel back and forth regularly go by carriage or wagon. Do they look at the scenery as they go? Stare into the waters? Survey the pathway and the foliage? I doubt it. They know it all too well. We will walk, and we will examine everything we see along the way. If Mr Gorrie did walk from the mill cottage to the town along that road, we may see some sign that he did so.'

As we walked, we glanced into the taverns and tea shops we passed, hoping to see a miserable mechanic sitting in a corner avoiding company, but there was no sign of him. Soon, the town gave way to country. The road by the millstream was well travelled. The trees, bushes and undergrowth alongside were abundant, but branches were cut back in places so as not to impede traffic. The ruts of carriage wheels and hoofprints were apparent, though not sunken too deeply as the weather had been mainly fine and warm in the last two weeks. There was little to see in the way of footprints. Holmes scanned our surroundings on the way, his eyes darting around, looking for anything unusual: crushed leaves, broken twigs, marks in the dry earth, abandoned objects, any sign of an accident or crime, but finding nothing. From time to time he used his walking cane to explore the undergrowth, lifting delicate fronds aside in case they concealed something. All the time, the waters of the stream flowed on their busy way, and it seemed as though they were mocking us. Whatever had happened here, wherever Gorrie had gone, they might have seen it all but were refusing to tell.

'I suppose he might have missed his way in the dark and fallen in,' I said. 'There was no-one near enough to hear him cry out. I doubt that such a fall would have left any obvious signs.'

Holmes nodded. 'He was not familiar with the way and if the moon was covered by cloud, yes that is a possibility. Or he might have been attacked and robbed. Did he beg a ride on a passing wagon going into town? If so, we might have found some evidence of him there by now. Further, more direct enquiries might elicit information. We have been too delicate in our questioning so far. Mr Young cannot hide from the directors much longer.'

I had heard stories of travellers who have been kidnapped and sold into slavery. I considered suggesting this as an explanation, but did not think Holmes would appreciate my theory. When I reflected further, I recalled that the kidnapped travellers were not usually middle-aged men with bow legs, and all the accounts I had read were works of fiction. I decided to hold my tongue.

We had almost reached our destination without result, and were not far from the little bridge over the stream that lay south of the mill, when Holmes, peering into the ripples at the water's edge, pointed and said, 'Can you see that, Stamford? In the reeds, just there.'

I followed where he was indicating, a tangle of discoloured vegetation. 'Fallen leaves, and — I am not sure.'

'I might hazard a suggestion,' said Holmes. 'Stamford, hold my wrist while I take a closer look.'

I took his wrist in both my hands. It was extraordinary to feel the power in the muscles and sinews of his arm, which appeared deceptively thin to the general onlooker. He ventured a step closer to the edge than might have been wise without my steadying support and leaned at a dangerous angle over the waters. 'Yes!' he exclaimed. 'There is something caught up in the reeds.'

'A body?' I asked.

'No, smaller than that.' To my relief, he easily righted himself. 'Come closer. Take a look.'

He took my wrist, and we changed positions, Holmes effortlessly holding me safe with one hand.

I was wondering if what he had seen might be some form of deceased wildlife, or just a mass of rotting leaves, but I was eager to look more closely. And I then I saw it. Something was there, an object, sodden and tangled in the matted material a few feet from the waterside, which was neither leaves nor branches, but appeared to be furry in nature. I was about to dismiss it as the corpse of a dog or a fox, when something unusual struck me about the reddish brown pelt — the indication of a pattern.

At this moment, Mr Young accompanied by Norris and Dr Baumann approached in the carriage, which was obliged to stop.

'Mr Holmes, Mr Stamford — what are you doing here?' asked Young.

'Perhaps Dr Baumann can enlighten us,' said Holmes. 'I have noticed something in the water. Are you able to identify it by colour and pattern as Mr Gorrie's carpetbag?'

Baumann stepped down from the carriage and came to look. 'I can't be sure,' he said.

'Lean closer, we will hold you,' said Holmes. He didn't wait for Baumann to agree or disagree but took him firmly by one arm.

I grasped the other and Baumann, probably realising we were not going to let go until he had complied, nervously leaned over the water's edge. As he saw what Holmes had pointed out, he gave a little gasp and lurched back, then he nodded. 'I think it is.'

'Really?' exclaimed Young. He jumped down from the carriage. 'Let me see.' Assisted by Holmes and me, he also took a look. 'It does look like some kind of carpeting,' he admitted. 'We had better bring it out.'

'It must not be touched,' ordered Holmes, so sharply that Baumann started at the sound and Young stared. Holmes turned to me. 'Stamford — take the carriage back to town and return with a policeman. Preferably Inspector Tubb. This not just a lost bag, it is evidence either of a serious accident or a crime.'

Young, while unused to persons abruptly commandeering his vehicle and servant, was nevertheless beginning to get the measure of Holmes. He nodded to the driver. 'Do as he says.'

I climbed into the carriage, and the driver obediently crossed the bridge to the open space where it could be turned about and then drove me back to Waltham Abbey as fast as it was safe to go. On the way, I wondered if Gorrie's body was under the water, clutching his bag, his bowed legs tangled in some tree roots. On reflection this seemed unlikely. I had seen no signs of any gases of decomposition rising to the surface, no shadow in the unmistakable shape of a corpse. I was taken to the police station and the carriage waited while I went in to make my report.

I encountered the same helpful desk sergeant as before and quickly explained that the man we were hoping to locate had still not reappeared, but we thought we had found his carpetbag in the millstream. We were naturally concerned that he might have come to some harm. The sergeant lost no time in summoning Inspector Tubb, a bustling kind of man in his forties, who agreed to accompany me, together with one of the younger constables, leaving the sergeant in charge of the station.

Young's manservant took his carriage home, while Inspector Tubb and I rode out to the mill in the police vehicle and conversed on the way. The market town of Waltham Abbey is not, as one might guess, a hotbed of serious crime. The police are kept busy enough with cases of drunken and disorderly conduct, pedlars vending their wares without a permit, persons allowing horses to stray, and all the usual varieties of petty theft. Tubb told me that he had just returned to the station that morning after interviewing a resident in possession of a dangerous dog for which he had no license. The inspector was naturally interested in what had brought me and Holmes to Waltham Abbey, and I decided to tell him about our commission from Mr Ineson, and that we were lodging at the New Inn. This led me to explain that Holmes was a consultant to Scotland Yard, and I was a junior surgeon at Barts who assisted him. Tubb absorbed this information thoughtfully.

'And you say that the bag has been left where it was?'

'Yes, Holmes prevented any interference with it.'

'Sensible man. Anyone else would have pulled it out, opened it, and left any useful evidence scattered about in confusion before they even thought of notifying the police.'

We arrived to find that Mr Young had summoned Jenkins, who had arrived at the waterside carrying a long pole with a useful-looking hook at one end. This well-worn implement was clearly what he employed for clearing debris from the waterwheel and the mill race. Tubb and the constable spent some time viewing the tangle of sodden material where it lay.

Finally, Tubb gave orders for Jenkins to retrieve the bag. Jenkins's experienced hands quickly released the bag from its nest of reeds, then he passed the hook through the handles, and drew it to the pathway. There was now no doubt at all that we were looking at a large carpetbag. Baumann stared at it. 'I think it is Gorrie's,' he said.

CHAPTER SIX

Inspector Tubb decided to remove operations from the roadside in case of passing traffic. He ordered the constable to remain at the waterside to see if there was any sign of Gorrie at the place where the bag had been found, and report to him at once if he discovered anything. He asked for a board to be fetched from the mill. Jenkins quickly obliged, and the waterlogged bag was laid upon it for carrying, much like a stretcher, that operation being achieved by Tubb and Jenkins. As we followed them, I told Holmes that I had informed the inspector of our mission for Mr Ineson and revealed that he was a consultant for Scotland Yard. As I did so, I feared that Holmes would think I had spoken too freely, but he simply nodded. I saw that he had no objection to his fame spreading to Essex.

At the mill, Jenkins went to fetch a packing case from the storeroom, which he placed on the pathway in front of the building. The board was then laid on top of it for ease of inspection, as if its burden had been a corpse. 'Good man,' said Tubb, 'I would be obliged if you could go and give the constable a hand.' Jenkins returned to the waterside without complaint.

'Before we open the bag,' said Tubb, 'tell me, gentlemen, are any of you familiar with the contents?' None of us were. Wet leaves and broken reeds were still clinging to the material of the bag. Tubb cleaned away the debris with a large and none too clean handkerchief, revealing a brass lock plate with a keyhole. On trying to open the bag, he found it securely closed and locked. 'I expect the key must be with Mr Gorrie,' he said. 'I'm afraid it will have to be forced.'

'Not necessarily,' said Holmes, taking a slender roll of cloth from his pocket. 'If I might be permitted to assist?'

'Please do,' said Tubb, eyeing the cloth roll with a curious glance, although I could tell that he suspected what was within.

Holmes carefully examined the lock through his magnifying glass before he attempted to open it. He then unrolled the cloth, revealing a set of delicate tools, and proceeded in his task with rather more confidence and expertise than might be expected of the average solicitor's clerk. Young and Baumann could only look on in astonishment.

I recalled when Holmes had first begun to acquire the skills of lock-picking during one of our adventures. Lacking tools, he had then been obliged to employ medical implements for strength and delicacy. The neat set of lock-picks, ones which no self-respecting burglar should be without, was a recent acquisition, and he had obviously been practising.

Holmes selected a suitable pick and introduced it into the lock. Mr Young turned his gaze to me, his expression a mixture of fascination and alarm. The fact that I regarded what Holmes was doing with perfect equanimity did not offer him any comfort.

It was not long before a slight click announced the success of Holmes's efforts and Tubb came forward and opened the bag. The contents, which he removed carefully and laid out on the board, were mainly sodden clothing, not folded but tumbled into the bag like so much tangled laundry. Gorrie had not been noted for his grooming, so I was unsurprised not to find the kind of combs and brushes many men often carried. There was just a razor and a small tin containing a piece of watery soap. Once these items had been removed, a packet remained at the bottom of the bag. It had been well wrapped in oilcloth, giving the contents several layers of protection. Tubb carefully eased back the wrappings and was pleased to find the contents undamaged. They consisted of a large leather-bound notebook and a document holder containing some newspaper cuttings folded into a bundle.

'How interesting,' said Holmes, as Tubb leafed through the notebook.

'Can you make anything of it?' asked Tubb.

'What do you think, Dr Baumann?' said Holmes. 'Do take a look.'

Baumann stared at the pages, which were a cluster of diagrams and mathematical calculations. 'I wouldn't like to say,' he said. He made no effort to touch the book or study it closely.

Tubb unfolded the cuttings and gave them a cursory look. 'These all come from American newspapers. They are reports about a man called Keely,' he said. 'I'll look into that New York address you gave us and see if I can learn more about him.'

'When we first missed Gorrie, I cabled my New York office to see if they could find out anything about that address,' said Young. 'They replied this morning. It's just a lodging house. Gorrie lived there alone in a two-room apartment.'

'The items in oil cloth have been very carefully protected before they were placed in the bag,' said Holmes, 'but everything else has been roughly tumbled in.'

'Which suggests that he left the mill in something of a hurry,' said Tubb. 'That would explain why he left the hidden money behind. Of course, this doesn't help us find him, but I fear that if the bag is in the water then so is he. I don't think he was attacked. A thief would surely have forced the lock, rifled through the bag, stolen whatever he thought worth keeping, then thrown the bag away. The fact that it is still locked means it is more likely that Gorrie met with an accident.'

'If a thief tried to force the lock, might he have thrown the bag away when he could not open it?' asked Young.

Holmes shook his head. 'There is no sign of any attempt on the lock,' he said.

'I'll take your word for that,' said Tubb. 'I'll get these things to the station and see about sending some constables to search the river for a body.'

'Do you think the place where the bag was found is where it fell in?' I asked.

'We are fortunate that the handles were tangled around some reeds, which prevented it from sinking out of sight,' said Holmes. 'Due to the weight of the contents, and the fact that the carpeting would quickly have become saturated with water, I think it cannot have been borne along by the current very far. If Gorrie is to be found, he might be further downstream. I suggest, Inspector, that Mr Jenkins who knows the waterways well, would be of valuable assistance to your search.'

'I agree,' said Tubb.

'And I would be obliged if you permitted me to examine the contents of the bag, in particular the notebook and newspaper cuttings,' added Holmes. 'They might throw some light on what motivated Mr Gorrie to leave the project.'

'Very well,' said Tubb. 'Call at the station this afternoon and ask for Constable West and he'll let you see it all, once we have listed what is there.'

Inspector Tubb headed back to town, promising an early return with a search party, and requesting Mr Young to make Jenkins available. Young was left contemplating the future of Baumann Motors. 'I do not wish to cancel the directors' meeting this afternoon,' he said. 'I shall advise them that it seems that Mr Gorrie may have suffered an accident, and we intend to engage another mechanic to work with Dr Baumann as soon as possible.' He turned to Baumann. 'Doctor, I must rely upon you to select the best candidate for your work.'

Baumann nodded agreement but looked extremely uncomfortable at the prospect. While Young was representing Gorrie's absence to the company directors as an event which should not arouse suspicion, it was clear that he was simply trying to prevent unease. I could not help wondering how much money the investors had placed into the business, which appeared to be on the road to collapse almost as soon as it had begun.

That afternoon, after sending a telegram to Mr Ineson, Holmes and I went to the police station, where the items found in the carpetbag had been stored and were made available for our inspection. Constable West informed us that Inspector Tubb and his fellow constables, as well as a number of volunteers, were busy searching the millstream for Mr Gorrie.

The clothing told us very little. They were of American manufacture, and such as a workman might have worn. All had been pushed roughly into the carpetbag, whether clean or soiled, with no attempt made to separate them, and careless of how creased they might be on unpacking. The apron worn by Gorrie in the workshop had been similarly treated. Holmes opened it out and searched the pocket on the front. It contained a number of simple tools, but the small notebook in which Gorrie had scribbled his record of readings during the demonstration was missing. Holmes searched every pocket in the clothing and the interior of the bag thoroughly, but it was not there.

The large leather-bound notebook which had been wrapped in oilcloth revealed several pages of scribbled calculations, and diagrams which appeared to show the apparatus we had viewed in the workshop. Disappointingly, there was no indication as to how the motor might operate, merely the dimensions of the construction, and notes of the type and weight of materials used. 'We still have no clues as to how the motor actually works,' I said. 'Do you think Dr Baumann knows?'

'I doubt it,' said Holmes. 'If Gorrie made any record of it, it might have been in the small notebook he kept on his person. It is not amongst the contents of the bag.'

'In that case, it was probably the most valuable thing he owned,' I said. 'He might have hidden it or passed it to someone for safekeeping.'

Holmes did not reply, but I could see he was concerned.

The press cuttings were of some interest. They came from New York papers and covered the last four years. All were on the subject of inventor Mr John E. W. Keely and his motor, which had been advertised as available for viewing on application to his workshop in Philadelphia. Several articles had described his demonstrations with great enthusiasm about the promised benefits to mankind. Other commentators were less kind.

In academic circles there had been furious debates. Two respected New York academics, Drs Nachtnebel and Klamm, had openly attacked each other in terms which suggested that old grievances and rivalries were boiling to the surface. The Keely motor appeared to be merely the most recent vehicle for their enmity. Nachtnebel, the more established man, maintained that Keely was an unrecognised genius, who had made an important discovery. Klamm, a recent appointment, asserted that the supposed inventor was a charlatan, and

Nachtnebel a victim of delusion bordering on insanity, who ought to resign his post. Questions had been asked by university management about the advisability of retaining Nachtnebel in his lectureship position because of his unorthodox beliefs, which did not meet with general approval. It was no surprise when his tenure was not renewed. A correspondent hinted that Klamm had been active in ousting him.

Meanwhile, the directors of the Keely Motor Company who had funded the ongoing work in the hope that a patentable machine would be provided, were becoming restless. Several of them had supported Keely financially since he first sought subscribers in 1872, and these were especially vociferous. They were openly demanding that even if Keely could not perfect the machine without delay, he should at least tell them the principle on which it worked. Their fear was that if he died before completing the motor, the secret would die with him. There had even been mutterings about taking out an injunction to force him to reveal his secrets to the directors.

Keely had repeatedly pleaded for more time, as there was always one more adjustment to be made, one more test to achieve perfection, but it was thought that he had had quite sufficient time and money already. By the spring of 1878, many of his supporters had deserted him, and were refusing to supply more funds. The company's work had ground to a halt and attempts to serve legal papers on Keely had failed, as the workshop was padlocked, and the man himself was nowhere to be found.

The behaviour of dead bodies in water is a fascinating subject which all medical men must study closely in case they are ever required to attend a scene at a river, lake or canal, where remains have been found, and then perform the post-mortem examination. My previous experience in Holmes's cases had led me to undertake further research in that area. I therefore felt well-equipped to discover what had happened to Mr Gorrie should his body be found, as Inspector Tubb anticipated. A corpse, even if unclothed, with air no longer in the lungs, is denser than water, and will soon sink into the depths, characteristically face down, with limbs dangling. If it does not become entangled in some obstruction, a current may carry it unseen far from the place of entry. Over time, the gases produced by decomposition will bring an unsnared corpse to the surface, and the warmer the weather, the more quickly this will occur. If Gorrie was in the water, and the weather remained fine, I knew we did not have long to wait.

Holmes and I returned to London and made a full report to Mr Ineson. His only comment was that the Baumann Motors company had been threatened with failure rather sooner than he had expected. He had been told by Mrs Beauregard that the directors' meeting at which Mr Young had revealed the possibility of an accident to Mr Gorrie had been fraught with anxiety and suspicion. Some of the investors, especially Mr Murray, who was short-tempered at the best of times, had announced that he was familiar with the warning signs of a company headed for an early demise, which included increasingly desperate efforts to keep it alive. Mr Young had eventually been able to soothe unrest with assurances that he would do everything in his power to minimise delays and would keep all investors informed of progress. Ineson had strongly advised Mrs Beauregard not to make any further investments to save the project, but held out no hope of her taking his advice.

I was able to pay a brief visit to St Bartholomew's Hospital to inspect the accommodation provided for junior surgeons and receive a schedule of work and a list of study papers. I had two weeks of supposed leisure before I took up my post, but idleness was not an option. I had new medical reading to pursue, and a mystery to solve. I began packing my effects prior to moving from my lodgings, but the next morning a telegram summoned Holmes and me back to Waltham Abbey.

Remains believed to be those of the missing mechanic had been discovered by a passing carrier, floating in the millstream about a mile downstream from Abbey Mill. The body had been taken to a nearby boathouse. A local practitioner who often assisted the police in drowning cases, Dr Henderson, had been appointed to make the examination and I was told that he would be happy for me to attend and assist. I decided not to ask for permission for Holmes to be there. I knew he would come with or without it.

Inspector Tubb arranged for the police trap to take us to the riverside location where Gorrie's corpse lay. I was pleased to see that Henderson, a young Scotsman with a brisk manner, who immediately assumed seniority, had come well equipped with all that was required. He had already ordered a coffin to be brought so the remains could be transported to the local cemetery once we had completed our work. The humble but conveniently arranged interior of the boathouse provided us with ample room for the procedure, and there was sufficient light and ventilation. Gorrie's body was laid out as decently as possible, and a workbench acted as a table for instruments and specimen jars.

Holmes and I had no hesitation in identifying the deceased as Edward Gorrie. His features, though bloated, were still recognisable, and his clothing was the same he had worn when we had seen him in the workshop at the mill. The shape of the legs confirmed identification. External abrasions on his hands were what one might expect on a body that had scraped along the shallows of a stream and encountered hard, uneven surfaces along the way. Dr Henderson had already been informed of the approximate last time the man had been seen alive, and on viewing the extent of decomposition, we both concluded that Gorrie had most probably died less than half a day after he was last seen. We hoped that further tests would allow a better estimate.

As we worked, Inspector Tubb was content merely to observe. Holmes took charge of the clothing as each item was removed, laying them out neatly on the bench and searching the pockets, arranging his findings on display. 'This is a man who liked to carry with him whatever small objects he would most find useful,' said Holmes. 'A cloth for cleaning his hands — there are traces of what appears to be machine oil on it — a box of matches, some of the smaller tools of his trade, a purse of coins and a stub of candle.'

Holmes examined the candle stub through his glass. 'The wick is sunk into the wax,' he said, 'this has not been lit recently. I would say that this is good for a few minutes' illumination but no more. Did he really set out to walk to town without anything better to light the way? In his place I would have taken the lantern with a new candle from the cottage and then handed it in at the railway station to be called for.'

'Might he have had one of those pocket lanterns?' asked Tubb. 'If he was robbed, a thief would have taken it.'

'But not the purse or tools?' said Holmes.

Tubb understood his point and grunted. 'Is there a carpetbag key?'

'No. I would have expected to find it on his person. And there was a small notebook he used to record readings taken during demonstrations. That is missing, too.'

'I suppose they might have fallen out of his pocket,' said Tubb. 'We won't find them now.'

Holmes examined Gorrie's boots, but the waters of the stream had washed away any traces of soil that might suggest where Gorrie had last stood. 'Candle wax,' said Holmes, suddenly. 'Not from the one in his pocket, which is undamaged. It looks as if he must have stood on one while it was still warm and some of the wax is impressed into one of the ridges of the sole.' He used a scalpel to ease out the sample of wax. 'Aha!' he exclaimed. 'There is some soil clinging to the underside, which may assist us.' He secured the material in a sample jar and labelled it.

I helped Henderson turn the body over, and that was when we saw the injury to the back of the head, a shallow depression in the skull, from which any blood or useful debris had long washed away.

'I think we have at the very least a contribution to the cause of death,' said Henderson, 'if not the primary cause. I often see injuries in drowning cases, where the head has struck a stone, but not like this. It is too regular in form.'

Holmes and Tubb came to watch as we moved aside the thin grey hair to fully expose the injury. The shape was familiar to us both. 'Clearly not a stone,' said Henderson.

'No,' I said, 'more like a bar, maybe some sort of club or iron pipe. Regular in diameter.' I made a careful probe of the area, under Henderson's keen but approving gaze. 'No splinters, so hardwood or metal.' We took a sample of the hair, in the hope that we might discover a weapon with blood and hair clinging to it so we could make a comparison.

'Would it have been a fatal blow?' asked Tubb.

'Not instantaneously,' said Henderson, 'but it would certainly have been enough to stun him. He might have been struck while standing on the path and then fell in the water, unconscious, and drowned. It will be hard to tell if he entered the water alive or dead, as he has been submerged long enough for water to seep into the stomach and lungs.'

'Either way, the man has been murdered,' said Tubb. 'He did not come by a blow like that by accident. He was attacked from behind.'

'There is a button missing from the shirt,' said Holmes. 'The third one down. The top two were usually left undone. The edges of the fabric above the third button are more worn than below. There is some thread remaining.' He made an intent examination using his glass. 'The button appears to have been torn off.'

'Which suggests a struggle,' said Tubb. 'Or the killer might have dragged the body into the water, grasping it by the shirt.'

'Was anything found alongside the stream to show where he entered the water?' asked Henderson.

'Nothing that we have found so far,' said Tubb.

'When you searched for the body, did you see anything that might have served as a weapon?' asked Holmes.

'No, whatever it was, the killer might have taken it away with him or thrown it in the water. There could be blood on his clothes,' said Tubb. 'I think he saw Gorrie alone on the road, carrying the carpetbag, and decided to rob him. Maybe he tried to open the bag and when he saw it was locked, he gave up and threw it in the river.'

Holmes shook his head. 'Even without tools he could have used a stone to break the lock. Why didn't he?'

'Perhaps he was disturbed and didn't want to be seen with it,' said Tubb. 'We might find a witness.'

'Have there been other similar crimes in this area?' I asked.

'Not recently,' said Tubb. 'In fact, I don't believe there's been a murder round here in living memory.' He shook his head. 'No, I think we should look for someone passing through, or new to the area. I'll make some enquiries. There's a pedlar who has been causing some trouble. I'll ask him a few questions. And we will have a further search for the weapon in case it's been thrown into the stream. I'll gather a team of constables.'

I could see that Tubb was feeling the burden of investigating the type of violent crime that was out of his experience. 'We will remain here to assist you in any way we can,' said Holmes.

The post-mortem continued with an examination of the heart, lungs and stomach, and the collection of organic samples. The stomach contents were of particular interest as there were identifiable undigested remains of Gorrie's supper. Dr Henderson said that he would examine all the material at his surgery, in anticipation of giving evidence at the inquest.

'Time of death, if possible?' asked Tubb, hopefully, as we washed our hands.

'Based on the stomach contents I would say most likely within an hour or two of his last meal,' said Henderson. 'That's as much as I can say for now.'

The coffin had by now arrived on a wagon, and we supervised arrangements for the body to be removed for burial.

'I had better inform Scotland Yard,' said Tubb.

'When you do, please mention my name,' said Holmes.

'You're a dark horse, Mr Holmes,' said Tubb. 'I shall certainly do so. But first, I had better go and see Mr Young and Dr Baumann and tell them that Mr Gorrie is deceased. The cause of death is not yet officially determined. I shall inform them only that the body was found in the river, and an inquest is to follow. Let's see what they have to say.'

The police trap took us up to Abbey Mill, where Tubb told Mr Young that Mr Gorrie's remains had been found in the millstream. Young sighed deeply, but the news was not unexpected. 'I feared that would be the result when the bag was found,' he said. 'Do you know if it was the result of an attack or simply an unfortunate accident?' he added plaintively.

'I can't say for now,' said Tubb. 'There is still much work to be done, and there will be an inquest which may provide answers.'

Young asked no further questions, and I sensed that his main concern was the loss of a mechanic and not how his death had occurred. 'I had better go and tell Dr Baumann,' he said, rising from his seat.

We accompanied him, all three of us interested to see Baumann's reaction to the news. He was not in the workshop but in a little kitchen where the staff of the factory could boil water for beverages and sit at a table to eat a cold luncheon. Baumann sat with a steaming mug before him, exuding a fragrance which suggested an addition of brandy. He looked up as we entered, and his face fell. 'It's not good news, is it?' he said.

'I am sorry,' said Tubb. 'Mr Gorrie's body was found in the millstream this morning. I can't say any more for now as there will be an inquest.'

Baumann uttered a little groan and took a gulp of his drink.

'Perhaps you can suggest where he might have been going, and what his purpose was? Was he on business for your company, or something else? Did he have personal reasons?'

'I had not sent him on any business,' said Baumann. 'He told me nothing of his intentions.'

'Had he quarrelled with anyone?' Tubb continued. 'Do you think he might have been going to seek other employment, or meet with someone? Did he have any family or associates that you know of?'

Baumann shook his head. 'I don't know. I really can't help you. I wish I could.'

He took a little flask from his pocket and charged his mug with more of its contents. We left him to his misery.

Before the day was out, we received a message from Inspector Tubb that Scotland Yard would be sending a man to arrive the following morning and assume charge of the enquiry. He was a recently promoted inspector by the name of Lestrade.

CHAPTER SEVEN

The next morning Inspector Tubb, Holmes and I were at Waltham Cross railway station to welcome the newly minted Inspector Lestrade. 'I volunteered to make the visit here, as soon as I knew you gentlemen were looking into the case,' he said, greeting us with a broad smile. 'When you take an interest, Mr Holmes, there is always something curious to find.'

'I am beginning to discover that for myself,' said Tubb, drily.

'The whole business is very peculiar,' said Holmes. He and Tubb proceeded to brief Lestrade on what we had discovered so far.

'I should like you to show me the places where the body and the bag were found,' said Lestrade. 'And I will speak to Mr Jenkins about the stream and its currents. We might be able to confirm where they entered the water.'

We used the police vehicle, alighting at the relevant places along the way to follow the banks of the stream on foot, pointing out locations of interest. Lestrade made careful observations, recording them in his notebook. 'Dry weather, unfortunately,' he said. 'Have you been able to discover anything new about Gorrie?'

'I am afraid not,' said Tubb. 'Dr Baumann who employed him can offer no information at all.'

Lestrade grunted. 'Well, we have sent a cablegram to the New York police to see if anything can be learned about him at the address you told us about.'

We reached the mill, where I thought we would go in and see Mr Young and Dr Baumann, but Holmes had another suggestion to make. 'Although the body and the bag were both found downstream, and it seems likely that Gorrie left his cottage and walked south towards Waltham Cross station, I would like to continue our survey upstream. He might have walked north towards Cheshunt, intending to take a train from there.'

Tubb nodded. 'Cheshunt police have confirmed that he was not seen there.'

'It is also possible,' Holmes continued, 'that he walked north by mistake, and encountered the signpost. It isn't far, so there might still have been enough light to read it by. If he had, he would have turned back. In either case, he might have gone into the water further upstream from the mill. At any rate, I wish to eliminate that as a possibility.'

'Of course,' said Lestrade, and we walked on.

The noise of the rushing waters over the weir could be heard long before we saw it. The cascade was more intense and determined than the comparatively lazy progress of the stream. The millstream itself was broader at that point, and one part of it, the part nearest to the bank along which we walked, was diverted from the weir and passed through a sluice gate. It flowed briskly into another channel, the one known as the head race that brought waterpower to the wheel. The sluice gate was a simple rustic affair, but no less effective for that. It controlled the flow of the water with a thick slab of hardwood set in a frame, the whole held between a stone wall on the bankside and the side of the weir on the other. This gate could be raised and lowered by a vertical pole operated by a crossways bar that could be turned on a screw, the metal components being painted bright green. A short way along the head race we saw a screen positioned across its flow. It was composed of what looked like a portion of galvanised fencing, and was there to capture any debris that might interfere with the operation of the mill wheel. Just before the screen, there was a short side channel, what Jenkins had called the 'fish pass' so any fish or river fowl that had been swept through the sluice gate could avoid being captured by the screen and return to the stream.

The old signpost stood by the side of the road, one arm pointing downstream to Waltham Cross and Waltham Abbey, the other upstream to Cheshunt. The lettering, which had been picked out in black paint, was clearly legible.

'You said, Mr Holmes, that although Gorrie most likely left his cottage after seven o'clock, which was near enough sunset, he didn't take a lantern with hm,' said Lestrade.

'It was found back at the cottage,' said Holmes. 'A small candle end was found in his pocket, but the wick was sunk into the wax. It had not been lit recently.'

'There was a good moon early on that night,' said Tubb. 'He might have thought he could see the path when he set out, but then, if he went the wrong way and turned back, it made him later than expected. It was darker, and of course he was a stranger to the place.'

Holmes was studying the ground at the bankside.

'I don't think you'll be lucky with any footprints,' said Tubb.

'No,' said Holmes, 'but there is something of interest here.' He knelt down. 'Look.'

We all joined him. Squashed into the dry earth was about three inches of candle, one end of which was cracked, and the other crushed flat.

'Now where did that come from?' said Lestrade.

'It might have been here for some days,' said Holmes. 'When I examined Mr Gorrie's boots I found candle wax on one sole. I will remove this for study.' No-one protested as he dug the item out of the ground with his penknife, taking care to preserve its damaged shape, together with a sample of the surrounding soil, and placed the whole into an envelope. He stood up. I saw his eyes carefully survey the area, and then he stepped off the bank and onto the stone wall by the sluice gate, walking with the balanced assurance of a gymnast. There he paused. 'I will need to know when Mr Jenkins last had occasion to adjust the height of the sluice gate,' he said.

'I can ask him that,' said Lestrade, looking puzzled.

'Come and see,' said Holmes.

Lestrade stepped onto the wall and shuffled along, a little awkwardly. 'What have you seen?'

'I have been told that it has not rained in the last week,' said Holmes, 'so any debris on the upper portion of the sluice gate will not have been washed away. Look at the turning handle. Do you see it?'

We all stared. There on the crossbar of the turning handle, at the end nearest the bank, was what looked like some wisps of grey hair attached by a smear of dried blood.

'Oh my word!' said Lestrade.

Holmes took some forceps from his pocket and leaned over to retrieve the material and place it in an envelope. 'I must convey this to Dr Henderson without delay,' he said. 'He may be able to determine the presence of blood and compare the hair to the samples he took from Mr Gorrie's head wound. If I am correct, we have found the bar which made the indentation to the skull.'

'Then it might have been an accident after all,' said Lestrade. 'He might have been standing on the bank and fallen backwards.'

'He was about the same height as Stamford, here,' said Holmes. 'I think we must make some measurements, but in my estimation, a simple fall would not have brought his head to that position.'

For a moment I worried that Holmes might ask me to demonstrate, but to my relief he did not.

'You mean he was pushed?' said Lestrade.

'I fear so.' Holmes pulled a coil of string from his pocket and, handing me one end to hold, he stepped back onto the wall and drew out the other end to the location where a small mark showed where the injury had occurred. Once satisfied with the tautness of the string he fashioned a knot to show the distance from a man standing on the bank. 'I think there was a struggle on the riverbank,' he said. 'I thought as much when I saw the missing button. It suggested that he had been grasped by the shirt. If Gorrie was stunned by the blow to the head, perhaps he recovered enough in the water to try and swim and was swept into the fish pass and carried downstream. It's a narrow channel but the waters run fast, and Gorrie was not a large man.'

'And the thief took the carpetbag,' I said. 'We still don't know where he threw it in.'

'What about that candle?' asked Lestrade. 'It can't have been Gorrie's as he already had one in his pocket. It might have fallen out of the attacker's pocket during the struggle.'

'I believe it has a tale to tell us,' said Holmes. 'An interesting one. Not everything here is as it seems.'

'I think,' said Lestrade, 'it might be to our advantage if you enlightened us.'

Holmes smiled. 'We have been discussing the theory that Gorrie, having decided to end his connections with the Baumann project, and leave the area, encountered a stranger who attempted to steal his bag. But there might be something more sinister involved. He might have been in company with or chanced to encounter someone he knew. If he revealed his intention to leave, that could have led to a quarrel. That would also fit the evidence we have observed here. Not a robber who struck him from behind, or an accidental fall, but a struggle with someone he was facing and standing near, who lost his temper, seized him by the shirt, perhaps to shake him, and then pushed him hard enough to propel him into the water.'

'That is certainly a possibility,' said Tubb reflectively.

'Gorrie's size and build, his bowed legs and unusual gait, suggest to me that he was not as secure on his feet as most men,' Holmes continued. 'Anyone, including a woman, especially an angry one, could have the strength to push him hard enough to unbalance him.'

'I cannot dispute that,' said Tubb. 'So, who amongst those who knew Gorrie might have quarrelled with him? I think I ought to be asking some questions, if only to eliminate suspects.'

'If he was intending to leave the project, which would have delayed the work and created more expense, then anyone with a financial interest in it would have been most unhappy,' said Lestrade. 'Perhaps someone tried to remonstrate with him and make him change his mind. Dr Baumann and Mr Young were directors of the company. They'll have to be interviewed first. But I'll get a full list of shareholders and how much they stood to lose.'

Lestrade decided to walk down to the mill, to question Young, Baumann and Jenkins. Our way lay several miles to the south, to Dr Henderson's surgery in Sewardstone Street, Waltham Abbey. Inspector Tubb took Holmes and me in the police trap, promising to send it back for Lestrade when we were done. The little envelope with its sample of blood and hair was in Holmes's pocket. I looked at him enquiringly, and he smiled. 'It is not the whole answer,' he said, 'but it is a fragment of the picture which will reveal all.'

Holmes was pleased to see that Dr Henderson's practice included a useful little laboratory with all the equipment and materials required for the most common tests a medical man might have to conduct. As I looked about me, I was inspired to think of a time when I would have a flourishing practice of my own, and my mind was filled with ideas of how it might be furnished, and the array of chemicals and instruments it would contain. Then I thought of the expense involved in appointing such a place and realised that such felicity lay far in the future.

Inspector Tubb stayed to watch our examination of the specimens with close attention, making notes of our findings and observations.

The first sample we showed Henderson was the hair and what appeared to be dried blood found on the handle of the sluice gate. We proceeded to make a comparison under a microscope with the hair taken from the wound on Gorrie's head. There was no significant difference between the two. Naturally it was impossible to declare the hair samples to be identical, no test could do that, but they were, as far as we could judge, alike in colour, length and thickness.

Given the nature of the material clinging to the matted hair on the sluice handle, there was a fair assumption from its appearance that it was blood, but nevertheless we conducted the usual tests and received the expected confirmation. Henderson said that he would now be able to tell the inquest that there was good evidence to suggest that Gorrie's injury had come about from striking his head on the metal bar. Whether this was an accident or the result of violence from another individual, he was unable to say. Either was possible, but given the distance of the impact from the riverbank, which he ascertained by measuring the knotted string, his opinion tended towards a violent projection from another individual.

Holmes showed him the crushed candle and under a good light we were able to observe the ridge marks of a boot sole. 'It looks like the sole of Gorrie's boot,' I said, 'although there may be many just like it.'

'True,' said Holmes, 'but observe the pattern of the crushing of the candle. Note how at one end, and this is the end where there are marks about the base, showing it has been in a candle holder at one time, the candle is merely cracked. At the far end the wax is very much flatter.' I wasn't sure what he deduced from this, and he did not enlighten me.

There were more samples to examine, and Holmes and Henderson took their time over them, pausing occasionally to confer. There was the soil which had been collected together with the crushed candle, the scrapings of wax from the sole of Gorrie's boots, and the material Holmes had collected from the interior of Gorrie's lantern. Holmes said nothing when his work was complete. When he enters that period when he has a great many facts to assemble, he will not speak until he has a complete picture, and it is pointless to interrupt him.

'May I make a note of your conclusions?' asked Tubb hopefully.

'I have conclusions, about which there is little doubt, but further work is required to confirm them. Dr Henderson is making those enquiries which will leave me in no doubts whatsoever. It will not take long, and then I will place all before you.'

And with that Inspector Tubb and I had to be content.

*

The inquest on Gorrie opened the following morning before Mr Lewis, the coroner for West Essex, at the cemetery lodge in Waltham Abbey, but a verdict was not yet asked for. There was just a formal identification of the body followed by an adjournment for three days to enable Dr Henderson to complete his report.

Holmes and I had received a note to meet with Lestrade, and he and Tubb joined us in the inspector's office at Sun Street station. Lestrade now had the full list of the directors and shareholders in Baumann Motors Ltd. In addition to Dr Baumann and Mr Young, the most important individuals were Mrs Beauregard, and Mr Herbert Murray, the husband of Mrs Beauregard's timid friend. The firms of Green and Co., investment brokers, and Jamison and Co., manufacturer of agricultural machinery, whose representatives we had also met at the demonstration, were substantial investors. Reverend Woodley had also ventured some funds. Several other individuals, including Mr Young's secretary, Norris, and a number of local businessmen and private residents, whom we had not formerly met, had subscribed for more modest amounts. None of the men who laboured at the mill had purchased any interest.

Lestrade had been busy interviewing the investors, starting with those who had most to lose, asking them to provide details of their whereabouts on the night Gorrie had last been seen.

'So far,' he said, 'the only person who has caused us any difficulty is Dr Baumann. Mr Young was at home with his wife that evening. Mrs Beauregard was at her home in Broxbourne, as confirmed by her servants, Mr Green and Mr Jamison were dining with families or friends, and Mr Murray was on a business trip to Paris. Baumann usually dines with the Youngs, but he had not done so that evening as he said he was meeting with some potential investors, whose names he thought it best not to reveal. I understand that many businessmen ask not to be named before they have actually signed the relevant papers. That is not usually a cause for concern. Now, however, I was obliged to point out to Dr Baumann that as a man was dead it was his duty to tell the truth. He was extremely unhelpful. He said that he knew nothing of Gorrie's death and whatever he might say regarding his location and companions that evening would not assist my investigation. He remained adamant that he had not harmed Mr Gorrie and had no reason to do so. I will continue to press him for details.'

'Do you notice a name missing from the list of subscribers to Baumann Motors?' asked Holmes.

This at least was apparent to me. 'Professor Novak,' I said. 'He showed a considerable interest at the demonstration but has not yet come forward in support.'

'Yes. He is staying at a hotel in London. Mr Young recommended I interview him the next time he is here,' said Lestrade.

'I should like to speak to him again,' said Holmes. 'He might have useful observations.' He looked at his watch. 'Young will be at the mill by now. Let us go there. I suggest we call on Mrs Young on the way. She might not have a direct interest in the motor, but its failure might have serious consequences for her family.' Lestrade and Tubb remained in town to continue their enquiries while Holmes and I went to see Mrs Young.

At the house in Sun Street, Mrs Young was taking tea with Mrs Murray, and they were discussing future works of the Essex and Hertfordshire Ladies' Philanthropic Society. Both were kind enough to speak to us about the night of Gorrie's disappearance.

'The inspector has already spoken to John, and all the servants,' said Mrs Young, with a soft smile. 'He is quite satisfied that we were here and had no warning or idea of what was about to happen.'

'My husband was in Paris on business,' volunteered Mrs Murray. 'He did not return until the Friday.'

'Inspector Lestrade has been interviewing everyone with a financial interest in Baumann Motors Ltd,' said Holmes. 'Was the Ladies' Philanthropic Society interested?'

Mrs Young smiled. 'No, we do not make investments of that nature. We collect donations for the poor and hold an annual bazaar to raise funds for the orphans.'

'But Professor Novak, despite his obvious interest and eagerness to see the project succeed, has not yet invested,' Holmes observed.

'He is more interested in principle than profit. And as a scientist he knows that experiments can fail time and time again before the one that finally meets with success. The path to innovation can be full of unexpected obstacles, setbacks which may result in delay and expense. Mr Gorrie's sudden absence is an example. When his bag was found we all feared that he had fallen into the stream and drowned, and now we have just heard the terrible news. Professor Novak has, however, volunteered his help to try and save the project. He will consult with Dr Baumann regarding his special requirements for a mechanic and will then make enquiries at colleges and universities to see if there is a trustworthy man with suitable experience to take over Mr Gorrie's position.'

'Professor Novak resides in London?'

'Yes, at a hotel. The Devonshire, in Liverpool Street. I have already told the inspector. The professor has been very busy, meeting with university gentlemen, and attending lectures. He comes up here for demonstrations of the motor and investors' meetings.'

'Has Professor Novak been told of Mr Gorrie's death?'

'I am not sure. I think he is coming to the mill for a meeting this afternoon about the new mechanic. Are you going up to see my husband? If so, I'll ask Saunders to take you there.'

'I think Professor Novak shows commendable restraint,' I said to Holmes as we rode up to the mill in Mr Young's carriage. 'He wants the motor to succeed but does not risk his own funds until he is more certain. And he is far better placed than the other investors to judge whether it will work as promised.'

At Abbey Mill we once again found Mr Young in his office.

'Is Dr Baumann here?' asked Holmes.

'No,' he replied wearily. 'I am not sure where he is. Drowning his sorrows somewhere I suspect. That Scotland Yard inspector interviewed him yesterday. The business of Baumann Motors will have to be suspended for the time being. I have notified the directors and will meet with them soon.'

'Baumann must have a key to the workshop?'

'He did have one, but after the inspector had finished with him, he returned it to me. I have it in the safe now. Then he went away. His effects are still at my house so I am sure he can't have gone far.'

'He has not revealed to you where he was at the time it is believed Mr Gorrie met his death?'

'No. Since the man likes a drink, I am guessing he might have been at a tavern. There are several in Sun Street.' He sighed. 'The man's interests have become apparent to me.'

'I take it you do not believe he was interviewing potential investors at the time of Gorrie's disappearance?'

'I hardly know what to think anymore.'

'Would you permit me to examine the apparatus in the workshop?'

Young looked shocked. 'For what purpose?'

'To learn more about it, and better judge the man who constructed it.'

Young considered the request but only briefly, then shook his head. 'I cannot permit it,' he said. 'Both Baumann and Gorrie were adamant that no-one else should be admitted apart from when the appointed demonstrations were held. The motor has not been patented, so its secrets are as yet unprotected. And they dare not risk unsupervised persons tampering with the machinery out of simple curiosity. It could set back years of work and might result in an action for damages.'

Holmes recognised an obstruction he was as yet unable to remove. Dissatisfied, we made our way back to town.

'What can we do now?' I asked Holmes.

'I do not intend to make a tour of the watering places of Waltham Abbey in the search for Dr Baumann,' said Holmes. 'Since his effects are at Mr Young's house he may reappear there in time. I am still waiting to hear from Dr Henderson. His reply may change things.'

'Can Lestrade not demand to see the workshop?' I asked.

'He can only override Mr Young if there is an emergency or evidence of a crime. I shall send a telegram to Mr Ineson to advise him of the present position and await any instructions. Later I shall go and see if Dr Baumann has made an appearance at Mr Young's house.'

That evening after a reflective supper we paid a call on Mr Young and found him and his wife in company with Professor Novak, all of whom were in poor spirits.

'Yes, Dr Baumann did return here for dinner,' said Young, 'but Inspector Lestrade has him now. He is at the police station being held for questioning. They think he murdered Mr Gorrie.'

CHAPTER EIGHT

The next morning Holmes received a message from Dr Henderson. It was handed to him at the breakfast table and caused quite a stir amongst the other residents at the inn as he crowed with delight.

'And now I have confirmation!' he exclaimed. He rose from the table in such excitement that he almost abandoned his breakfast, pausing only to thrust some bacon between two slices of bread to eat as he walked. I knew better than to demand an immediate explanation and kept him company on his way to the police station.

Lestrade had not long arrived, and was also looking pleased with himself, having news of his own to communicate. He asked for Tubb to be summoned at once to a meeting. This was not, as it transpired, difficult as Tubb and his family occupied living quarters on the station premises.

We gathered in Inspector Tubb's office, over generous supplies of coffee and buns.

Holmes, in triumphant mode, could hardly remain still, and paced about the office, chewing on an unlit briar, which seemed to help his thought processes. Lestrade sensibly decided to allow him to speak first. 'I can now put before you all my thoughts on the question of the death of Mr Gorrie,' Holmes announced. 'Firstly, I do not believe that Gorrie was actually intending to leave Abbey Mill that night. His intention, when he left his cottage, was to conduct a meeting with an individual to whom he wished to express his concerns about the future of the Baumann Motor.'

'What were these concerns?' asked Tubb.

'The time required to complete the work, I am sure of that, but possibly even the feasibility of the entire project. I may know more in time, but at present I can only speculate with the information already in my possession. Mr Gorrie had recently told Mr Young that in his opinion the motor was a long way from completion, and he thought that Dr Baumann's confidence was unwise and misleading to the investors. He might even have feared that the principle on which the motor was constructed was flawed. But this alone was surely insufficient to make him take any unusual action. He was, after all, merely an employee, presumably in receipt of a wage, without any personal responsibility. If the project failed, he would simply be obliged to seek another position. So, why was the meeting to be held in secret in the semi-darkness?'

Tubb nodded. 'That is suspicious, I agree.'

'The signpost by the weir was a good location,' Holmes continued. 'It was only five minutes' walk from the mill, without passing the other cottages on the way, and the sounds of water cascading over the weir would prevent anyone who approached the spot overhearing the conversation from a distance. I can only conclude that what Gorrie had to impart was some information which was only in his possession. Facts which, had they been revealed, would have had serious consequences, quite probably threatening the entire project. The result would have been a collapse of the company, a substantial loss of funds for the investors, and damage to several reputations. There might even have been criminal charges.'

'Do you know who he met?' asked Tubb.

'It would not have been with Dr Baumann — at least not him alone,' said Holmes. 'Had Gorrie and Dr Baumann wished to converse with each other secretly there was ample opportunity for them to do so behind the closed doors of the workshop. If Dr Baumann was there then another individual, whom I cannot yet say, must have been involved.'

'But if he was not intending to go away that night, why did he pack his bag in such a hurry and carry it with him?' asked Lestrade.

'He didn't,' said Holmes. 'The only thing he carried with him was the lantern he brought from the cottage, with a lit candle.'

'But wasn't the lantern still in the cottage?'

'It was when I searched there.'

Lestrade scratched his head. 'Did someone find it and return it?'

'It was returned, yes.'

'And the candle — are you suggesting that it was the same candle we found by the weir?'

'It was. The marks on the base of the candle where the wax was merely cracked, showed that it had been in a holder. And the fact that the other end was crushed showed that the wax there was softened. It was a burning candle. It had not fallen from a pocket, as was suggested, but from the lantern.'

'And that happened during a struggle?' asked Lestrade.

'I think so,' said Holmes. 'At the meeting, on the path by the sluice gate, Gorrie revealed what he had to say. The result sadly was an altercation which became violent. He dropped the lantern on the path. The catch is old, the gate came open, and the candle fell out and was extinguished, trodden into the earth during the scuffle.'

Lestrade nodded. 'And how did Gorrie fall?'

'There must have been an angry push. His balance was poor, as we have seen. He fell backwards onto the sluice gate, striking his head on the handle. He might have tried to save himself, but we don't know how good a swimmer he was, or how conscious he was at that point. He probably drowned quite quickly, and his body was borne downstream.'

'But the bag — how do you explain that?' asked Tubb.

'His killer had not expected what happened, and hoping that the body would not be found, or at least not for some time, he decided to make it seem that Gorrie had gone away. This was not, as we know, an unlikely event, given the doubts that he had already expressed to Mr Young. The killer picked up the lantern, not perhaps noticing that the candle had gone. He — I am assuming it was a man, but that is not certain — took the lantern back to Gorrie's cottage. If the candle was missed, it was probably too dark to go back and look for it. And a dropped candle would not have been thought especially incriminating. Gorrie's carpetbag and its key were in the cottage. The killer must have lit a candle to look about him. That was the light seen by Phillips later on, a candle in its holder moving about. Not carried by Gorrie, as Phillips assumed, but by Gorrie's killer. The killer gathered up Gorrie's clothes and other effects and pushed them into the carpetbag. This already had the wrapped papers lying at the bottom, but in the dim light, he might not have noticed them. He locked the bag and threw it and the key into the stream. He could also have taken the little notebook. It might hold Gorrie's secrets. Something he could sell, or if too incriminating, destroy. He did not, of course, know about the money hidden under the mattress or the workshop key under the pillow. By now there was only moonlight, and it was growing darker. If he knew the path, it might have been possible for him to walk back to wherever he lodged, and not be seen, or at least, recognised.'

'Can you explain how you came to your conclusions, Mr Holmes?' asked Lestrade. 'I mean, it's all very well, but you know what judges and juries are like. They want to see proof.'

Holmes smiled. 'When I first examined the lantern, I noticed there were splashes of candle wax inside which suggested it had been dropped, and there was also dried soil in the hinges and base. I took a sample of the material. The candle found near the sluice gate suggested to me that it had fallen from the lantern. I collected some of the soil there and asked Dr Henderson to compare both samples. What we saw under the microscope encouraged us to believe that we might be able to conclude that the soil in the lantern came from near the sluice gate. You recall that the sluice gate was painted green to protect the metal components from rust. The paint looked quite fresh. Dr Henderson has spoken to Jenkins who confirmed that the gate was recently repainted. He still has some of the paint in his toolshed. The soil in the immediate vicinity of the sluice gate contains small flecks of green paint. The soil in the lantern and on the candle also has those flecks. I later sent Henderson a sample of soil taken from the path nearer the mill. That has no paint at all.'

'Was it the same paint?' queried Tubb. 'Could you even tell?'

'I suspected as much, but as Lestrade said, courts like to see proof. Dr Henderson has provided confirmation by consulting an expert friend of his. He contacted the manufacturers of the paint, who agreed to carry out their own tests. I had a message this morning. Given time I would have been able to do the work myself, of course. The manufacturers are prepared to certify that the samples found near the sluice gate, on Gorrie's boot, and in the lantern are of their paint.'

'And the name of the killer?' demanded Lestrade. 'Come now, Holmes, you must have a suspect!'

'That is harder,' said Holmes. 'Especially if he has cleaned his boots. If not, there might be traces of candle wax and soil with flecks of green paint.'

'But — here's a question,' said Tubb. 'If your theory is correct, Mr Holmes, and the killer went to Gorrie's cottage, how did they know which cottage was Gorrie's? He wouldn't have knocked on each door asking after him, or we would have been told that. The investors who came to the demonstrations — I can't imagine they knew or cared to ask where the mechanic was lodging. Who did know? Could someone have guessed?'

Lestrade nodded. 'That is a good point. Mr Young and his secretary, Norris, would have known, but they were both in Waltham Abbey at the time of Gorrie's death. The workmen occupying the other cottages would have known, but I can't see that any of them had a reason to quarrel with Gorrie. None of them had any interest in the motor. I can interview them again, of course.'

'Which leaves us with Dr Baumann,' said Tubb, 'who most definitely knew, and is currently here, in a cell, contemplating his future.'

'Is he still refusing to speak?' I asked.

'I am afraid so,' said Tubb.

'Well, I have some information to share,' said Lestrade. 'You said just now, Mr Holmes, that the fact that Gorrie and his killer met in secret away from the mill did not necessarily absolve Baumann from suspicion. Baumann is the principal man behind the motor; he worked with Gorrie and knew where Gorrie was staying. He has no alibi for the probable time of death and is undoubtedly concealing something.'

'I agree' said Tubb.

'Well, the Yard has followed up on Gorrie's address in New York. The police there have confirmed it is a lodging house, and Gorrie left the address several weeks ago. They have interviewed some acquaintances of his, who have said that he was very interested in the motor invented by Mr Keely. That fact is borne out from the newspaper cuttings found in his bag. It seems that Gorrie had decided that he wanted to work for Keely. He told friends that he was going to Philadelphia to see Keely and offer his services. Now whether he did so or not, we can't at present say. And it appears that Mr Keely — who is in dispute with the directors of his company over lack of progress — is not available for interview.'

Lestrade sat back with a satisfied smile which suggested that he had reached a conclusion.

'You think Baumann is your man?' asked Tubb.

'He is, and I propose to have a talk with him. Mr Holmes, Mr Stamford, you may join us if you wish.'

I though Tubb might protest at our presence, but on a quick assurance from Lestrade, consented, and we made our way to the cells to confront the suspect.

'I am glad we still have him,' said Tubb. 'I thought it best to hold him for the time being in case he fled. But if we find nothing to charge him with soon, we will have to release him.'

'We may have to apply for more time,' said Lestrade, 'especially as some of the information we require may be in America.'

Before we reached the cells, we heard a strident voice coming from the direction of the public desk that was all too familiar. We went to investigate. There, standing immovably in front of the desk, and engaging the duty sergeant with a torrent of demands, was Mrs Beauregard. The sergeant, who was a little pink about the ears but using all his experience of dealing with difficult lawbreakers and outraged residents in order to remain calm, looked up as we approached. 'Inspector —' he began.

'That's all right,' said Tubb, with a dismissive wave of the hand. He approached the irate visitor. 'Now then, Mrs Beauregard, what can I do for you?'

She turned on him and if this mysterious etheric force really did exist, it was certainly glinting in her eyes. 'Ah, there you are! What is this I hear about you questioning Dr Baumann? Don't deny it; Mr Young told me he has been here since last night! To speak plainly, Inspector, I insist that you release him at once. An innocent man, a man of science and vision who will confer unimaginable benefits to society, should not be imprisoned without charge!'

'Ah, well,' said Tubb, blandly, 'I am afraid there are one or two things we need to sort out before we can release him. Such as where and in whose company he was on the evening that Mr Gorrie was killed, and why he refuses to tell us. He didn't dine with the Youngs, we know that much. And you have already told us he did not dine with you. But perhaps you know where he was? If you do, I would be most grateful if you could let us know.'

I did wonder for a moment if the lady's infatuation might lead her to give Dr Baumann a false alibi, but she did not. Instead, Mrs Beauregard assumed a posture and expression of dignified respectability. 'I assure you, Inspector, I do not. As you know, I dined alone at my home that evening and then spent some hours at my writing desk. I am preparing a pamphlet about the motor. I understand that Dr Baumann was at a meeting with new investors; at least that is what I have been told. It is all I can tell you.'

'Well, as soon as he tells us the truth and we are satisfied he had nothing to do with Mr Gorrie's death, he will go free,' said Tubb. 'This is a serious case, and Inspector Lestrade has come from Scotland Yard to speak to Dr Baumann. If you have any influence over Dr Baumann, you might use it to urge him to do the right thing.'

'I have every confidence that he will,' said Mrs Beauregard. 'I have summoned Mr Ineson, the senior partner of Ineson and Randall, my London solicitors, to represent him, and I expect him to be here without delay. He will be sure to do what is necessary.'

Unable to resist a smirk of triumph, she sat down on a bench facing the desk and appeared to have every intention of remaining there until Mr Ineson arrived.

Inspector Tubb decided to let her remain there and asked the sergeant to send a constable for the cell keys.

We were taken to see the prisoner, who was in a small but clean cell. The newly built station certainly had amenities that London stations would have envied. There were rented lodgings in the capital which were far worse places to reside in than the free and secure custodial accommodation at Waltham Abbey. As the door was unlocked, we found Dr Baumann sitting despondently on the edge of a low bed. He was no longer in possession of a cravat or shoelaces. He looked up, hoping perhaps for a friendly face, or even an announcement that he could go, but his shoulders slumped in despair as he saw the constable usher in the four of us.

Lestrade took the lead. 'Dr Baumann, I am Inspector Lestrade of Scotland Yard, and I have come to look into the death of Mr Gorrie.'

Busman sighed wearily. 'I have already said, over and over again, that I know nothing of that,' he said.

'Before we begin,' said Holmes, 'I would like to examine Dr Baumann's boots.'

Lestrade ordered Baumann to remove his boots. The prisoner looked surprised, but complied, and passed them to

Holmes. My friend took some trouble turning them over in his hands, examining the soles very closely with his magnifying glass. 'Do you have any others?' he asked.

'I travel light; my only other footwear is a pair of indoor slippers. They are at Mr Young's house where I have been staying.'

'When were these boots last cleaned?'

'Er — yesterday. Mr Young's servant who cleans his boots does mine also.' Holmes handed back the boots.

'Anything?' asked Lestrade.

Holmes shook his head.

Lestrade addressed the prisoner in friendly fashion. 'I only wish, Dr Baumann, that you would tell us where you were and in what company on the evening of Mr Gorrie's death, and we could settle that point straight away,' he said. 'You were absent from Mr Young's house for a number of hours, and he tells me that you did not appear to be especially inebriated on your return, so I am quite sure that wherever you were you were fully competent to know your location and recall your movements.'

Baumann was silent.

'You see it is my experience,' Lestrade continued, 'that when I question a suspect, even if a man is not guilty of the crime I am investigating, he may well be guilty of another he is unwilling to admit to.'

Baumann shook his head. 'That is not the case here.'

'No?'

'No. I can say no more.'

'Very well, we will leave that point for the moment,' said Lestrade, 'but I can promise you we will continue to return to it until I have received a satisfactory reply. I have a few simple questions for you, which you ought to be able to answer.'

Baumann still appeared nervous.

Lestrade opened his notebook and poised a pencil over a clean page. 'First of all, I would like to know your date of birth, where you were born, and where you were educated.'

'Is that important?'

'It could be. I have been told you claim to be Swiss. Is that so?'

Baumann gulped and nodded.

It was then that Holmes spoke, addressing Baumann in fluent German.

'What did you just say?' asked Tubb.

'Perhaps Dr Baumann can translate,' said Holmes.

Dr Baumann clearly could not.

'I advised Dr Baumann that I was quite certain that he was not Swiss,' said Holmes. 'His boots are of American manufacture, and I believe the man wearing them is also American.'

'And we know that Mr Gorrie was American, so, Dr Baumann, I suspect that your story about meeting him in England was a lie,' said Lestrade.

Baumann said nothing.

'I think you met in America,' Lestrade continued, 'where Gorrie offered to work for you. Philadelphia to be precise.'

'I have never been to Philadelphia,' said Baumann, in astonishment.

'No? But that was where Gorrie told his friends he was going. He went to meet Mr Keely, the inventor.'

'Yes, he told me he had gone there.' Baumann sighed, and all traces of a continental accent vanished. 'All right, I admit it, I am American. I thought it would improve my chances of acquiring investors if I told people I was Swiss. Gorrie said he had met with Keely and offered to work for him, but was rebuffed. Keely would not allow any other man to work on his motor.'

'I don't believe that is true,' said Lestrade. 'I think that Gorrie and Keely struck up a business arrangement. Keely was in trouble, the directors of his company were withdrawing their support, refusing to supply more funds for his work. They were demanding to know his secrets. There was even talk of an injunction. It suited Keely to disappear and start up somewhere else, under another name. Admit it Dr Baumann, you are John Ernst Worrell Keely!'

Baumann's expression of incredulity told me what I needed to know, but before anyone could say more, there was a rap on the door and a constable peered in. 'Excuse me, but there is a gentleman just arrived, a Mr Ineson. He says he is Dr Baumann's solicitor.'

'Very well, admit him,' said Tubb, reluctantly.

Mr Ineson appeared, looking brisk and official. 'I have come to speak to my client,' he said. 'If I might be permitted to see him in private?'

'Of course,' said Tubb, nodding at us. We filed out, leaving Ineson alone with Baumann. The door was very firmly shut.

'And now,' said Mrs Beauregard, who had been lurking in wait, the fire of victory in her eyes, 'we shall see some sanity applied!'

Tubb did not respond, but motioned Lestrade, Holmes and me in the direction of the offices, and we were soon assembled once more in the inspector's room.

'Permit me to offer an observation,' said Holmes.

'Of course,' said Lestrade.

'I suggest that Scotland Yard contact the authorities in Philadelphia and ask for a description of Mr Keely. His age, stature, build, and any distinguishing marks. And whether or not he is or has ever been a married man.'

Lestrade nodded and made some notes. 'I will do so, and that should settle the matter.'

'But I have to say,' Holmes continued, 'that Dr Baumann, whoever he might be, cannot be Mr Keely.'

'But if you have never seen that gentleman, how can you be so certain?' asked Tubb.

'What do we know about Mr Keely?' asked Holmes. 'Very little, I fear, but that little may be enough. He is American and a mechanical engineer. When I examined the body of the unfortunate Mr Gorrie, I saw the very obvious signs of his daily work on his hands. Now take a look at Dr Baumann's hands. He has never claimed to be a mechanic, and had he said so I would have disbelieved him. His hands are unmarked by a mechanic's work. I do not think he has ever laboured with his hands. The only other things we know about Dr Baumann is that he is — or has been — married, as the mark of the wedding ring is on his finger, and he is not, as he had claimed, Swiss.'

'Then who is he?' asked Tubb. 'And why is he promoting this motor? Is he a businessman who has invested in it?'

'I have my suspicions,' said Holmes. 'I only hope Mr Ineson can persuade him to speak.'

And that was when the idea struck me. The only man we knew for certain to be a mechanic was the late Mr Gorrie. I almost blurted out that perhaps Mr Gorrie would prove to be the elusive Mr Keely, but on further thought, I decided to say nothing. Even if my inspiration proved to be correct, I knew that Holmes would always claim it as his own.

Lestrade spent a few moments giving Holmes's words some consideration, then he said, 'I had best send a cablegram. I will be back shortly.' He hurried away.

'How much longer can Dr Baumann be held here?' I asked.

'I think that depends on whether anything new can be found to establish a case against him,' said Tubb. 'Two days in total if we have nothing to charge him with.'

Soon after Lestrade returned from his mission, Mr Ineson emerged from the cell. 'I have questioned my client very thoroughly,' he said. 'While he is not very forthcoming about his origins, he assures me that he has committed no crime of any kind. And I believe you have no evidence to suggest that he has. If a man wishes to change his name and start a new life in another country, he is perfectly at liberty to do so. If he works to patent an invention that he believes will benefit the world, that is not against the law. If he has no alibi for the time a crime was committed, that is not proof that he committed it. You must release him forthwith.'

Tubb grunted.

'I have not yet completed my enquiries into Dr Baumann,' said Lestrade. 'I am expecting to receive a cablegram with further information. I cannot approve his release at present.'

Ineson nodded. 'You have another twenty-four hours before I make an application to secure his release,' he said. 'I will return if required.'

He turned to Holmes. 'Twenty-four hours, Mr Holmes.'

I saw that Holmes understood his meaning.

Ineson went to speak to Mrs Beauregard.

'All we can do now is wait,' said Lestrade.

Tubb nodded. 'I will try and see if I can persuade him to say anything that might assist us. Are you remaining in Waltham Abbey, Inspector?'

'I am,' said Lestrade. 'Scotland Yard will contact me here. And then we will see. What are your plans, Mr Holmes? I am sure you have them.'

'Tomorrow morning I will return to the mill,' said Holmes. 'It is high time that the Baumann motor's mysteries were unlocked.'

CHAPTER NINE

The next morning, Lestrade secured the Waltham Abbey police vehicle to take us to the mill.

'What do you intend to do?' I asked Holmes, a little nervously. I had seen the determined expression on his face before and it usually meant he was about to engage in hazardous behaviour.

'My intention, as it has been for some time, is to obtain entry to Dr Baumann's workshop and examine the motor,' said Holmes.

I glanced at Lestrade, who gave a little cough. 'If you don't mind my saying so, Mr Holmes, I appreciate that your methods may be a little unorthodox sometimes, and while the results are often quite useful to the police, your proposal does concern me. At present I am not sure I have grounds to obtain a warrant to gain admission to the workshop.'

'My first step,' said Holmes, 'will be to make a close examination of the area outside the building, for which neither permission nor acts of burglary will be required. We will then take a view on what further action is possible.'

Lestrade looked relieved. I saw Holmes's long fingers play over the weighted head of his walking cane, which was for him far more than a gentleman's fashionable accoutrement. It served him both as a weapon and a tool, for sounding and prodding when investigating locations. I hoped it was the latter use he anticipated.

Arriving at Abbey Mill, all appeared peaceable, with the steady creaking of the great wheel and the grind of industry. A carriage emblazoned with Mr Herbert Murray's initials was waiting outside with a groom in attendance, and two smaller vehicles were also there. The directors of Baumann Motors Ltd hoping for reassurance, or at the very least information, had arrived well in time for another meeting. I wondered what story Young was planning to tell them to soothe any anxieties about the future of the company. Mr Green, leaning against the wall beside the entrance, was in deep conference with Mr Jamison, who was pacing back and forth in an agitated manner. They looked up as we approached, exchanged a few words, and hurried indoors.

'The workshop is the last room at the rear of the building on the right-hand side,' said Holmes. 'Let us proceed.'

We walked around the side of the mill, encountering the hardwood water chute. As we stood by the rear wall, the busy waters passed at a level well above our heads. 'The penstock,' Holmes explained to the inspector, 'brings water from the channel that is diverted from the millstream, the one you have seen flowing through the sluice gate. It carries the flow to the waterwheel, which causes it to turn.'

'What is your interest in this?' asked Lestrade.

'Its possibilities,' replied Holmes. 'Is Jenkins about? I am rather hoping he will supply us with a ladder.'

I took this as an order, and went to find Jenkins, discovering him at the back of his cottage tending his small vegetable patch. 'Jenkins, I hope you can bring us a ladder, Mr Holmes wants to take a look at the penstock.'

'Oh yes?' said Jenkins. 'Is there something the matter with it?'

'I'm not sure,' I said.

'I've got a small ladder in the shed, that should be enough.' He went to the back door of his cottage, leaning his spade against the wall, and called inside. 'Maggie, I'm just going out for a while.' A quavering voice came from within, followed by racking coughs.

'Your sister sounds unwell,' I said. 'How long has she had that cough?'

'Oh, a good few days now. Hardly gets a wink of sleep. I give her warm drinks, but it doesn't help much.' He went to open up the toolshed, and I followed him.

'I don't know if you know, Mr Jenkins, but I am a surgeon. I would be happy to take a look at your sister and see if she needs anything.'

He looked dubious. 'Oh, I'm not sure about that.'

I recognised at once the probable reason for the hesitation. 'I wouldn't charge you for the consultation. We are grateful for your help.'

I had obviously identified the difficulty, for his expression brightened. 'Well, if that is the case, yes, I would be much obliged to you.'

'Once you have helped us look at the penstock, I will come back with you and if you agree, I will examine her.'

'That is very kind of you, sir. I do appreciate it.'

Jenkins extracted a ladder from his toolshed, and we brought it back to where Holmes and Lestrade were gazing up at the penstock.

'Is there anything the matter with it?' asked Jenkins. 'It looks right to me. I don't see anything that needs mending.'

'I should be able to tell you soon,' said Holmes, placing the ladder against the wall. 'I am just curious about this section of it, which travels past the last room in the building.' He handed me his cane. 'Pass it to me when I require it,' he said and climbed up the ladder. There was a narrow gap between the penstock and the wall, not enough for a man to put his head through to look, so he stared up at it. Holmes spent some time gazing along the length of the penstock, then he reached out for his cane, which I handed up to him. He let it travel through the gap, then moved it back and forth. We heard it strike metal. The penstock, being quite heavy, was fastened to the wall at intervals on iron brackets but not at that point. 'Have there been any repairs here, Mr Jenkins?' asked Holmes.

'Just there? No. Why, what have you found?'

'I am not sure.' Holmes passed his cane back to me, took a candle end from his pocket, lit it and held it up. 'I see what appears to be two pipes, quite narrow, obviously metal from the sound, and they seem to be hollow, but they have been painted dark like the wood. They travel from the penstock and appear to pass through the wall.'

'You mean there is a water flow going through the wall?' I asked.

'Just so.'

'Into the workshop?'

'Precisely.'

'But surely we would have seen these pipes when we were in the workshop?'

'Not if they were hidden by the framed drawing that hung on the wall. Mr Jenkins, I take it you know nothing about this?'

'Nothing at all, sir.'

Holmes blew out the candle and climbed down. 'Best leave the ladder there for the time being. Mr Young should be invited to take a look. He might have an explanation. I had better go and see him.'

'If you don't mind, I have to see Mr Jenkins's sister on a medical matter,' I said. 'I will join you as soon as I can.'

Poor Miss Jenkins, who appeared to have aged several years since I last saw her, was in a bad way. What had begun as a cough had taken a hold within her frail body and was in danger of advancing to pneumonia. My instinct was that she ought to be removed to an infirmary for nursing care. I said so and offered to ask Mr Young if he could make the arrangements. He seemed like a considerate employer, and I hoped he would be willing to help. In the meantime, I advised nourishing drinks and propping the patient up on pillows to help her breathe more easily.

Mr Jenkins thanked me. He asked me what I thought her outcome would be, and I did my best to be truthful while offering some hope. He nodded as I spoke. I think he already feared that due to her age and condition her life was in danger if she could not improve.

I was about the take my leave when he said, 'Mr Stamford, I've been thinking about that night Mr Gorrie went missing, when I saw him coming out of the workshop just after six o' clock.'

'Have you remembered anything?' I asked hopefully. 'Did you see him again after that?'

'No, but there was a man on the path outside the next morning. Of course, he could just have been a passer-by. But I don't often see anyone about so early. Not a man walking alone.'

'Early?'

'Yes, it was around first light. I woke because I heard Maggie asking for a drink of water and I got out of bed and went to her. I heard a noise outside, footsteps. Wouldn't have heard them if I had been asleep. I looked out of the window, and there was a man walking down the path.'

'Which way was he going?'

'Downstream, towards the bridge. I didn't see where he came from.'

'Can you describe him?'

'Just a man, in a coat and hat. I only saw him from the back. Not enough light to see much more.'

'But it wasn't Gorrie?'

'Oh no, I'd have known him by the walk.'

'Might it have been someone you have seen before?'

He mused for a while. 'I don't think I have.'

'Well, what I would advise, Mr Jenkins, is for you to think about it, and try to recall as much as you can, perhaps how tall the man was, whether he was thin or stout, that sort of thing. Holmes has gone to see Mr Young about the penstock, but once he has done, I will ask him to come and talk to you. Would you be happy to speak to him?'

'Oh, yes, I would.'

'And I will do all I can to help your sister, I promise.'

Jenkins stayed by his sister's side to look after her and I returned to the mill. I found Holmes and Lestrade in the waiting area outside Mr Young's office. The meeting of the directors and subscribers of Baumann Motors was in progress and was not to be disturbed. I described what Jenkins had told me, and Holmes agreed that he would go and talk to him as soon as he could.

At length the office door opened, and Mr Norris emerged holding his notebook. 'Gentlemen,' he said, 'would you like to come in?'

We entered the room, which was already somewhat crowded. Mr Young was seated behind his desk and there were a number of attendees, most of whom we already knew — Mr Green and Mr Jamison, Reverend Woodley and Professor Novak. There were three other gentlemen: the director of a market garden, a corn merchant, and Mr Herbert Murray, a stern-looking man with a red face and dark grey whiskers.

'Is Mrs Beauregard not here?' asked Holmes.

'She has an important meeting with Mr Ineson,' said Young. He did not need to elaborate.

Norris introduced Inspector Lestrade of Scotland Yard and also gave out our names to the men we had not previously met, saying we were from the solicitors Ineson and Randall.

Young looked weary and strained but gathered his strength. 'How may I help you, Inspector?'

'I have been asking some questions of Dr Baumann in the hopes of learning more about Mr Gorrie,' said Lestrade. 'I am still awaiting further information before I can permit him to return here. However, there were some issues I wish to ask you about, and if you don't mind it will have to be done soon, and in private.'

'Very well,' said Young with a sigh. He addressed the members of the meeting. 'Gentlemen, if you would be so kind as to withdraw. This should not take long. Norris, could you go and see where Jenkins is, and ask if he can take our visitors on a tour of the factory? I am sure you would all like to see how a waterwheel when supplemented by steam power can be a benefit to industry. Mr Jenkins knows all its history and secrets and can show how easily it can be made to run smoothly.'

The visitors obligingly withdrew and were conducted away by Norris.

Holmes, Lestrade and I took the seats before Mr Young.

'I have discovered,' said Holmes, 'that there are two metal pipes which appear to be channelling water between the penstock and the workshop where the Baumann Motor is located. Are you aware of this?'

Young looked mystified. 'I — no, but surely Jenkins will know about it. '

'I have shown him the pipes and he knows nothing about them.'

'Oh. Well, Dr Baumann ought to be able to advise you.'

'I have not yet had the opportunity to question him on the subject,' said Holmes. 'But it would be interesting to know what explanation he can come up with. He has claimed that any power created in the workshop is generated only by his motor. But we can clearly see that there is another potential source of power — water. From the very flow that powers the watermill.'

'Do you know that the water flows *in*?' asked Young. 'Perhaps the power the motor generates flows *out*.'

'Then why the secrecy?' asked Holmes. 'The metal pipes have been concealed and painted so they cannot be seen against the wood of the penstock unless one examines them closely. During the demonstrations Baumann has failed to mention their existence. Those facts alone must arouse suspicion.'

'I am at loss to explain it,' said Young. 'Perhaps we could ask Professor Novak for his opinion?'

'I would prefer at this stage not to involve anyone with an interest either financial or scientific in the Baumann motor,' said Holmes. 'I ask you because you have custody of the keys, and I wish to ask politely for your permission to enter the workshop and examine its contents. If all is well, then we need not inform the investors at all. And if one of them happens to notice anything out of the ordinary in future, then we will have the explanation to hand.'

'But Dr Baumann —'

'I believe that his fate and that of the company may hang upon what we discover,' said Holmes, stonily.

'The thing is,' said Lestrade, as Mr Young battled with his dilemma, 'since I suspect that something may be happening in that room which is against the law, I am empowered to obtain a warrant to enter it. That may take a day or so, of course. Why not let us in now, and we can settle the question without any more delay? If, however, you oblige me to apply for a warrant, I shall have to insist that while we wait, the room is kept locked and the door guarded by a constable.'

Young looked horrified at this prospect. He rose to his feet and took a key from the safe. 'Let us go,' he said.

Mr Young was now a very worried man, but there remained in his eyes a little flicker of hope that our proceeding would put an end to all doubts and enquiries. Before we entered the workshop, we invited him to take a look at the penstock and the hidden pipes, so he might understand the nature of our concerns. He had no suggestions to offer as to the purpose of that arrangement, about which he assured us he knew nothing. Returning indoors, he unlocked the workshop, and we followed him in. Within, all was as it had been before. Lestrade stood quietly for a few moments, looking about him. 'So where is this wonderful motor that can power whole factories?' he asked.

Holmes lifted the cloth from the apparatus. 'This, Inspector, is the Baumann motor.'

Lestrade stared. 'It's very small,' he said.

Holmes smiled and handed his cane to Lestrade. 'Before we examine it, Inspector, kindly use this to tap upon the pipes we saw outside so we may be in no doubt as to the place of entry.'

'Right you are, Mr Holmes,' said Lestrade. He took the cane and left us, Mr Young glancing after him, as if he had never before seen a Scotland Yard inspector do the bidding of a junior clerk without question.

'These pipes — they may not be pipes at all,' said Young hopefully. 'They may just be supports, and quite solid inside.'

'That will soon become clear,' said Holmes. While we waited, he lit the lanterns. Soon we heard a metallic tapping sound. It was coming from a section of wall directly behind the framed drawing. 'Thank you, Inspector!' Holmes called, and we waited until Lestrade returned to the workshop.

With care, we lifted the drawing away from where it hung on the wall and rested it on the floor against the shelf. Two thin pipes emerged from a small hole in the stonework, and travelled down the wall, disappearing behind the shelf, where they were hidden from view by the canisters stored there. We pulled the canisters aside, and saw the pipes continue their descent until they plunged into the flooring.

The floor of the workshop was composed of small stone slabs. Holmes took his penknife from his pocket and knelt down. 'This floor was laid a good many years ago,' he said, tapping the mortar between the slabs with the tip of the blade. 'But look here — some of the mortar is lighter in colour, and — yes, you can see where my knife has left an impression — these slabs have been lifted and re-laid quite recently.'

'Do you think the pipes run underneath the floor?' I asked.

'I think so, although I do not plan to lift the slabs at present. We may however follow the path of the more recent mortar to see where the trail leads.' Lestrade and I watched in fascination as Holmes followed the new mortar. Young also watched the proceeding apprehensively.

The trail ended at the base of one of the stout wooden legs of the table which held the various sections of the Baumann motor. Holmes got to his feet. He walked about the table, tapping the other supports with his cane. He nodded. 'These are plain wood,' he said, 'but this one, where the pipes end, sounds different. I think the pipes are encased in it, concealed by it.' He fetched a lantern and crouched down, looking under the tabletop. 'Yes, here they are, they come out of the support and lead across the underside of the table. Then they go up through it and —' he peered over the tabletop so his eyes could survey the apparatus — 'they must plunge straight into Dr Baumann's amplifimoderator.'

Holmes stood up. 'Mr Young?'

'Yes?' responded Young with what sounded like a nervous squawk.

'Kindly assist me with an experiment. I would value your observations.'

'Very well.'

'I would like you to examine the contents of the canister which Dr Baumann fills with air and water for his demonstrations.'

Young unscrewed the top of the canister. 'It is empty,' he said. 'Do you want me to put any water in it?'

'No, please leave it empty. I do not wish our demonstration to be affected by any excitement of the etheric force by a combination of air and cold water in the vessel.' Sometimes it is hard to know if Holmes is being serious or not. On this occasion I am sure I detected a note of mockery in his voice, which someone less acquainted with him would not have noticed. Holmes pressed the lever to activate the beam engine as Gorrie had done, then turned the little stopcock which led from the canister to the amplifimoderator. There was no detectable result.

'There,' said Young, 'surely that proves it. There must be both water and air in combination for the motor to work.'

'Indeed,' said Holmes, closing the stopcock. 'Do you agree that with this closed nothing may flow from the canister?'

'It appears so,' said Young.

Holmes cast his eyes over the amplifimoderator. 'When we witnessed the demonstration, we did not see precisely what Mr Gorrie did,' he said. 'All eyes were on Dr Baumann. Before activating the beam engine, Mr Gorrie moved about, appearing to do no more than observe and check that all was well.' Holmes walked about the table, then he made an exclamation and bent down. 'Yes, I see something here, in the base of the amplifimoderator. A little lever. Let us see what it does.'

'I really think you ought not to —' began Mr Young but Holmes took no notice and depressed the lever.

For a moment there was nothing to be seen or heard. Then there was a faint rushing sound, and the brass wheel on the amplifimoderator began to turn, and we heard a low hum. The beam engine came to life.

'How elegant!' said Holmes. 'The lever must open a valve which allows water diverted from the penstock to enter the apparatus. If I was to take it apart —'

'Oh, please do not!' begged Young.

'It may not prove necessary — yet. If I was to explore the interior of this mystery machine, I think I would find a paddle driven by waterpower coming from the penstock, through one of the hidden pipes, supplying the motion to the beam engine. The water then returns through the second pipe to the penstock and passes innocently on its way. Mr Young, we have good reason to believe that the Baumann motor is not a scientific miracle, but a simple and blatant fraud.'

Our host's face suddenly drained of colour. 'You must be mistaken! There must be a reasonable explanation!'

'I fear not,' said Holmes calmly.

'Baumann! I must go and see him at once!'

'That will not be possible as he is in police custody,' said Lestrade, 'and about to be charged with a crime.'

'Mr Young, I beg you to accept the truth,' said Holmes. 'You and your fellow investors are the victims of a clever deception.'

Young tried to make for the door, but his legs shook, and he clutched at the bench for support. I thought he was about to faint and took him by the arm. 'I think,' I said, 'that we should take Mr Young back to his office where he may sit down and take a glass of something strong.'

Holmes and Lestrade agreed, and we took charge of Mr Young. After restoring the room to the way it had been, Holmes locked the workshop door behind us.

We sat Young down at his desk, where he groaned and bent his head, resting his forehead on a folder bulging with company paperwork. I poured a glass of Canadian whisky and pressed it into his hands. He drank it at a gulp, looking none the better or worse for it. 'What have I done?' he said. 'What have I done?'

I saw now that the full extent of his misery and guilt had struck home. In supporting Dr Baumann's motor, he had involved his business, his family, his friends, and his reputation. The fact that his motives were of the highest would earn him little support or sympathy from the investors who had lost their money.

Mr Norris came in to report that the factory tour was underway but hesitated when he saw his employer's obvious distress. 'Sir?'

'Mr Young is feeling unwell and should rest,' I said.

'And I think the directors had better leave once their tour is done,' added Holmes, 'They can be summoned to another meeting in due course.'

'Mr Young, sir?' asked Norris, seeking confirmation.

'Yes,' Young gasped. 'Do as he says.'

'Please don't worry yourself, sir, I will attend to everything necessary,' said Norris. He looked at Holmes. 'Perhaps I ought to fetch a surgeon?'

'I am a surgeon,' I said. I was still not used to saying this, and it felt satisfying every time I did so.

'Very well.' Norris turned back to Young. 'If there is anything you require, sir, please let me know. I will go and speak to the directors now.'

Norris left us. 'I think once Mr Young has rested, he should be taken home,' I said. 'Inspector Lestrade, can you take him? I will suggest a suitable draught Mrs Young can obtain from the chemist. And if she could also send a cough syrup for Miss Jenkins, I would be most obliged.' I started to write a note of what was required.

Lestrade nodded. 'Mr Young, I have no questions for you at the moment, but there will be a serious interview in due course.'

'Baumann and Gorrie!' exclaimed Young. 'They are the villains! They lied to us. I will see Baumann rot in prison!' He was trembling with fury and reached out for the whisky bottle. I permitted him another small glass, then carefully removed the bottle from his reach before he took too much.

'It strikes me that if Baumann was not in on the fraud and he found out about it, that gives him a strong motive to murder Gorrie,' said Lestrade.

I went to assist Young to the waiting vehicle when we suddenly heard a loud cry from the direction of the factory, followed by a general commotion.

'Stop the wheel!' someone shouted. 'Stop the wheel!'

CHAPTER TEN

Before we could discover what had occurred, the foreman come running, his face slick with perspiration and his eyes wide and staring.

'What is it, Phillips?' Young demanded.

'Sir, there's been a terrible accident on the wheel. We've stopped it, but...' He trailed off and shook his head.

'Jenkins is there. Can he do anything?'

'Ah, no, sir, he can't,' said Phillips and drew the back of his hand across his forehead. 'It's Jenkins — he fell.'

'Should the sluice gate be shut down?' asked Holmes.

'We have stopped the wheel from inside, but it's best to be safe and close the gate,' agreed Phillips.

'I'll attend to that,' said Holmes, and dashed away.

'I'm a surgeon,' I said. 'Let me see what can be done.'

'Right you are, sir, but —' the distressed foreman gave a little gasp that was almost a sob — 'I don't think there's much that can be done.'

Norris arrived at a run, his face pale. 'Mr Young, sir,' he exclaimed, then choked on his words.

I glanced at Young, who looked so distraught by the day's events that he was barely able to stand. 'Mr Young is unwell. I think you should stay here with him,' I said to Norris.

'And neither of you should leave the building,' added Lestrade.

Norris, with some relief, nodded agreement. I followed Phillips along the corridor, accompanied by Lestrade. A double door linked the company offices to the factory, which was noticeably quieter than usual. Phillips threw the doors open, revealing the long grinding room with its high ceiling supported by iron pillars. At one end was a heavy door, which, judging by the sounds that issued from it, was the entrance to the engine room and coal store.

There were two rows of heavy benches, with a series of workstations provided with tubs of blunt knife blades and trays to receive the completed items. Here, the men, with shirtsleeves rolled past their elbows, would normally have sat hunched on wooden stools to labour at the grinding wheels, which were driven by thick belts. The machinery rumbled and wheels turned, but the work had fallen still, and the men stood as if frozen. The shareholders and supporters of Baumann Motors Ltd who had attended the meeting and had been enjoying their tour were now huddled in a group by the far wall, shocked and silent.

Halfway along the room, a set of wooden steps led up to a high platform. 'Up there, sir,' said Phillips, pointing. 'That's where we go to see to the wheel and do any repairs when it has stopped. Jenkins used to go up there and take out any weed that had got onto the struts.'

I climbed the steps to the platform where the access doors had been opened for viewing the wheel. I looked down. Inside the wheel, lying on the lower struts, was Jenkins. His skull was broken, neck awry, and his face was a mass of blood and bone. Phillips had accompanied me, but stayed back to avoid looking at the remains. He must already have seen enough.

'Do you know how it happened?' I asked.

'I wasn't up here at the time; I just heard the shout. He was showing the visitors around the factory and then took them up to see the wheel at work. They were all crowded up here.' He looked about him. 'Dawson, you were nearest, did you see what happened?'

A young workman stepped forward. His eyes were bright with tears, and he wiped a rag across his face and steadied himself. 'No, but one of the gentlemen said that someone on the platform felt a bit uneasy, what with it being high up, and then there was some moving about, and then Jenkins —' the boy's lips trembled '— he just fell. He didn't give any warning or cry out. There wasn't anything could be done to save him.'

'Did he stumble or lose his balance?' asked Lestrade.

'Not that I know of, sir.'

'Well, I won't take any chances,' I said. 'The sluice gate must be closed before we can even think about the best way of recovering the body. There'll have to be an inquest.'

'No doubt about that,' said Lestrade. 'I'll need to take statements from all the witnesses.' He turned to address the room. 'I am Inspector Lestrade of Scotland Yard. No-one should leave before I have spoken to them.'

Holmes returned and confirmed that the sluice gate was down, and all was safe. Lestrade, meanwhile, had made a start on gathering information from the witnesses, noting their names and addresses, and promising that they would be informed when they were required to give evidence at the inquest.

Norris came to tell us that Mr Young was so distressed that he thought he should be driven home. He wanted to ask permission from Mr Murray to use his carriage.

'Does he require any medical attention?' I asked.

'No, sir, I think Mrs Young will be able to look after him.'

Lestrade grunted. 'Very well, but as you are a witness you must stay here until I have spoken to you.'

'Since I did not witness the tragedy, I will undertake to deliver Mr Young to his home,' said Holmes. 'I will return as soon as that is done.'

'Please do,' said Lestrade, 'and kindly advise him that he is not to attempt anything foolish like trying to see Dr Baumann.'

'I shall make sure that Mrs Young also knows,' said Holmes. I thought that both he and Mrs Young would have a firmer hand and more persuasive manner with Young than Norris might have exerted.

'And call on Inspector Tubb. He is to send a police surgeon as soon as he can. I'll be along to brief him fully as soon as I have finished here.' Holmes took the note I had made for Mrs Young about medicines and made a swift departure.

'The body should not be touched until the police surgeon has seen it and given permission,' said Lestrade.

'Is there anyone who can look after Miss Jenkins?' I asked. 'I saw her earlier and she is very unwell. She can't look after herself.'

'She has a married niece in Cheshunt,' said Norris. 'A Mrs Cooper. I'll see she is sent for.'

My thoughts inevitably turned to my last conversation with Jenkins and the stranger he had seen on the path the morning after Gorrie's death. We would now never have his further thoughts on the sighting.

While we waited for the surgeon, and Lestrade continued his interviews, I mounted the platform once more. Gazing on the sad remains of Jenkins I wondered how best to recover the body from its awkward location and pondered on how and why he had fallen. Jenkins had many years' experience of looking after the wheel and ensuring its smooth operation. This time, he had merely been showing it to visitors.

'Can I help you with anything, sir?' asked Phillips, who had come up the steps behind me.

'Yes, thank you. Can you tell me if the wheel was in need of repair?'

'No, it was all working well.'

'Was there any debris on it which needed to be cleared away?'

'Not that I know of, but if there had been, Jenkins would have stopped the wheel and used his staff to remove anything.'

'Did he have his staff or any other tools with him during the tour?'

'No, sir.'

There was a mystery on my mind. Somehow, Jenkins had slipped between the struts of the wheel and the hinged containers, plunging into the centre, where his head must have impacted the powerful iron cog. Death had occurred in an instant. I wondered why, if he had simply lost his balance, or been accidentally tumbled from the crowded platform, he had not managed to save himself by gripping a strut. Had he done so, he would have been carried around the outside of the wheel and fallen into the tail race. He could very well have survived such a fall and swum to safety or been rescued.

Holmes returned to the mill having seen Inspector Tubb and reported that Mr Young was now under the care of his wife. He brought the medicine I had ordered for Miss Jenkins. I took it to her and made sure she was comfortable. There would be time enough to tell her of the tragedy, but not yet.

Soon afterwards, Dr Henderson drove up in his little equipage. His surgery was not far from the cemetery, where he had already ordered a coffin for the remains. Lestrade briefed Henderson on what had happened. I said that I had spoken to Jenkins shortly before his death, and he had not appeared to be unwell or under the influence of alcohol. I did think he might have been distracted by worry over the illness of his sister. Henderson promised to call on Miss Jenkins once he had seen the body.

Henderson climbed up to the platform to view the body and eventually gave permission for it to be removed. A robust figure, he was obliged to be content to be merely an onlooker for the actual recovery. Young Dawson, who was a capable-looking lad, said that he had often helped Mr Jenkins when he repaired the wheel, and knew it well. He volunteered to assist me, and Holmes stood by to offer a hand if needed.

To make our way easier, some tools were brought to detach one of the containers from its hinges, leaving a clearer space for access. Together Dawson and I slipped carefully between the struts, which offered good handholds, the exterior of the wheel serving almost like a curved ladder. We worked our way down to the base where poor Jenkins lay. Most of his face had been crushed and some portions of skull had become detached, exposing the brain. Fragments of bone were missing. They must have fallen into the water below and I was not sure if they could be retrieved.

We were able to balance by standing on the lower struts and lifted the body, raising it up to the helping hands reaching down to us. To my great relief, the task was completed without accident, and we clambered safely out of the wheel and onto the platform. Someone had brought a trestle to lay the body on. Most of those present who had not seen the body turned their heads away. The body was carried to an adjacent storeroom where Henderson said he would complete the post-mortem before removing the remains to the cemetery.

Once again Holmes and I assisted Henderson, but the damage to the skull made some of our investigations inconclusive.

'His hands show no sign of fresh injuries, only the usual marks of a workman,' Holmes observed. 'He made no attempt to stop his fall.'

'I was told that he did not carry his tools with him and did no work on the wheel,' I said, 'so his hands were free to try and save himself had he been able to.'

'I believe the man was nearing eighty years of age,' said Henderson. 'He might have suffered a sudden failure in the brain or the heart. It can happen even in a man who otherwise might appear to be in health. If in the brain, we will not be able to determine anything.'

'You think he might have died before he fell?' I asked.

'Yes, that is very possible.'

Henderson took the usual samples, and after arranging for the body to be removed, went to see Miss Jenkins.

We returned to the grinding room, where Lestrade was completing his notes. Holmes mounted the steps to the platform and looked keenly about him. I decided to join him. 'What are you looking for?' I asked.

'I agree that a death of a man Jenkins's age can happen suddenly, but it might be precipitated by exertion or a shock. I wonder, did he see or hear something unusual?'

It was a fine, bright day, the sun was up and the sky clear, and there was a view across woodlands and fields, but we saw nothing that might have unsettled an onlooker.

Holmes descended the steps and had a word with Lestrade. 'Henderson thinks that Jenkins might have suffered a sudden bleed in the brain or a spasm of the heart, which caused him to fall,' he said. 'I can see nothing that might have given him a shock which could have caused the event, but I cannot help but be concerned at a sudden death which took place so soon after a murder and before the deceased could tell us something that might have been of importance.'

*

Lestrade finally permitted all the witnesses to depart. Before Dr Henderson left, he said in a sombre tone that Miss Jenkins should not be told of her brother's death and her niece should be fetched as soon as possible.

Lestrade, Holmes and I took the police vehicle back to Waltham Abbey, leaving foreman Phillips in charge of the factory.

'It is a pity we will never know what Jenkins had to tell us,' I said. I told Lestrade of the stranger on the path and he agreed to make enquiries in the vicinity of the mill to discover if anyone else had seen or could identify the figure.

'Oh, and I have a theory about that motor,' said Lestrade. 'But I shall wait to hear from Philadelphia before I put my case together. Don't worry, Mr Holmes, I won't keep you in the dark much longer.'

Holmes nodded, his expression showing no great curiosity to know Lestrade's theory.

When we arrived at the station no-one objected when Lestrade asked for strong coffee and rolls to be brought from the kitchens. There would be time for brandy later on. We met with Inspector Tubb in his office where Lestrade was about to deliver a full briefing on the current position, when we heard a commotion at the visitors' desk and a loud and insistent voice. A harassed-looking young constable knocked at the door and looked in. 'It's Mrs Beauregard again,' he said. 'She has heard a rumour that Mr Young arrived home early looking upset and she wants to know what is happening. She went to the house, but his wife turned her away, saying he is too unwell for visitors. She also demands to see Dr Baumann. In fact, she insists on his being released. What shall I tell her?'

'Tell her to sit down and wait, and I will speak to her,' said Tubb. 'And no-one except his solicitor is permitted to see

Baumann.' He sighed. 'I want to tell her to go home but I know that won't wash.'

'And this telegram has arrived for you, Inspector Lestrade,' added the constable, handing it over.

'Ah!' said Lestrade, with a broad smile. 'From Scotland Yard. This was what I was expecting.'

The constable left us, bracing himself for another attempt to calm Mrs Beauregard, and Lestrade perused the telegram, which was of some length. 'Excellent!' he announced. 'They have heard from Philadelphia. Keely is described as being about forty years old, medium height and build, no distinguishing features. That is a good fit for Baumann.'

At that moment I was thankful I had not suggested that Gorrie might have been Keely.

'Oh,' said Lestrade, as he read on, his face dropping in disappointment. 'And it seems that two days ago, Mr Keely held a meeting of the directors of Keely Motors, in Philadelphia, assuring them that his motor would be ready in three months, when he would apply for a patent.'

'Then we now know for certain that Baumann is not Keely,' said Holmes, making no attempt to conceal his lack of surprise, 'even if we still do not know who he is.'

'But we can still charge him with fraud,' said Lestrade.

'If I know his kind, he'll claim that he started out with honest intentions,' said Tubb. 'He'll say he only turned to trickery to gain time and funds to make a genuine working machine. I wouldn't believe him, no policeman would, but he might hope a jury will, if he plays it right.'

'I have seen that story tried before,' said Lestrade.

'What was your theory, Lestrade?' asked Holmes. 'You were going to reveal it once you had heard from Philadelphia.'

Lestrade grunted. 'Well, it did rather depend on Baumann being Keeley,' he admitted, 'but you know, I was right in a way. Baumann may not be Keely, but I think he was inspired by Keely's example.'

'I wonder how long he might have been able to continue the imposture,' I said. 'It's a good thing Mrs Beauregard consulted Mr Ineson, who engaged Holmes, or it might have gone on far longer.'

'Every time it looks like they might be found out, these criminals tell another lie, and their victims are fooled again,' said Lestrade. 'If they realise that they are about to be exposed, they clear out the bank accounts and disappear. Then they start up again somewhere else.'

'Yes, we were fortunate to discover Baumann as soon as we did,' said Tubb to Lestrade. Holmes raised an eyebrow but refrained from comment. 'But now his game is done. I will be charging him with fraud and will resist any request for bail. A slippery type like that can't be trusted.'

'We may find that he has committed other frauds in other countries under other names,' said Lestrade. 'He might even have served time in prison.'

'I can believe that,' I said. 'He has a very persuasive manner. I think he could convince anyone of anything and become a completely different person if he chose to.'

'And what about the death of Gorrie?' asked Lestrade. 'Do we think he had a hand in that?'

We all fell silent. Finally, Lestrade capitulated. 'What do you think, Mr Holmes?' he asked.

'It is a possibility,' said Holmes. 'Let us look at the position. Baumann promoted a fraudulent scheme. He is neither a scientist nor a mechanic. He employed Mr Gorrie, a mechanic with an interest in the Keely motor, who would do what he asked. But the association turned sour. And Gorrie knew too many damaging secrets to simply be dismissed.'

'Gorrie was not happy when Baumann promised the investors a motor in six months, and he didn't try to hide his feelings,' I said.

'Young tried to encourage Gorrie by telling him about future demonstrations and potential new investors,' said Holmes. 'But of course that did not help matters, since Gorrie knew that the motor would never be patented.'

'Yes,' said Lestrade, thoughtfully. 'I think I can see what happened. If Gorrie was afraid that the investors would rebel, like they did with Keely, he would have told Baumann he thought their game would soon be up, and they might be arrested. They probably quarrelled about whether they should give up the motor idea and move on.'

Tubb nodded. 'I don't think they trusted each other. It was all very well while the money was coming in, but as soon as the scheme was threatened, it was every man for himself.'

'Just suppose,' said Lestrade, 'that Baumann was afraid that Gorrie would reveal the fraud to the police before it was discovered and turn Queen's evidence to avoid conviction. Now that is a motive to commit murder.'

'But why did they meet at the signpost?' I asked.

'Perhaps Baumann might tell us that if he confesses,' said Tubb.

'It must have been part of his plan,' said Lestrade. 'That's why the meeting had to be by the stream, in darkness. He was going to strike Gorrie on the head with something and then throw the body into the water above the weir, thinking that if it went over the weir that would account for the injury. But there was a struggle by the waterside which was where it went wrong. What do you think, Holmes?'

'It is certainly an elegant theory that accounts for the circumstances,' said Holmes. 'There was enough time for Baumann to come up from Waltham Abbey on foot, commit the crime, dispose of the carpetbag, and return.'

'There, you see,' said Lestrade triumphantly. 'You are very clever, Mr Holmes, I grant you that, but sometimes I am ahead of you.'

'While Baumann's inability to provide an alibi is damaging to his case, I would advise you not to ignore the investors,' said Holmes. 'Any of them might have a motive if they suspected fraud, and it would only take the failure of one alibi to place that individual under suspicion.'

Lestrade chuckled. 'No, no, Mr Holmes, I know you like your mysteries, and you do occasionally come up with some helpful suggestions, but sometimes you must admit the obvious answer is the right one.'

'Well,' said Tubb, rising to his feet, 'I shall advise Dr Baumann of his present position. We can certainly hold him until he appears before the magistrates. I can only hope he sees sense and tells us about himself.'

'I am happy for Mr Holmes and Mr Stamford to accompany us,' said Lestrade.

Tubb did not disagree, and we went to see Baumann in his cell.

The prisoner was not a small man, but as he sat hunched dejectedly on the edge of his bed, he looked smaller than he was. He looked up at us piteously. 'Can I go now?' he asked.

'No, Dr Baumann, if that is your real name, which I doubt,' said Tubb. 'Are you ready to tell us who you really are?'

Baumann said nothing.

'Very well, I shall have to charge you under the name you have given which is all I have at present.'

'Charge? With what?' said Baumann. 'I haven't done anything!'

'I have more than enough evidence to charge you with fraud,' said Tubb. 'Other charges may follow.' He proceeded to make the formal charge in face of a man who was either astonished or extremely good at pretending to be.

'I don't understand,' said Baumann. 'What fraud is this?'

'The Baumann motor,' said Tubb. 'The whole scheme has been shown to be a fraud. Now we know why the room was kept under lock and key and no-one was allowed to examine the apparatus. This morning, Mr Young kindly permitted Inspector Lestrade and these gentlemen to conduct an inspection, and the trickery has been revealed.'

'What trickery?' exclaimed Baumann. 'The machine worked. It did everything it was supposed to do. The combination of air and water passed through the amplifimoderator, which released the etheric force.' He turned to Holmes and me. 'You were both there, you saw it!'

'It delivered power,' said Holmes, 'but we now know that there was no etheric force involved.'

'How can you possibly know that? You have heard what Professor Novak said. He understands the principle. Ask him!' Baumann frowned. 'You've not damaged the motor, have you?'

'No,' said Holmes, 'although it will have to be dismantled and displayed at your trial.'

'Trial?' gasped Baumann incredulously.

'The machine was connected to a hidden pipe which diverted water from the course which powered the factory's waterwheel. It was that which caused the beam engine to move.'

Baumann was silent while he tried to understand what Holmes had said. 'So — you are saying that it was just waterpower? And a hidden pipe, you say? Hidden how? I saw no pipe!'

'It was well concealed,' said Holmes. 'But I was able to follow its course from the exterior to your motor.'

'Come now, are you saying you don't know about the pipe?' demanded Lestrade.

'Of course I don't know!' cried Baumann. 'I didn't build the motor! Gorrie built it!'

'On your instructions.'

'No! I am not a mechanic, I don't know how these things work.'

'And neither are you a scientist, as we have already established,' said Holmes. 'So what are you?'

'A trickster, nothing more,' said Tubb. 'I'll see the constable keeps a regular watch,' he added.

'What is your real name, Baumann? And where were you on the night that Gorrie was killed?' asked Holmes.

Baumann hid his face in his hands. 'I can't tell you!' he moaned.

'I think you murdered Gorrie,' said Lestrade. 'You planned to deprive people of their money by inviting investments into a machine for which you made elaborate fraudulent claims. And you hired Mr Gorrie to build something that would convince people to part with their money. You didn't need to know how to build it, you just told him what it was supposed to do. And when he threatened to expose your little scheme, you killed him.'

'No, it wasn't like that,' said Baumann. 'Gorrie built the machine, all of it. It was all his idea from the start. And I didn't hire Mr Gorrie. Mr Gorrie hired me!'

Despite our surprise, Baumann refused to say any more, and we left him alone to consider his options. At the duty desk, Mrs Beauregard was demanding to see Inspector Tubb. As soon as he appeared, she turned and advanced upon him like a ship of war, her eyes blazing like twin cannons.

'You have no right to hold Dr Baumann any longer!' she exclaimed. 'You must free him at once so he can continue his vital work on the motor!'

Tubb uttered a small groan of despair, then steadied himself. 'Come to my office, Mrs Beauregard, and we will discuss the situation,' he said. 'I promise I will tell you everything I know.'

'I do not envy him,' said Holmes, as the office door closed behind Tubb and his demanding visitor.

Lestrade looked at his watch. 'A long day,' he said, 'and I for one am ready for my dinner. Would you care to join me, gentlemen? We don't want to be here when Mrs Beauregard explodes.'

We took up his invitation with some alacrity. At one of the many inns not far from the police station, we were once again to enjoy simple but abundant country food.

'I am not yet in a position to charge Baumann with Gorrie's murder,' Lestrade admitted, as dinner was brought to the table. 'I can't prove that Gorrie threatened him, and lack of an alibi will not be enough to convict him. If he is innocent, and was simply alone that night, out walking maybe, then there is no reason for him not to say so. But he might have been with bad companions and therefore cannot expect them to come forward in support of his story, especially if they were planning another crime. If he offers them as alibis and they refuse to confirm where he was, he will seem to be a liar, and it will be worse for him than if he offered no alibi at all.'

CHAPTER ELEVEN

The inquest on Jenkins was opened the next morning. The hearing was a simple formality. It lasted only a few minutes, sufficient to attach a name to the body, and hear a brief report from Dr Henderson, describing the examination he had made and what tests were still to be completed. The next session would receive the evidence of all the witnesses and, we hoped, return a verdict as to the cause of death and determine if there were any suspicious circumstances. I could see that Holmes was not yet ready to accept that Jenkins's death was due to natural causes or accident.

This hearing was followed by the resumed inquest on Edward Gorrie. The approximate time of death, based on the stomach contents, was believed to be between seven and ten o'clock on the night he disappeared. Death was caused primarily by a blow on the head from a fall on the sluice handle, which might have rendered him unconscious, followed by immersion in water resulting in drowning. It was not possible to rule out foul play. The inquest was closed, the remainder of the investigation being a police matter.

We returned to the police station, to learn that the prisoner was still refusing to reveal anything about himself or his movements.

Inspector Tubb's recent interview with Mrs Beauregard had been a turbulent one. Still convinced of her favourite's innocence, she had flounced away in a fury of frustration, to summon Mr Ineson.

'Baumann's attitude won't go down well with the magistrates,' said Tubb. 'Even Ineson couldn't prise an alibi out of him, and he will have to work very hard to ensure that Mrs Beauregard does not appear to speak for his client.' He looked at his watch. 'I am due to see him again very shortly. There's talk of having the trial moved to London. He's about as popular as Dr Palmer round here.'

A telegram arrived for Lestrade. He opened and read it, his eyebrows climbing as he did so. 'How interesting,' he said. 'I am told that two Pinkerton detectives will be arriving at Waltham Cross station today and I should go and meet them. Newman and O'Hara. I wonder if they have any more information about Gorrie. Gentlemen, you had better come with me.'

The railway station was not busy, and we waited on the platform for the two Pinkerton men. Pinkertons, from the many exciting tales told of their exploits, are considered to be the most thorough and indefatigable agents there are when in pursuit of wrongdoers. They have earned the respect of police forces worldwide. It was not unusual, Lestrade told us, for Scotland Yard to collaborate with visiting Pinkertons.

When the train drew to a halt we saw families, a number of gentlemen travelling alone, and one couple alight, but not the two detectives we had been anticipating. Lestrade glanced at the telegram. 'Mr Newman, Mr O'Hara?' he called out.

The couple who had been strolling amicably towards the exit turned to us, smiled, then approached.

'And you may be...?' asked the man in an American accent.

'Inspector Lestrade of Scotland Yard,' replied Lestrade, producing his warrant card, 'and these are my associates, Mr Holmes and Mr Stamford.'

'Frank Newman,' said the man, holding out his hand in greeting. He was a broad-shouldered man of about forty, with tanned skin and generous crinkles about his eyes. We shook hands.

'Kitty O'Hara,' said his companion, offering a gloved hand. She was a striking woman of about twenty-five, with copper-coloured hair and green eyes. Although dressed in travelling clothes designed for practicality rather than fashion, she was still a vision to be admired. I confess that I glanced quickly at Holmes to see if he was impressed by her appearance, but if he was, he gave no sign. I like to think that sometimes he does encounter young ladies who engage his interest, but his iron control and determination to remain single allow for no outward suggestion.

Lestrade was less surprised than I to see a female detective. He smiled as he shook her hand. 'I have heard tell of lady Pinkertons but have never until now been privileged to meet one.'

'Do you employ lady detectives in England?' she asked.

'Not directly, but the private agencies employ them with great success, as they are never suspected of being secret spies.'

I thought from Holmes's expression that lady detectives did not meet with his full approval, but he refrained from comment.

'Why don't we stop for some refreshment,' said Lestrade. 'I would be interested to know what brings you here.'

'Travelling is thirsty work,' agreed Newman, with a hearty smile.

The Queen Eleanor Inn was close by, and we found a quiet table where Lestrade ordered a large pot of tea, and a plate of bread and butter, with jam. The inspector, being on official duty, was not about to drink anything stronger than tea. I knew Holmes would not drink beer at such an early hour, but I sensed that Mr Newman might have liked a beer, and ordered a small glass for myself, and a larger one for Newman, with a beef sandwich. Miss O'Hara expressed a curiosity to sample English tea, which she did, showing commendable appreciation.

'We have travelled to England because we have been employed by a prominent businessman to trace his daughter's husband, who has deserted her,' said Newman.

'What is the husband's name?' asked Holmes.

'I can show you both his name and his picture,' said Miss O'Hara. She carried a leather travelling bag, which was a rather more capacious and useful item than the customary ladies' reticules. She unlatched it and extracted a folded paper which she opened out and handed across the table. It was a poster of the kind seen outside theatres, and advertised a production of a drama entitled *Davy Crockett, or Be Sure You're Right, Then Go Ahead* at a New York playhouse. The leading man was a popular star of the American stage, Jackson Bourne, heroically portrayed in buckskins and fur hat, brandishing a rifle. We had no difficulty in recognising him.

'Dr Baumann,' said Holmes. 'He is currently being held in custody at Waltham Abbey police station. His hair and beard are a little longer, but it is undoubtedly he. He and his associate, a mechanic called Edward Gorrie, have been demonstrating a machine that they claimed produces power from a mixture of air and cold water. They formed a company called Baumann Motors which has been attracting investors. Inspired by Mr Keely's example, I imagine.'

Miss O'Hara had taken a notebook and pencil from her bag as Holmes spoke and was writing rapidly.

'The machine has been proven to be a fraud, and Dr Baumann — Mr Bourne — has been charged with the offence,' Holmes continued. 'Unfortunately, Mr Gorrie is recently deceased, and it is suspected that he was murdered. The prisoner refuses to supply an alibi for the time of death. Has Mr Bourne been involved in previous crimes?'

'Not as far as we know,' replied Miss O'Hara. 'During the last ten years he has had a very successful career in the theatre. He has no criminal record. It is his private life that is in question.'

'Mrs Bourne's father was not happy about the marriage,' said Newman, 'but he found it hard to deny his daughter, who was very much in love and begged for his approval. They have been married for seven years and have three children.'

'Yet he has deserted her,' said Lestrade, shaking his head sorrowfully.

'Was he a cruel husband?' I asked.

'It appears not. Mrs Bourne says that he was kind and affectionate, and a fond father,' said Newman, 'but it seems that other ladies found him interesting. Some, even those who knew his married state, clamoured for his attention, and put temptation in his way. Unfortunately, he has a great weakness in that area of his life, and he succumbed.'

'At least four times that we know of,' said Miss O'Hara, bluntly. 'That is the number of paternity claims that have been made against him. Our client is determined that his daughter should sue for divorce. A legal separation will not satisfy him, he wants the connection to be completely severed, so there can be no claim on any property. That is not usually an easy matter for a woman, which is why so many wives are obliged to endure bad husbands. When one's father is a wealthy man, however, a way can be found.'

'Will her position as a divorced woman not diminish her standing?' asked Holmes. 'How can her father countenance that?'

Miss O'Hara nodded emphatically. 'It is vital that the divorce should be concluded in strict confidence, or she may not be able to appear in society again. There will simply be an announcement that they are living apart and she will in future devote herself entirely to the upbringing of the children. We have come to find Mr Bourne and serve papers on him.'

'Given his betrayals and desertion, Mrs Bourne will undoubtedly gain her freedom, and if her father has his way, Bourne will be ruined,' Newman added. 'There have already been rumours in the press of his impending difficulties, which were not described, although those who know of his weakness can guess the position. He was obliged to leave the theatre production, and his agent, Mr Danielson, issued a statement to say that his client was convalescing after an illness. Once Bourne's situation is exposed, the public will learn the truth.'

'How did you know he was here?' asked Holmes.

'It was his friend Mr Gorrie who led us here,' said Miss O'Hara. 'We spoke to Mr Danielson, and while we were sure that his client was not convalescing but in hiding, he refused to tell us where he was. We discovered, however, on speaking to some of Bourne's theatrical friends, that "Jackson Bourne" was only a professional name, although he has used it for some twenty years and is not known by any other. His birth name is Howard McGuckin. We checked the passenger lists on the steamships leaving New York, and there was a man on an Atlantic crossing by that name, about two months ago.'

'We interviewed the captain and a steward,' said Newman. 'Mr Bourne feared being recognised and was in disguise, at which he is naturally adept. He was travelling as an invalid, appearing older than his years, his face muffled. He was accompanied by a valet named Edward Gorrie. We traced Gorrie's address and obtained a description from his neighbours. A man with bow legs who spoke with a Scottish accent.'

'That is the man,' said Holmes.

'We learned of his interest in the Keely motor, about which he made no secret,' Newman continued. 'The captain and the steward confirmed the description.'

'At Gorrie's address in New York we found that enquiries had recently been made about him by the office of Young's Toolmakers, and they informed us that Gorrie was working at Mr Young's Abbey Mill factory in England,' said Miss O'Hara. 'We took the fastest steamer here.'

'Excellent work,' said Holmes, approvingly. 'While here, Gorrie built the motor which his confederate claimed could generate power, but it was actually connected to the millstream by concealed pipes.'

'Do you know how Gorrie and Bourne met?' I asked.

'We are not certain,' said Newman, 'but if Gorrie was hoping to find a man of favourable appearance with the skills he lacked to attract investment, he might have read of Bourne's rumoured scandal in the newspaper and seen Mr Danielson's statement. If he approached the agent, he would have found that his client was more than willing to secure work that would take him to Europe.'

There was a certain air of satisfaction as we finished our refreshments and proceeded to Waltham Abbey to pay a visit to the prisoner.

'Mr Bourne is claiming that he knew nothing about the fraud, it was all down to Gorrie,' said Lestrade. 'I suspect he murdered Gorrie to conceal the crime.'

'Does he have a lawyer?' asked Newman.

'His solicitor is one of the best in England,' said Holmes. 'I think he will be crucial to his client's fate.'

At the police station we briefed Inspector Tubb and introduced the two Pinkertons, who were taken to see the prisoner.

'Visitors for you,' announced Tubb as the two detectives entered the cell. The prisoner looked surprised, but Miss O'Hara took the lead in the interview. He rose to his feet. She smiled at him in a disarming fashion, and his manner at once softened.

'I don't know who you are, Miss, but I am happy to see you,' he said.

'I am Kitty O'Hara, and I am very happy to see you too,' she said. 'I have something for you.' She took an envelope from her bag. 'Please accept this,' she said, holding it out to him.

'Why thank you,' he said, and took the envelope. 'What might this be?'

'Mr Jackson Bourne, you have hereby been served with papers in the proceedings commenced by Mrs Emily Bourne in the matter of your divorce,' said Miss O'Hara.

He whimpered and fell back onto his bed.

Before the day was out, Lestrade received another note from Scotland Yard, which created a new situation. Since the fraud charge involved a company registered in London, and there was the potential for a murder charge as well as considerable local prejudice against the prisoner, it had been determined that Jackson Bourne, formerly calling himself Dr Baumann, should be removed to a secure custody cell in the capital. He was now destined to appear to answer the charge of fraud before a bench of London magistrates. A sergeant and a constable were being sent to accompany Lestrade, and arrangements had been made to transport the prisoner by the earliest train leaving Waltham Cross the following morning.

Holmes and I made sure to be up with the lark so as to be there to watch the departure, and Miss O'Hara and Mr Newman were also in attendance. Bourne and his escort arrived by police trap. He looked dishevelled and miserable. Once he had stepped down, he stumbled along in shoes without laces, while handcuffed between the two junior officers.

The stationmaster, who had been alerted to what was planned, came out to the forecourt. 'The train is on time, sir,' he said. 'It's due in ten minutes. You'll have a carriage to yourselves.'

'Thank you, Mr Block,' said Lestrade.

The prisoner was being led across the forecourt, towards the station entrance, when a light trap carrying two men arrived. At first, they appeared to be merely early travellers, but the trap circled about, and drew up in a very deliberate manner, stopping in front of the entrance to the station and blocking it from the approaching police party.

Lestrade and the officers, scenting danger, backed away, pulling Bourne with them, but linked as they were, the movement was a little awkward to achieve quickly. In moments, the two men had jumped down from the trap, striding purposefully towards Bourne, drawing guns from inside their coats as they did so.

'Take cover!' yelled Newman. A gun appeared in his hand. 'Cassidy — stop right there!'

The two gunmen paused in surprise while the police hustled Bourne away. There was no available cover nearby, and they could only retreat around the side of the station building, where a fence prevented access to the railway lines. Holmes, who was unarmed, went with them, and I followed him to safety.

I was unable to resist peering around the corner at the scene. That was when the shooting started.

Both gunmen fired at Newman, who returned fire. At first the flying bullets whined astray, then I saw Newman hit in the forearm. He dropped his gun and collapsed with a groan. The gunmen now turned towards Bourne again, but Miss O'Hara, who had also drawn a gun, had quickly seized Newman's fallen weapon. Planting her feet firmly apart, she raised the guns, one in each hand, and blazed away at the would-be assassins with them both.

I don't know why I did what I did, but it must have been my surgical training that was uppermost in my mind. Crouching low to avoid any stray bullets, I ran out across the forecourt and threw myself to the ground beside Newman, to see what I could do for him. His lower arm bones were shattered, and his hand was limp and useless. It was not a fatal wound, but the bullet had passed through the arm and had continued on its path, lodging in his body. All I could do for the moment was try and stem the bleeding.

I looked up in time to see Miss O'Hara shoot one of the gunmen in the chest. He went down with a gasp of surprise. The other man hesitated, then decided, in the face of flying lead and a two-gun opponent, to abandon his stricken accomplice and make a run for the trap. Before mounting the vehicle, he made the error of turning to point his gun for another shot at Miss O'Hara. She fired again, and he cried out, having been hit in the thigh. Limping, he was just able to scramble into the trap, where he tried to control the horse, which was plunging in panic at the noise, making a fast escape impossible. With one hand on the reins, he turned his gun on Miss O'Hara once more. At that moment, Holmes arrived at a sprint, bounded onto the trap, seized the man's arm and twisted it, making him drop the weapon. He then wrestled the screaming gunman to the ground and subdued him, forcing him to lie face down. One sharp knee in the small of the back was a powerful inducement to remain still.

Newman was moaning with pain, and Miss O'Hara hurried to his side.

'I'm — all right,' he gasped. 'Just help me up.'

'No, Frank, you lie right there,' commanded Miss O'Hara. She glanced at me as I worked.

'Are you unhurt?' I asked.

'Yes, though I might need a new bonnet,' she said. There was a clean bullet hole in the brim. She must have felt it strike.

'See if the station has any medical supplies,' I said. 'I need a firm bandage. Then we can get him some help.'

The stationmaster had very sensibly dived indoors when the shooting started. Miss O'Hara went to find him and returned with a tin box of medical materials. 'The stationmaster says he has wired to Cheshunt for the police and a doctor, and they should be here soon,' she said. To my relief, Miss O'Hara knew how to help tie a good bandage without fuss and proved to be a valuable assistant.

'You're going to need surgery, Mr Newman,' I said as I secured the bandage, 'that bullet will have to come out, but we'll have you right again soon enough. Just try not to move.'

The police had by now handcuffed the wounded gunman and secured him to a tether rail. Holmes took a bandage to tie up the man's thigh. 'Just a flesh wound,' he said. 'His friend is dead. There are no other injuries.'

'How is Bourne?' I asked.

'Shocked but unharmed. He won't be trying to escape.'

Cheshunt was only about a mile away, and it was not long before a Hertfordshire police inspector called Moore arrived together with a Dr Evans. I consulted with Evans and there being no hospital or infirmary nearby, it was decided in view of the seriousness of Newman's injury to convey him on the police trap to the nearest inn, the Queen Eleanor, where he and I would operate. The wounded gunman would be taken under arrest to Cheshunt police station, where his injury would be seen to. The body would be removed to a medical practice in Cheshunt for later examination.

'Should we report to Inspector Tubb?' I asked.

'In due course,' said Lestrade. 'He is Essex police, and Waltham Cross is Hertfordshire. They're very particular about things like that round here.'

'I think we should,' said Holmes, who had been examining the vehicle the men had arrived in. 'That trap is painted with a sign, the White Lion Inn, Waltham Abbey. They must have hired it from there, and may have been staying there, waiting for their chance. We should make enquiries about them, and might learn something useful, especially if they have been sending and receiving messages.'

'Very well, Mr Holmes, I deputise you to carry out that duty,' said Lestrade. Inspector Moore looked a little surprised at this but said nothing.

'Does Bourne know why the men came to shoot him?' I asked.

'If he does, he is not saying,' said Lestrade. 'And the man with the leg injury is saying nothing either. One interesting thing, though. I went over to look at the man shot in the chest. He spoke one word before he died. It sounded like "ruby". Maybe Bourne stole some jewels. I'll find out if there have been any robberies in New York recently.'

The stationmaster had been holding the train for the police, but it had to depart soon, and Lestrade and his men assisted their prisoner into an empty compartment, which the stationmaster obligingly searched for them before they occupied it. It was with some relief that they were able to depart without further incident.

'One of the men was called Cassidy,' I said. 'Newman recognised him.'

Inspector Moore was taking statements, and once he had spoken to Miss O'Hara, I asked her about Cassidy.

'A New York criminal,' she said. 'Small fry. That's all I know.'

When I was questioned, I made sure to tell Moore that Miss O'Hara had only fired in self-defence, after the gunmen had shot first. She was adamant that she would accompany Newman to the inn to look after him. The injured Pinkerton was in great pain, and in no condition to be interviewed. Once I was satisfied that it was safe to move him, a makeshift stretcher was created from some boards. There was just enough space in the police trap for him to lie still. Inspector Moore said he would head back to make a report at Cheshunt station and return to question Newman when he had recovered from the surgery.

Miss O'Hara and I brought the patient to the Queen Eleanor as gently as possible, accompanied by Dr Evans who drove his own gig.

The innkeeper was unused to admitting gunshot injuries, but he granted us a good-size room with a bed, where Newman was made as comfortable as possible. I introduced Miss O'Hara as a nurse, which was partly accurate in that situation, and there was no objection made when she said she would sit by the injured man until he was well. Dr Evans laid out his materials and was extremely pleased when I revealed that I had several years' experience in operating theatres in Barts

Hospital. He had brought a wire mask with a flannel cover, and chloroform in a dropper bottle. Once I instructed Miss O'Hara on applying the anaesthetic safely, she continued giving it drop by drop onto the material, watching carefully for any signs of distress, and tilting the patient's chin to assist his breathing. Newman took it well, while I saw to the broken arm and Dr Evans tried to track the course of the bullet. At length Evans stepped back and said, 'Mr Newman is a very lucky man.'

'Oh?' I said.

'Yes, it is not an injury one sees often; in fact, I have only ever read about such an incident. The bullet struck the arm first, which is where most of the damage has been done. He will keep the arm, but he may not have use of it for some time. That injury, however, slowed the bullet and when it entered his body it struck a rib, but did not go through. Instead, it glanced off and passed around the fleshy part to lodge somewhere in the back.' He felt around the man's body. 'Yes, here it is. Just under the skin. No vital organs have been damaged, so I will remove the bullet and close the wounds.'

I was pleased to see that Evans had adopted Lister's antiseptic methods, which gave Newman an excellent chance of recovery. He supplied us with clean dressings, a draught to relieve the pain should the patient require it, and the usual advice on a light diet. He then left us to continue the care of Mr Newman, promising to return in the afternoon.

'I can't thank you enough, Mr Stamford,' said Miss O'Hara. 'I am sure it would have been much worse for Frank if you had not been there. He is a fine man. We have worked together for four years, and he has taught me all I know about being a Pinkerton.'

I made the usual modest response, but to my surprise she took my face in her hands, leaned forward, and kissed me on the lips. She smiled at my startled expression. 'Why Mr Stamford, I do believe you are blushing. Anyone would think you had never kissed a woman before!'

I was about to protest that she was mistaken, but then I thought that a chaste peck on the cheek of a female relative was not the kind of kiss to which she was referring. 'You should thank Holmes, too,' I said, 'he disarmed the gunman. I mean — not that I am suggesting you kiss him,' I added hurriedly. 'In fact, I would advise against it; he is very easily embarrassed.'

At this awkward moment I was glad to see that Newman was beginning to regain consciousness, and Miss O'Hara went to sit beside him, reassuring him that all was well. So gentle and calming was she that I was obliged to remind myself that only a short while before she had shot a man dead without compunction or remorse.

Holmes returned to see the patient, and report on his findings. 'I have briefed Inspector Tubb on what has occurred,' he said, 'and we went to the White Lion Inn to make enquiries. As I suspected, the two men had been lodging there. They arrived yesterday, giving the names Cassidy and Jones. They spent a great deal of time in the bar listening to local gossip. The landlord, noticing their accents, asked if they were American and they said they were, and asked if there were any other of their countrymen in town. Of course they were told there were none. They showed him a *carte de visite* with a photograph of Jackson Bourne and said they had heard that the famous actor was visiting Waltham Abbey. No-one knew the name, but the landlord said the picture was of a Swiss scientist, Dr Baumann, who had drunk at the White Lion on occasion. We also learned that the news of Baumann's arrest had spread though the town. Perhaps someone had talked too freely, and there was a rumour that he was due to be taken to London by the morning train.'

'Cassidy was a small-time crook,' said Miss O'Hara. 'I don't know the other man.'

'They must have been sent here expressly to murder Mr Bourne,' said Holmes, 'in which case the person who sent them will be expecting a response and might become impatient. The landlord of the White Lion has been told to keep a watch for any telegrams or letters arriving for either of the men, and if any should arrive, they are to be handed to the police unopened. Inspector Tubb is going to do his best to keep this incident out of the newspapers so as not to alert their employer. He fears that there may be officers who speak too freely when off duty. All his men have been warned. He knows Mr Block the stationmaster to be reliable.'

'Good thinking,' said Miss O'Hara.

'I did learn one interesting thing,' Holmes continued. 'Apparently, when talking in the barroom, the men asked if Bourne, or Baumann as he was known, had been seen about in the company of a lady. They implied that she was not an Englishwoman and thought he had arrived from abroad in her company.'

'And had he?' I asked.

'He has not been seen publicly in female company the whole time he has been here,' said Holmes. 'Miss O'Hara, when you questioned the captain and steward of the steamship which brought Mr Bourne and Mr Gorrie to England, they told you that the two men travelled together as master and servant.'

'Yes, that is correct. Mr Bourne in his guise as an invalid was not inclined to spend too much time with the other passengers. He was afraid he might be recognised.'

'But there might have been a lady on board who was known to him, and they had decided mutually to pretend to be strangers,' said Holmes. 'Stewards tend to notice things of that nature, and of course they will be discreet.'

'That is true,' said Miss O'Hara. 'The steward told us that the only person they conversed with to any extent was a gentleman. He thought he was a medical man, which was understandable as Bourne was assumed to be an invalid. I might have the name here.' She brought a notebook from her bag and leafed through the pages. 'Yes, his name was Dr Nachtnebel.'

'Nachtnebel?' exclaimed Holmes.

'I have heard that name before,' I said.

'Indeed. You recall the newspaper cuttings in Mr Gorrie's bag? Dr Nachtnebel was the supporter of Mr Keely's principle who lost his tenure as a lecturer because his views were considered unacceptable.'

'It is quite a coincidence that he and Gorrie were travelling on the same vessel,' I said.

'Coincidences may occur, but in this instance, I doubt it,' said Holmes. 'Gorrie might well have wanted to approach Nachtnebel, to ask for his support, or advice. Whether they met before the voyage, we cannot be sure, but if Gorrie learned that Nachtnebel was travelling to England, then securing a berth on the same ship would be a good opportunity for a meeting to discuss their shared interests.'

'Perhaps Nachtnebel has been trying to find a new lectureship here,' I suggested. 'The universities and colleges may have heard of him. He might have something useful to tell us about Gorrie.'

'I don't doubt it,' said Holmes, pensively. He refused to say anything more on the subject until he had made further enquiries. I suspected that he did not want to describe his thoughts until he had proof that he was right. Being proved wrong was something he disliked, and it was only with greater maturity that he was able to tolerate it with the appearance of good humour.

Inspector Moore returned to the Queen Eleanor Inn for further interviews, and Holmes told him what he had learned at the White Lion. Newman, who had supped rather well of the doctor's draught, was sleeping.

'The man we are holding, who simply gave his name as Jones, has not been informative,' said Moore. 'There is no doubt that Bourne was the intended target, but we have yet to establish a reason. Jones has denied that he came to kill Bourne, claiming that the intention was simply to frighten him, and he did so at the request of his associate Cassidy, who is not, of course, able to enlighten us. Inspector Lestrade told me he thinks Bourne may have been a jewel thief. I leave that enquiry to Scotland Yard.'

'I do not think Bourne is a jewel thief,' said Holmes. 'Such persons are usually highly intelligent, adept at planning their crimes, and skilled at carrying them out. They often exhibit a strange fascination amounting to an obsession with jewellery. Bourne does not fit that description.'

Moore stared at Holmes. 'I would agree. Perhaps the man had unpaid gambling debts and was to be shot as an example.'

'From what we know of him, he is more likely to have been the target of an outraged husband, whose wife was Bourne's mistress,' said Miss O'Hara, displaying her Pinkerton agent's card. 'He had come to England to escape his angry father-in-law whose daughter had been made miserable by his behaviour. And there were paternity suits which might have ruined him. His father-in-law engaged us to follow him here so we could serve legal papers, which we have done.'

'Bourne's weakness was not jewels, but women,' said Holmes. 'Cassidy and Jones had been asking if he had arrived in England accompanied by a woman, but it appears he did not.'

At this point, Newman stirred in the bed and mumbled. Miss O'Hara went to him and helped moisten his lips from a sponge dipped in water. 'It's all right,' she said, softly. 'The operation has been successful and all you need to do now is rest and get strong again. I'm here to look after you.'

'May I ask him something?' said Inspector Moore.

'I think I know what you want to ask,' said Miss O'Hara. 'Frank, can you tell me about Cassidy? Do you know why he came here?'

Newman sighed and tried to move but gave a little groan.

'There, my dear, don't try to move.'

'Delaney,' he murmured. 'He is Delaney's man. Killer for hire.'

'And Cassidy's friend Jones?'

'I don't know.' He gasped in pain, and she pressed a damp cloth to his forehead.

'I think that had better be all for now,' I said.

'Who is Delaney?' asked Moore.

'There is a criminal gang in New York, the Delaney gang, responsible for many of the biggest crimes there,' said Miss O'Hara. 'Robberies, extortion, swindling. They won't hesitate to murder anyone who tries to stop them. The gang is run by brothers Eddie and Jimmy Delaney. Eddie is the elder and gives the orders. He's not a man you should cross. If Cassidy was sent to kill Bourne by Eddie Delaney then he must have done something very serious, and he is lucky to still be alive.'

'How did Delaney know that Bourne was in England?'

'He has informers everywhere. Someone must have talked. Maybe he found out that Pinkertons were after him and had us followed.'

'Inspector Tubb told me he has heard from Lestrade, and Bourne is now in safe custody,' said Holmes. 'And I think I know why Delaney wanted to kill him.'

CHAPTER TWELVE

The next morning, Lestrade returned to Essex to make further enquiries concerning the murder of Mr Gorrie, and we attended the resumed inquest on Jenkins. It was well attended, given the shocking nature of the death which had been widely reported by word of mouth with varying degrees of accuracy.

Mr Young, who was still distressed at recent events, was unable to attend, but since he had not been present at the death his presence was not thought to be necessary. Mrs Young was there in his place with Norris, to make notes on the company's behalf.

The post-mortem, which had been completed by Dr Henderson, had revealed no suspicious findings regarding the cause of death. He was certain that Jenkins had not been inebriated but knew that the deceased had been concerned about his sister. The coroner asked if he thought this worry might have been a distraction, making him less careful than usual, and Henderson replied that he could not rule this out. He had not been able to gather anything from an examination of the brain, which was too damaged, but he thought the heart and blood vessels serving it — which he had examined under the microscope — showed a weakness which might have caused a failure at any moment, especially at times of exertion or distress. In view of the fact that the deceased had made no attempt to save himself, it was very possible that Jenkins, who had just climbed a flight of steps to the platform over the wheel, had expired almost instantly from natural causes before he fell.

Mr Phillips told the court that his last impression of Jenkins was that the man looked troubled, but he had been as active as usual. Jenkins had shown interested visitors the wheel on previous occasions. Phillips had not been on the platform at the time of the fall and had not seen what happened. There was nothing on the platform that might have caused anyone to trip or lose his footing.

The party of gentlemen who had been on the platform at the time of Jenkins's death next proceeded to give evidence. Understandably, most testified that their attention had been on the action of the turning waterwheel, and they had not seen what had caused Jenkins to fall.

Reverend Woodley testified that everyone on the platform had taken care as it was so high up. No-one had bumped into anyone else, or made any comment that might have been startling or distracting. The visibility on the platform had been good. Professor Novak, the market gardener, the corn merchant, and Mr Herbert Murray all gave similar accounts.

Mr Green, who said he had been standing close by the deceased, said that he had heard Jenkins give a little gasp and had turned to look. He saw a curious expression pass over the man's features just before he fell. He was not aware of anything that had actually made the deceased fall. Jenkins had just tumbled backwards without warning.

Mr Jamison was somewhat reticent about his testimony. 'Yes, I saw Jenkins was upset by something. And I heard him gasp, but it sounded like words to me — it sounded like "the demon" or something similar. He wasn't looking out at the wheel. Someone had asked him a question, I think it was about when the wheel had been installed, and he looked round to reply. And that was when it happened.'

I was asked to testify, since I was the first medical man to see the body, and I did so to the best of my ability. I described the last conversation I had had with Jenkins and confirmed that he was worried about the health of his sister. I also said that he had been intending to speak to Holmes about the man he had seen on the path outside his cottage on the morning after Gorrie's death, but that he had only seen a back view of the man, who he thought was a stranger, and did not think he would know him again if he saw him. The coroner nodded at the completeness of my testimony, but I could see that he did not think the sighting had any relevance to the tragedy. As I returned to my seat, I saw Mr Phillips give a thoughtful little frown.

After due consideration the coroner's jury brought in a verdict of death by natural causes.

I agreed that the sighting of the man on the path was unlikely to have given anyone a motive to murder Jenkins, and I said as much to Holmes. He, however, did not accept that there was nothing further to be done. 'Let us pay a visit to Miss Jenkins. I am sure you will want to see her again, and she might have something to say. Perhaps her brother shared something of note with her.'

Since the members of the tour at which Jenkins had died were assembled, it made sense to hold a business meeting at the mill that afternoon. Mrs Young, of a calm and practical disposition, had decided on her husband's behalf, to advise all persons concerned with Baumann Motors of the results of the examination of the workshop. Also to be present were Professor Novak, for his scientific expertise, and Mr Ineson, who had requested that Holmes and I should attend as independent advisors.

Mrs Young took us up to the mill in the carriage, and on the way, I asked her about how poor Maggie Jenkins was doing. I said I had hoped to be able to see Miss Jenkins again, and in preparation had purchased a small item I hoped would benefit her if she was well enough to use it. Mrs Young told me that the niece, Mrs Cooper, had come from Cheshunt to care for her, but she was still very weak. 'She has been told of her brother's death, but I am not sure that she took it all in,' said Mrs Young sadly. 'She did speak kindly of you, Mr Stamford, and I am sure she would be pleased if you paid her a visit.'

When we arrived, Mrs Young went to consult with Mr Norris about arrangements for the meeting, and Holmes and I knocked on the door of Jenkins's cottage. The lady who opened it was in her middle years, and tidily dressed, with a large apron over her dress. 'Yes, sirs, how may I help you? Miss Jenkins is asleep just now and I wouldn't like to disturb her.'

'I am Surgeon Stamford,' I said. 'I examined Miss Jenkins recently, shortly before her brother died, and as I was here, I thought I should come and see her again. I have brought some Friar's Balsam. You just need a few drops in a basin of hot water — if she can inhale the vapour, it might ease her breathing. I am not making a charge for my visits out of gratitude to Mr Jenkins. And this is my associate Mr Holmes.' I was, I must admit, rather tempted to describe Holmes as my assistant, since he did not have any qualifications, but I didn't want to disgruntle him.

'Oh, please do come in,' said Mrs Cooper, accepting the balsam gratefully. 'Might I offer you some tea?'

'Thank you,' said Holmes.

I wasn't sure I wanted tea, but then I thought that a friendly conversation around the table might be more revealing than a series of questions.

'We have just attended the inquest on your uncle,' said Holmes.

'Ah yes, my brother was there,' said Mrs Cooper sadly. 'It was such a shock. I hope they thought that it was quick, and he didn't suffer.'

'I was here on the day he died, and helped recover his body,' I said. 'I can reassure you it was quick, he would probably have known nothing. The inquest has found natural causes most probably due to a sudden failure of the heart.'

While Mrs Cooper made the tea I went to see Miss Jenkins, who was sleeping peacefully in her bed. She looked comfortable and was wrapped warmly. I thought her breathing was less laboured than before and entertained the hope that despite her advanced years she might recover.

'Your aunt is doing well,' I said, as Mrs Cooper bought the tea things to the table. 'She doesn't appear to be in any pain. Continue to keep her warm and make sure she has soothing drinks, and whatever nourishment she can accept. Beef broth, with a little bread soaked in it, if she can manage it.'

Mrs Cooper thanked me. As she poured the tea she sighed. 'Such troubles, recently. Aunt Maggie so ill, and now poor uncle gone. And there was that man who died in the river not so long ago. Aunt Maggie told me about it. Everyone saying he must have been robbed on the path, and thrown in. I think it must have been a stranger, someone passing through, because no-one round here would do a thing like that.'

'The last time I saw your uncle, he told me he had seen a man on the road outside the cottage,' I said, 'but it wasn't anyone he recognised, and he only saw him from the back. Of course, that man might have had nothing to do with the body found in the millstream, as he was there the morning after the man died.'

'Oh yes, Aunt Maggie mentioned that. Uncle told her he thought the man was one of those pedlars.'

'What made him think that?' asked Holmes, suddenly alert.

'I'm not sure,' said Mrs Cooper. 'But there was another man on the road as well. It was the same day, but a few minutes after. Aunt Maggie saw him.'

'Could she describe him?' asked Holmes.

Mrs Cooper shook her head. 'No, only that she didn't like the look of him.'

'If she is able to recall anything,' said Holmes, earnestly, 'anything her brother might have told her about the first man, and what she saw of the second one, I would like to hear it.' Holmes produced his card and wrote on it the name of the inn where we were lodging.

'Do you think it might be important?' she asked, dubiously

'If not, there is no harm done, but I like to look at every possibility,' said Holmes.

We thanked her for the tea and took our leave, returning to the mill for the meeting which was to take place in Mr Young's office.

'There is something missing from the inquest,' said Holmes.

'Oh?'

'Evidence was given of what happened on the platform, and also Jenkins's health and state of mind beforehand. All very important, of course, but no-one described the tour of the workshop.'

'Perhaps we should speak to Mr Phillips,' I said.

'Yes,' said Holmes. He looked at his watch. 'I think we have a little time before the meeting.'

We sought out Mr Phillips, who was in the factory telling the other men about the result of the inquest.

'Mr Phillips, I know you did not see what happened to Jenkins, but I could not help wondering if you had anything else to say about the proceedings,' said Holmes.

'Yes, well, it was what you said, Mr Stamford, about the man Jenkins saw the morning after Gorrie died.'

'Did he tell you what he had seen?' asked Holmes.

'No, he never said anything to me,' said Phillips. He glanced at the other men who all shook their heads. 'But while he was down here, showing the gentlemen how we make our knives and such, there was some talk about Mr Gorrie's death and whether that matter had been resolved. Jenkins said there had been a lot of talk in the town about how Gorrie might have been attacked by a stranger passing through, as there had been some pedlars in town and some of them had looked disreputable and been questioned by the police. He said he had seen one going past but that was the morning after Gorrie was thought to have been killed, and then there was another man who passed by later on. He thought he ought to report it.'

'Did he describe either of these men?'

Phillips shook his head. 'No, at least not to any of us.'

'If you don't mind,' said Holmes, 'might I ask if you or any of the men who work here have an interest in Dr Baumann's motor?'

To our surprise Phillips laughed. 'No, sir,' he said. 'Round here we all think it's nothing but a lot of nonsense. I wouldn't trust that Baumann an inch. He'll be selling sunlight in a box next. And there'll be rich fools who'll buy it, too.'

Holmes thanked him, and we went to the little luncheon room where Mrs Young had kindly arranged for some tea and simple refreshments. I didn't say so, but I thought that the directors would require some strengthening food before the meeting and a glass or two of best Canadian whisky afterwards.

As we took our places in the office, I looked about me at the assembled persons, wondering who of those present knew about what we had discovered in the workshop. Rumours of Dr Baumann's arrest had been rife in Waltham Abbey, and many people were thinking that he had quarrelled with Mr Gorrie and was suspected of murder. Only Holmes and I, Mrs Young and Mr Ineson were well informed, and we still had much to learn. Mrs Beauregard had arrived; her features and posture were an unshakeable barrier to any criticism of her favourite. Messrs Green, Jamison and Murray, Professor Novak and Reverend Woodley all appeared concerned, but were simply waiting to hear the news. Perhaps, I thought, they were hoping for no more than a formal change in the board of directors of Baumann Motors.

'Before we begin,' said Mrs Beauregard, and all heads turned in her direction, 'I feel I should express my shock at the treatment of Dr Baumann. It is impossible for anyone who truly knows him to imagine for a moment that he can be responsible for what happened to Mr Gorrie.'

'I heard a rumour that he has been taken away by Scotland Yard to be charged with a very serious crime,' said Reverend Woodley.

'Outrageous!' exclaimed Mrs Beauregard.

'I never liked the fellow,' said Green. 'I always thought there was something off about him. And that Gorrie? He was a strange one.'

'Genius is often misunderstood by fools,' said Mrs Beauregard, sharply.

'Can we please proceed with the meeting?' snapped Mr Murray impatiently.

'Yes, please do,' said Professor Novak, mildly.

'But Mr Ineson must advise us on the current position of Dr Baumann, as he is Mr Young's co-director,' said Mr Jamison anxiously.

'In view of the current legal proceedings I am not bound to say anything on that subject,' said Ineson. 'The subject of this meeting is the future of Baumann Motors Ltd.'

'I am pleased to hear it has a future,' said Mr Green. 'But I assume that Baumann cannot fulfil his duties on the board.'

'That is to be decided,' said Ineson.

Mrs Young tapped the desktop with a pencil. 'Let us begin,' she said gently. 'Mr Ineson, I would be obliged if you were to take the lead.'

Ineson made a little bow of agreement. 'Mrs Young was kind enough to allow me to view the workshop just now, and while I am no mechanic, I was able to understand what I saw. In due course, you will all be able to see for yourselves. Those of you who have been present at demonstrations of the motor have been led to believe that the action of the beam engine was powered by the Baumann motor, using no more than a mixture of air and cold water, without any fuel, and no application of heat or pressure. That, I can tell you now, is not the case.' He paused to allow this news to be absorbed by the members of the meeting, then turned to Holmes. 'Mr Holmes, since you were instrumental in the discovery, would you be so kind as to describe what you found?'

Holmes nodded. 'I am sorry to have to tell you that the Baumann motor does not provide any power. The power you saw at the demonstrations was produced by water pressure, passed into the workshop through a concealed pipe going from the penstock outside — that is the chute taking water from the mill race to power the waterwheel. This water entered the part of the apparatus described as the amplifimoderator, which we were told was instrumental in some way to transferring and enhancing the etheric force. What it actually did was to convey the waterpower to the beam engine. The water was then carried away to return to the penstock by another concealed pipe. The Baumann motor in its current form is a fraud.'

There were expressions of shock, surprise and disbelief around the table. There was a little wail of despair from Mr Jamison, and a groan of disappointment from Professor Novak. Only Mr Green seemed unmoved.

'Are you quite certain of this?' asked Reverend Woodley. 'You have not made a mistake?'

'I am certain,' said Holmes.

'But the principle — that is still sound? I refuse to believe otherwise!' exclaimed the reverend.

'The principle must hold true, of course it must,' said Novak.

'Well I for one want to see this proof of fraud, before we talk any more,' said Murray. 'The truth! No arguments!'

'I think we should all go and see the evidence before the meeting continues,' said Mr Green.

Mrs Beauregard pressed her lips firmly together and gave a sharp nod.

'I agree,' said Mr Ineson. 'Mrs Young, you have the key.' He rose from his seat. 'Follow me.'

The gloomy little assembly was conducted on a tour of the abandoned workshop. Holmes pointed out the trail of the hidden pipes, and showed how the beam engine could be made to work without any obvious power. 'It is apparent to me, as it should also be to yourselves,' he said, 'that the pipes which were installed to give the motor the appearance of working without a supply of power, were not a recent addition but must have been a part of the structure from the start.'

Mrs Beauregard remained silent during the procedure. I was worried she might level accusations against Holmes, but she said nothing, simply staring at him with a gaze dipped in vinegar.

Mr Green uttered what sounded like a self-satisfied laugh. 'There!' he exclaimed, clapping his hands together, 'I had my suspicions. It all seemed too pat to believe. When Gorrie's bag was found I knew something was up and I took out a wager to cover my expenses if the company collapsed.'

'You might have told us to do the same!' exclaimed Jamison angrily, and Murray bellowed agreement.

'You knew everything I did,' said Green, unrepentantly. 'It was up to you to decide what to do. My advice doesn't come free of charge.'

'But the principle!' declared Reverend Woodley. 'The etheric force is proven by science! It is given to us by God, for the good of man! A motor that used it could be made to work! We cannot abandon the effort. The company ought to continue under another director.'

'I am so sorry to see this,' said Professor Novak, sadly. 'I agree with you, Reverend. It will work, and I look forward to that day. Dr Baumann always believed in the principle, but it seems to me from what we have been shown that he must have made a great error of judgement. He wanted to raise sufficient money to create a working motor. Perhaps the demonstrations were only to illustrate what it would be capable of.' He sighed heavily. 'If it hadn't been for Gorrie's death we might never have learned about this strange deception. The work would have gone on, and in a year's time or less, we would be seeing the fruits of Dr Baumann's labours.'

'Well, I shall have nothing more to do with this or any other such venture!' barked Murray. 'I resign from the board at once!

In my opinion, Baumann is nothing more than a mountebank, and I hope he gets his just deserts in prison! As for you, Mr Green, I find your behaviour shocking, and I shall be having a word with your father!' He walked out of the room and a minute or two later we heard him outside ordering his carriage to depart. Mr Green said nothing, but I could see that Murray's threat was not without some weight. We left the workshop, and Mrs Young locked the door.

It was a miserable assembly that returned to the office. Jamison was stricken with emotion, struggling not to dissolve in tears. 'Baumann should be asked to explain himself,' he said.

'He has been questioned and denies all knowledge of the fraud,' said Mr Ineson. 'He blames it all on Gorrie.'

'Easy enough to blame a dead man,' observed Mr Green.

'Well of course it was Gorrie!' declared Mrs Beauregard, seizing upon the suggestion triumphantly. 'Dr Baumann is a man of science. He is not a crude mechanic. The motor was built by Mr Gorrie, who must be held wholly responsible. If he introduced anything he ought not to have, then he did so without the knowledge of Dr Baumann.'

'There may be some truth in that,' said Mrs Young, mildly. 'My husband did mention to me that Gorrie told him that while he had made the motor to his employer's specifications, he introduced some changes to improve its operation.'

'If it was Gorrie alone who resorted to fraud it was surely only to gain more time and investments to make a working motor for his employer,' said Professor Novak. 'Dr Baumann's promises concerning completion time were simply too ambitious. The project can still succeed,' he insisted.

Reverend Woodley nodded agreement, but the other directors did not appear to share his optimism.

'I am obliged at this juncture to mention one other issue,' said Ineson. 'I don't know whether this will improve your understanding of the situation or add to your woes, but it must be aired.'

'Oh dear!' said Mr Jamison, dejectedly. 'Well, let us know the worst.'

'The director known as Dr Baumann is not, as he has claimed, a scientist, or indeed Swiss,' Ineson began. 'Neither is he a mechanic. He is an American actor who performs in the New York theatres under the name Jackson Bourne.'

Mr Jamison slumped miserably in his chair, grey-faced. 'I'm not sure I can bear any more,' he muttered but made no effort to move.

'Mr Bourne has claimed that so far from employing Mr Gorrie, that Mr Gorrie employed him to promote his motor,' Ineson continued. 'I have never met Mr Gorrie, but I am told he was a softly spoken man with a Scottish accent, and of unprepossessing appearance, so there may be some truth in his employing another man as a kind of showman, although we only have Mr Bourne's word for it.'

'What an extraordinary allegation!' exclaimed Mrs Beauregard. 'Do you have proof that Dr Baumann is Bourne the actor?'

'I do,' said Ineson. 'I cannot discuss that proof, which may be disclosed in time.'

I had thought to mention the theatrical poster, but on reflection felt that even if permitted, I doubted the advisability of showing Mrs Beauregard an engraving of Bourne posing heroically as Davy Crockett.

'Well,' she said after a moment's consideration, 'if that is true, it must exonerate him from all suspicion. After all, he only did what he was engaged to do, and it is not against the law for an actor to play a part.'

'My advice to the Board, therefore,' said Mr Ineson, 'is that the company should be dissolved forthwith. Mr Young has a London solicitor who would be willing to advise you.'

The investors decided to consult their own legal men before that step was taken, but none of them objected. There was nothing more to add at that juncture. The meeting was formally closed. Mrs Young offered the members refreshment, but they all seemed eager to leave.

'Well, Mr Holmes, do you still believe that Gorrie was murdered?' asked Ineson, as he collected his papers.

'I do,' said Holmes.

'If Mrs Beauregard agrees, I will continue to act for Mr Bourne on the fraud charges. He may also be charged with Gorrie's murder.'

'She will not abandon him?'

'I am not certain of that. She has still to be told he is a married man, although that situation may not last much longer. But I do not think her standing in the county would be improved by a connection with a divorced actor, and in her position, she will be very well aware of that.'

'Is he still unable or unwilling to provide an alibi for the time of Gorrie's death?'

'I am afraid so. He is clearly concealing something.'

Outside, Mr Murray's carriage had gone, and Mrs Beauregard had also departed. Professor Novak and Reverend Woodley remained and appeared to be offering each other words of comfort and reassurance. Mr Green and Mr Jamison had not been so amicable. Mr Green was clutching a bloodstained handkerchief to his nose and Mr Jamison was sporting the makings of a black eye. Neither was willing to receive my offered help or discuss the reason for their altercation.

Holmes proposed we make another visit to see how Frank Newman was doing and Mrs Young kindly lent us her conveyance to take us to the Queen Eleanor Inn where Miss O'Hara remained, tending the invalid. Newman was conscious, still in pain but on the mend. I examined him and thankfully saw no signs of infection or fever.

'Mr Newman,' said Holmes, 'does "ruby" mean anything to you?'

Newman smiled weakly. 'Yes, it does, why do you ask?'

'Inspector Lestrade told us that as Cassidy was dying, he said the word "ruby" which has led him to believe that Mr Bourne was being pursued due to some stolen jewellery. He is even now trying to discover if there were any jewel robberies which Bourne might be guilty of. But "Ruby" is also a name, and when lodging at the White Lion, Cassidy and Jones asked whether their quarry had been seen with a woman, who they thought had accompanied him from America. If she did, she has yet to be found.'

'I will tell you about Ruby Chavez,' said Newman. 'I have never seen her, but I have been told that she is young and exceptionally beautiful, with hair as black as night and dark eyes. For some years she has been the mistress of Eddie Delaney, who commands the Delaney gang, an association of criminals in New York. He did not always treat her kindly. He is a jealous and violent man. She has a scar on her left cheek, which I was told he gave her, the result of a blow with his right hand on which he wears a heavy ring. Strangely, it does not detract from her beauty. Some weeks ago, I heard a rumour that she was missing and had not been seen for some time. It was thought that she had been so badly beaten by Delaney that she was having to heal in private before she could be seen in public again. It has also been rumoured that he has killed her and hidden the body, or that she has run away with another man.'

'Do you think she might have run away with Jackson Bourne?' I asked.

'I can't say, but if she did then I am sure that Delaney would have thought nothing of sending two of his men here to bring her back and kill Bourne — or perhaps to kill them both.'

'Now that we have a description, and a name, it might be possible to discover if Miss Chavez has made her escape to England,' said Holmes. 'She might have travelled on the same ship. Miss O'Hara, might I trouble you to enquire again with the ship's steward should he be on shore? And it would also assist me if he was able to provide a description of Dr Nachtnebel.'

Miss O'Hara promised to make enquiries for us, although since the persons she wished to question might be at sea she thought it might take some while to contact them for a reply.

'I will send a telegram to Lestrade,' said Holmes. 'He will have his own channels of enquiry and will be grateful for the information, since he is currently wasting time trying to connect Bourne to a jewel robbery.'

The carriage took us along the sunny streets of the little town to our lodgings, and we sent it back to Mrs Young at the mill. We were just ordering a light luncheon, when the landlord came to speak to us. 'I have a note for you,' he said. 'It was delivered to Mr Young who is a friend of yours but addressed to Mr Holmes and Mr Stamford, so he had it forwarded.' He handed over an envelope, which was of that fashionable hue often seen in garments of silk and satin, called eau-de-nil.

Holmes stared at the envelope, then he held it to his nostrils. 'It is undoubtedly from a lady,' he said. 'This is a warning to you, Stamford. Whenever there is trouble, there is always a lady in the case!'

I did think to mention that Miss O'Hara was far from being troublesome but decided against it. We retired to a quiet corner of the lounge bar with our beer and sandwiches to study the letter.

To Mr Holmes and Mr Stamford.
Dear Sirs,

I have heard that you are very clever gentlemen and have been enquiring into the death of Mr Gorrie. I know that Dr Baumann the scientist has been questioned concerning this and has not explained where he was on the night Mr Gorrie was killed. I must tell you that he was in my company that night, so cannot have been responsible for what happened to Mr Gorrie. I am maidservant to a great lady and would suffer ruin if he named me.

The letter was unsigned.

'Scented and best quality,' I said. 'She must have used her mistress's paper.'

Holmes said nothing but finished his repast and rose to his feet. 'Let us go to Mr Young's and see if he is able to receive us. We may learn more there.'

We walked to the Youngs' home in Sun Street, where a maid admitted us. 'Master is at home,' she said, 'but I am not sure he is able to receive visitors today.'

'Perhaps you could enlighten me,' said Holmes. He showed the maid the envelope. 'This was forwarded to us at our lodgings today. Do you know how it was delivered?'

'Oh, yes, that came by hand,' she said. 'The girl said she would not wait for a reply, so I took it to Mr Young, and he said to take it to you at the New Inn.'

'Was the girl known to you?'

'I don't know her name but have seen her before. I think she is in service with Mr Murray.'

Before I could comment, Mr Young came into the hallway to join us. He looked tired and dispirited. There were dark shadows under his eyes which told of sleepless nights. 'Ah, I thought I heard your voice, Mr Holmes. Come through to the drawing room. Mary — please be so good as to bring us some coffee.' The maid bobbed a curtsey and left us.

In the drawing room we sat comfortably although Young looked crumpled into his armchair rather than alert. There was a low table at his elbow with a decanter and a glass of whisky. 'I could offer you something stronger if you like?' he said.

'Thank you,' said Holmes, 'coffee will be more than adequate.'

'It has been a hard few days,' said Young with a sigh. He reached for the whisky glass but thought better of it. He rubbed his eyes. 'I have had letters from lawyers I cannot bear to look at. My wife has borne the burden for me, and Norris is always a diligent assistant. I am hoping that when all is done, the company — Young's Toolmakers — will survive and move on. Is there anything I can do for you? I heard you asking Mary about that letter. From the Ladies' Philanthropic Society, I assume? I have seen that notepaper before.'

'Indeed,' said Holmes. 'But I was wondering if I might have a word with your father-in-law. Is he here?'

'No, not at present,' said Young. 'Was he not at the meeting?'

Holmes was silent, but he smiled.

Young stared at Holmes and uttered a low groan. 'Oh dear!' he said. 'I fear I have revealed what I should not. Please forgive me. Can you forget what I have just said?'

'I am afraid I cannot,' said Holmes. 'You have only confirmed what I suspected, or I would not have asked the question.'

'But — how did you know?'

'There were a great many clues which, once assembled, gave me the picture,' said Holmes airily. I said nothing, since I had no idea what he alluded to.

'We have done nothing wrong,' said Young. 'Please believe me. But there were good reasons, business reasons, for our secrecy. Promise me you will say nothing until the truth is out, which it may be in time. I fear that an honest man will be made to suffer!'

'I remain to be convinced,' said Holmes. 'But to do so, you must tell me all.'

Young nodded. The coffee arrived and he drank it gratefully, before he assembled his thoughts. 'My wife Erna is, as you rightly guessed, the daughter of Professor Novak. That is not his real name, although that is how he wishes to be known here. He is Dr Helmut Nachtnebel, a respected man of science, author and lecturer. Like so many of his profession he became interested in the etheric force and hoped that one day man would be able to use its power for the benefit of society. He was planning to go and examine the Keely motor, but that has recently been studied by experts who have expressed doubts as to its future. He remains, however, a firm believer in the principles expounded by Baron Carl von Reichenbach. I believe you read his book, Mr Holmes.'

'I did,' said Holmes. 'It was very curious.'

'The late baron is the only man who has ever conducted studies that prove the existence of the force. So far, all efforts by others to replicate his results have failed. As a result, his work has fallen out of fashion with younger men. One such, a Dr Klamm, openly criticised my father-in-law on the subject, often in quite insulting terms. Klamm actually campaigned for my father-in-law's tenure as a lecturer not to be renewed, claiming that his teachings were outdated and wrongful. Sad to say, that is what occurred. My father-in-law decided to use his retirement to come to England and see us. It was on the voyage here that he was approached by Mr Gorrie.'

'Had he met Mr Gorrie before?' asked Holmes, as Young poured more coffee.

'No, but Gorrie knew him by reputation and made sure to establish an acquaintance and introduce him to his travelling companion. He claimed that the man calling himself Mr McGuckin could not travel under his real identity as there were jealous persons who might attempt to rob him of some valuable papers. Of course, they had much to talk about. Gorrie hoped that my father-in-law would advise and support him in his intention to construct a motor, and that the name of a distinguished scientist might attract investors. But of course, that was precisely what he could not do.'

'I see why, but kindly explain,' said Holmes.

'Dr Klamm is taking an interest in the Keely motor, which he believes to be a delusion, if not an outright fraud, and he is alert to any attempts to create similar devices. If he was to hear of the Baumann motor and found that Nachtnebel was involved in the company, he would use all his influence to ensure that it did not attract investors. The name Nachtnebel must never be associated with the company. My father-in-law would not be a director or employee of the company; he would not accept any fees from it or make any public pronouncements on its work. He would, however, under the name Professor Novak, be happy to give informal advice, attend demonstrations and make suitable observations. That is all.'

'And it was he who introduced Mr Gorrie and Dr Baumann to you?'

Young nodded. 'Yes.'

'And suggested that you provide space at the mill for their work?'

'Yes.'

'He has not invested any of his own money in the Baumann motor?'

'No. Not a cent. Of course he is disappointed at recent developments, but he remains optimistic that it is only a matter of time before the principle is vindicated. We have heard that Dr Klamm may be coming to England next year for a lecture tour, and it would be good to be able to advance matters so as to challenge him.'

'Who would you say are the greatest losers?'

Young sighed and absentmindedly added some whisky to his coffee. 'Mrs Beauregard of course. She still thinks her shares will recover if the right man can be found to take over the company. It will be a brave man who tells her otherwise. Mr Murray invested a large sum on the advice of his wife. He is angry with her and with me. But then he is angry with most people. Mr Green's company is in the business of taking risks, and he seems to have covered himself financially, although I understand that Mr Murray has lodged a complaint against him and withdrawn his portfolio.

'Reverend Woodley is being asked some very hard questions by his bishop. He has been preaching some stirring sermons on the power of the force to demonstrate God, and members of his flock have invested. I fear his enthusiasm may have caused him to risk church funds.

'Mr Jamison has been demoted by his father, who is furious with him. And I have recently learned that when Mr Norris purchased some shares, he used funds he was saving towards marriage. Only a small sum, but it was all he had. I am getting letters in every post asking where compensation is going to come from. I am sure I don't know.'

'Thank you for enlightening us, Mr Young,' said Holmes. 'Might I request you inform your father-in-law of what has passed here and ask him if he would agree to talk to us? There are a few small details I am sure he could supply so I have the complete picture of what has occurred.'

Young agreed, and we left him to his contemplation and his whisky. 'I know the police have established alibis for those persons who might have taken against Mr Gorrie with the exception of Mr Bourne,' said Holmes, 'but I feel that a closer look might be advisable in all cases.'

'Do you think the letter from the maidservant might be genuine?' I asked. 'She may not want to come forward.'

'She will not,' said Holmes, 'I am sure of that.'

'You know who she is? The girl who delivered the letter perhaps?'

'No. You have already observed that the writer must have used the mistress's notepaper.'

'Yes.'

'I think she also used the mistress's pen and ink, and it should also be possible to prove the lady's educated style of lettering,' observed Holmes drily. 'If there was an intrigue, it was with a woman who had far more to lose than a servant's position.'

'You mean the lady herself?'

'Yes.'

'Not Mrs Beauregard?'

'No, her blushing friend, Mrs Murray, who favours that delicate shade of green and whose husband, you may recall, was in Paris at the time of Mr Gorrie's death.'

'Oh!' I exclaimed.

'Whether Mr Murray's French visit was for business or pleasure, we can only surmise. If this letter is to be trusted, however, Mr Bourne may indeed have an alibi for the time of Mr Gorrie's death, but he will never be able to use it.'

CHAPTER THIRTEEN

'I regret to say,' said Lestrade when we met with him at the police station the following day to enlighten him on our progress, 'that this letter is not the only one purporting to be from a woman who offers a scandalous alibi for Mr Bourne. The Yard has received several, which means that they will most likely all be ignored. I have however received a letter from Mrs Bourne, who is on her way to see her husband. She may be able to extract some truth from him.'

'He has not attempted to claim that he struggled with Gorrie and the fall was accidental?' said Holmes, drily.

'No. And I can see what you are thinking. That is often the claim of a guilty man who has no alibi and is trying to escape the noose. Bourne flatly denies being anywhere near the weir.'

'I feel that the police suspicion of Mr Bourne, which is wholly understandable, has diverted enquiries from the other possible suspects,' said Holmes. 'The investors in the company who have lost money and reputation due to Gorrie's fraud. Any one of them might have learned of the fraud before Gorrie disappeared and entertained a strong desire to wring the neck of the perpetrator. My advice is to examine their alibis once more. They may not stand up to a close examination.'

Lestrade frowned but said nothing.

'Let us list them,' said Holmes. 'We may begin with Mr Murray who claimed to be in Paris on a business visit. Has he supplied the name of his hotel?'

Lestrade coughed. 'I believe he has a little apartment there — with a lady housekeeper. I am sure she will vouch for him.'

'I am sure she will,' said Holmes. 'Mr Green?'

'He lives in Cheshunt, and he is married with one child. His wife and servant confirm that he was at home on the evening of Mr Gorrie's death.' Lestrade glanced through his papers. 'Mr Jamison is a single man, and lives with his parents in Waltham Cross. He was dining away from home with some other gentlemen that evening. Oh, that is interesting.'

'What is?'

'Mr Jamison is a director of a company that makes agricultural equipment, of which his father is the main shareholder. He, Green and Young are members of a businessman's club. And Jamison's company owed money to Green and Co., a loan to fund improvements to the factory. Jamison arranged the loan from Green without his father's knowledge. And now he is unable to repay the first instalment. Or possibly any of them.'

'I assume he was hoping to repay the loan from profits on the Baumann motor,' said Holmes.

'Just so. I think he is being sent abroad. Somewhere inhospitable.'

'What of Mrs Beauregard? I do not exempt her from suspicion.'

'Yes, she has quite a temper,' said Lestrade. 'She has a manor house in Broxbourne. Dined alone that evening, according to her maid. No visitors. She is writing an appreciation of Dr Baumann and his work. At least, she was. Then there is Professor Novak who was in London, dining at his hotel in London, the Devonshire. I confirmed that by examining his account. Mr Young was dining in Waltham Abbey, with his wife.'

'Have you questioned Mr Norris, Mr Young's secretary? He lodges in Waltham Abbey.'

'Yes, he called on his sweetheart and was walking out with her before returning to his lodgings for supper. But his investment was not very great, compared to the others.'

'It might have been great to him,' said Holmes.

'Ah, I see your point.'

'Reverend Woodley?'

'A man of the cloth? You don't seriously suspect him?'

'I suspect everyone. And Woodley, who has announced to the world that the Baumann motor is proof of God, has more to lose than his own, the church's or his parishioner's money.'

'That is true. I did speak to him. He lives with his widowed sister who keeps house for him in Waltham Cross and was there that night.'

'These alibis mostly rely on family, friends or servants for confirmation,' Holmes observed.

'So many alibis do,' said Lestrade.

'And I ought to point out that the murder of Gorrie occurred within an easy walk of Cheshunt, and Broxbourne is not far distant. Neither is Waltham Cross. I assume you have made enquiries of drivers who may have taken someone to the signpost or hired out a vehicle or given someone a ride on a wagon? Or discovered anyone who might have seen one of our suspects on a train?'

'If nothing else comes to light I shall have to check them all again,' said Lestrade. 'Oh, and thank you for letting me know about Professor Novak. We have examined the company papers, and he is not mentioned anywhere either as Novak or Nachtnebel. All the moneys at the mill are accounted for, and I am satisfied that he has no financial interest in the Baumann motor. I asked Bourne about him and he has confirmed that he first met the professor on the voyage, and he offered his advice but nothing more. I also asked Bourne about Miss Ruby

Chavez, and he admitted that she was a friend of his in New York, whatever that may mean, but he had never even thought to run away with her. As far as he was aware, she is still in America. But you may have something there as I understand her gentleman friend Mr Eddie Delaney is the jealous type, and likely to jump to conclusions. I am still waiting to hear if she has been seen recently. Of course, she may have followed Bourne without his knowing. I am looking into that.'

He leafed through his notes. 'On that subject, a telegram has just been received at the White Hart from Delaney addressed to the late Mr Cassidy asking if his business had been successfully concluded. We will have to respond. We don't want more of Delany's gang over here.'

'If I might make a suggestion,' said Holmes. 'Mr Frank Newman, the Pinkerton detective, is the best man to compose a reply that will convince Mr Delaney that it comes from his gunmen, and he has no need to send others.'

'Ah, yes, I shall see it done.' Lestrade wrote in his notebook.

'Are you satisfied with the verdict on Jenkins?' asked Holmes.

'I have to be, for now,' said Lestrade. 'Why do you ask?'

'When Jenkins took the visitors on a tour of the factory, they asked him if Gorrie's murder had been solved,' said Holmes. 'Jenkins told them that local gossip attributed Gorrie's death to a pedlar, and that two such men were seen on the road outside the mill cottages on the morning after Gorrie was killed. He was thinking of reporting them to the police.'

'Did he describe them?'

'No. I was intending to interview him, but he died before I had the chance.'

'Perhaps it was Jenkins who quarrelled with Gorrie,' suggested Lestrade. 'And he was trying to deflect suspicion from himself by blaming some unknown pedlar.'

'But why would Jenkins quarrel with Gorrie?' I asked.

Lestrade shrugged. 'I don't suppose we will know that now. But it was Jenkins' business to see to the sluice gate and keep things running. He might have been up there and seen Gorrie doing something suspicious. The way I see it, Jenkins might have made up this pedlar story to avoid blame, or, if he really did see someone, whoever it was might have had nothing to do with Gorrie's murder. Would any of the persons with possible motives have been out on the road alone at first light? It doesn't seem likely. Dr Henderson can't have been so far wrong about the time of death.'

'Time of death is never precise,' I said, 'especially when a body has been in water. But the stomach contents and when the man was last seen are our best guidance in this case.'

'Perhaps the killer dropped something that would identify him, and had to come back for it,' said Lestrade. 'Not that that helps us without a description.'

Holmes did not reply to this, but I could see that a new thought had struck him which he needed to pursue.

A brief note invited us to take tea with Professor Novak at the Devonshire Hotel where he was staying. We caught a train to London and found him in affable mood, doing his best to mitigate the problems besetting the Baumann motor.

The dining room was quiet and elegant. The dinner service was yet to begin. We took a table in one corner, and Novak ordered tea and pastries.

'If you don't mind,' he said, 'I wish to be called by my *nom de guerre* while here. If Dr Klamm should be aware of my involvement in any project, he will do what he can to put an end both to it and my career.'

'But you are confident of victory?' asked Holmes.

'I am indeed. The science cannot lie. Klamm is a fool. If it means starting afresh then that is what must happen. Then I will publish the results, which will vindicate Baron Reichenbach and put Klamm to shame.'

'From what I have been told,' said Holmes, 'you first encountered the man calling himself Dr Baumann when on the voyage to England. He was introduced to you by Mr Gorrie.'

'That is so. Gorrie was a strange fellow, but he cut a more respectable figure when travelling, and he was skilled in his work.'

'The motor he constructed was also strange,' I said. 'I couldn't make out what it was supposed to do.'

'I think that was deliberate,' said Novak. 'It had to appear mysterious, as we were told it generated power by a method new to science. As we now know, Gorrie had us all deceived. I still think he had the best of intentions and would have succeeded in time and with the right funding.'

'I must ask,' said Holmes, 'how it is that you were you deceived by Baumann? It must have been very apparent to you during your first conversation that he was a charlatan. Surely you saw through him?'

Novak smiled. 'I perceived very quickly that he was no scientist,' he said. 'I thought he might be one of those unqualified dabblers, who think they can make money from inventions. But there was something about him that struck me. Something that I knew would make him very useful.'

'Go on,' Holmes prompted.

'You see,' said Novak, 'for Gorrie's enterprise to bear fruit, one must consider what kind of men are required. I believe there are three. First of all, the man of science. He understands the principles involved and can compute what is required to construct a device that will deliver the result. Secondly the mechanic. Skilled with his hands, he can follow directions exactly and manufacture the apparatus. But such a project is expensive, so thirdly there is the promotor, who can speak convincingly and demonstrate the device to interested parties to attract investments.

'I maintain that where Keely has made his mistake is that he has tried to be all three at once. Now, the man may exist who can be all three such things at once, but Keely is not that man. He is no scientist. He must have read some scholarly works, but he may not have grasped them fully, and he proceeds in ignorance, concealing his lack of understanding with flamboyant words that impress only those ignorant of what they mean. Thus, he has attracted the money of persons who wish only to become rich and are likely instead to lose all their funds.

'Keely is a mechanic, and he has a convincing way of speaking, but how long mere words have lasted we have seen. Science has declared his motor to be a humbug, half his investors have deserted him, and the rest remain only to clasp at straws in the hope of future success, which I do not think he is capable of delivering, or at least not for many years.'

'So you took the role of man of science,' said Holmes, 'for which you are well qualified.'

'I am. But for reasons you already know, I could not openly support the project. Mr Gorrie, while skilled with his hands, was no speaker. He could converse quietly but not address a gathering. Baumann was a man of charm, easily able to memorise the material given to him and deliver it with energy and confidence.'

'And Mr Young's factory was a ready-made location for a workshop where the motor could be constructed,' said Holmes.

'John is a dear fellow and let us have the use of the room at no cost,' said Novak. 'I knew, given the nature of his business, that he would be amenable, and so he was. He knew my reputation at least. Once we arrived, I introduced him to Dr Baumann who I said was a man with an important venture to pursue. I maintained that I was retired from the academic life, but Baumann was the coming man and should be encouraged. It went on from there. I suppose in a sense I attributed to Baumann the qualifications I had gained. I know it was a deception, but the important thing was the success of the project and the benefits to mankind.'

'You had a central role which you kept well hidden,' said Holmes.

'Naturally I wished to maintain a close eye on the operation. I coached Baumann on what to say. I attended the demonstrations under the name of Professor Novak of Prague, and added comments which would encourage investment. I was obliged occasionally to provide information where Baumann appeared to hesitate and conceal his lack of knowledge.'

'Inspector Lestrade told me he has been asking everyone with an interest in the Baumann motor where they were on the night when Gorrie was killed,' said Holmes. 'I believe you were included.'

'Yes, I was able to provide him with my information,' said Novak. 'I keep a diary of my travels and visits.' He took a small leather-bound notebook from his pocket. 'That day I attended Mr J. L. King's afternoon lecture at the Royal Polytechnic. I conversed with several persons there. The inspector has their names. It was a pleasant day, so I took a walk and returned here for my dinner. I spent the evening in my room, reading papers and making notes for my publication. I then retired for the night.'

Holmes was studying the menu on the table. 'I see dinner service begins at seven,' he said. 'Do you recall what you ate that night?'

'The Russian salad with beef, it is very good.'

'Served here or in your room?'

'In my room. Alone. I like to dine quietly. There is too much clatter of dishes during the dinner service. Not conducive to my work at all.'

'Professor, I thank you for your time. Can you advise me how much longer you intend to remain in England?'

Novak smiled. 'I begin to like it here,' he said. 'And I have so much work to do. I think I might cease to be a visitor and become a resident. My dear daughter has already suggested I come and live with her. There is ample room for me, and Waltham Abbey is such a delightful place. Once the new motor has been built and patented, I will write and lecture, and if Dr Klamm dares to visit, I will send him back to America an unhappy man.'

We left Novak finishing his pastry anticipating a happy future. As we left, I noticed that Holmes had slipped the menu card into his pocket.

Lestrade had been diligent in his searches for Ruby Chavez. As far as he had been able to discover she had not taken passage on a ship under that name, and no-one recalled seeing her. 'Until she turns up somewhere I don't think Delaney will give up the hunt,' he said. 'We are being very careful who we allow near Bourne. Oh, and Mrs Bourne is arriving in London tomorrow. Perhaps I need to keep an eye on her as well. She might not be pleased with her husband. Some women can turn very nasty, you know. I shall get a lady to search her in case she has a gun.'

'I would like to speak to Mrs Bourne if I may,' said Holmes.

Lestrade was a little surprised but agreed. 'She is going to see Mr Ineson and then talk to her husband,' he said. 'But I'll see if she will talk to you.'

As it happened, Mrs Bourne was willing to talk to anyone who had met her husband while he was in England, in the hopes of finding someone who would support her endeavours to free him.

She was a modestly dressed lady of about thirty years, careworn but eager to do her best.

'I have seen Jack and he is trying to keep his spirits up,' she said. 'Mr Ineson feels sure he can have the fraud charges dismissed. And the idea that Jack has killed someone is just nonsense. He has never attempted violence on a living soul. It is not in his nature.'

'You are very forgiving of his bad behaviour,' said Holmes.

She smiled. 'I am his wife and intend to remain so,' she said. 'The divorce petition was at the insistence of my father, who would do anything in his power to part us. He has never trusted Jack, who he thinks married me only for money. He only agreed to the wedding if my private fortune was placed in trust and my jewels kept under lock and key. But during my voyage here, I had time to think. I still love my husband and would not want to see him ruined. He is a fond father to our children. I am sure I can persuade my father that the divorce petition should not proceed and will never even be spoken of. I have told Jack that in view of his wayward manners we cannot live as husband and wife. My proposal is that we have separate establishments but appear together in public in a harmonious fashion. He will return to the stage, and I will take care of the children's upbringing and education. That way we will preserve our standing in society.'

This plan did of course depend on her husband not being in prison, or hanged for murder, but I decided not to mention that.

Bourne was soon to appear before the magistrates in London on a charge of fraud, relating to Baumann Motors Ltd. It was accepted that Mr Young had been an innocent dupe, and he had not been charged with any offence. In view of the perceived danger to the defendant, the public was not to be admitted to the hearing and the case was not to be reported in the newspapers.

In the event, as we were told later on, Mr Ineson made a compelling submission that there was no case to answer since his client had not been aware that a fraud was taking place. His client, who was an actor by profession, had simply been employed as such. He had been engaged by the late Mr Gorrie to play a role, to learn lines supplied to him, and perform them before an audience. Mr Bourne was no scientist and no mechanic. The fraudulent apparatus had been devised and constructed by Mr Gorrie alone. The pipework which had made the motor appear to generate power had been so well hidden that it had deceived all onlookers. His client had no knowledge of it and would have been unable to detect anything unusual. After some careful consideration, the court decided that there was no case to answer and Jackson Bourne was discharged.

Bourne had not yet been charged with murdering Gorrie. Although suspicion remained, the case against him now looked even weaker than before. If his part had been such a minor one, and he had known nothing of the fraud, then where, observed Holmes, was his motive to kill Gorrie? Lestrade confided to us later that he had received a visit from a lady who refused to remove a heavy veil but described an intrigue with Bourne while her husband was from home. She had described a small detail, a scar on the gentleman visitor's shoulder from an old injury, which it was possible to confirm by inspection. Lestrade thought it unlikely that Bourne would be charged with any crime. The enquiry into Gorrie's murder continued; however, Lestrade felt that he needed to keep an eye on Bourne in case new evidence should emerge, in which case he could be arrested once more.

Bourne, now a free man, albeit a very nervous one, was quickly taken from court in the company of his wife and transported to a quiet hotel. There we met with him and Mr Ineson.

When we congratulated Bourne on his freedom, he sighed unhappily. 'I am glad to be declared innocent of that crime, but I do not know what the future holds for me,' he said. 'I cannot return to America, not with that madman Delaney looking for me. I must stay in hiding and only go out in disguise. I can only hope that Miss Chavez reappears and convinces him that I am blameless. I cannot pursue my career until she does.'

'I will advise my father of the position and see if there is anything he can do,' said Mrs Bourne.

Her husband patted her hand, but he was clearly not convinced that any assistance from his father-in-law would be forthcoming.

'Now that all is in the open,' said Holmes, 'I would be grateful if you could tell me the full story of how you were hired to play the part of Dr Baumann.'

'As you know, there were a number of lawsuits against me; there still are I expect. I haven't the funds to fight them all. My career has suffered mainly due to some sensational reports in the newspapers. I was obliged to leave the cast of the *Davy Crockett* play and lost all my income. Mr father-in-law had been making me an allowance but that ended too. My money was running out and I was wondering what to do when I received a letter from my agent, Mr Danielson. He told me he had met with a Mr Gorrie who wished to employ me. Apparently, Gorrie had designed a motor which he wanted to market and hoped to make a substantial profit. But he did not have the skills to promote it, due to being shy and softly spoken. I was to play the part of the inventor and demonstrate the motor. The invention was so advanced, the details had to be kept secret, and Gorrie was afraid his plans would be stolen, so he wanted to establish a company in Europe. Of course, I was attracted by the sea voyage and the opportunity to escape my difficulties. I decided to travel under my birth name, which few people know of, and he would accompany me as a valet, and coach me on what to say. So I signed up. I had to borrow what I needed to pay the passage.'

'From Mr Danielson?'

'Er — no, from Miss Chavez.'

'And you met Professor Nachtnebel on the way?'

'I did.'

'I can't believe that was by chance.'

'No. Well, it was none of my business, was it? I didn't ask him, but I rather suspected that Gorrie had discovered that Nachtnebel was planning a journey and booked a passage on the same voyage to try and get an introduction to him.'

We left the happy couple to enjoy a quiet dinner in their hotel. Holmes had a brief conference with Lestrade, who went to make his report at Scotland Yard. We then had what I thought would be our final interview with Mr Ineson, whose representation of Jackson Bourne was now complete.

Holmes had absorbed the new information, but I could see that he was still not content. Ineson, like Lestrade, had the feeling that Mr Bourne would cross his path once more.

'There is one item of information I require to complete my case,' said Holmes, 'and for that, I require Inspector Lestrade and the authority of Scotland Yard. I have asked for a cablegram to be sent to New York. I feel sure I know what the answer will be, but I cannot proceed without it.'

'What is the information?' I dared to ask.

'Quite simply, I need to know how Mr Gorrie, a man of no theatrical experience and unconvincing manners, succeeded in engaging Mr Bourne? Of course, Bourne was eager to hide from the various persons trying to sue him, and his source of income had ended. But how did Gorrie convince his agent, Mr Danielson, that this was a genuine offer? I still feel that I am not being told everything. I am hoping that now Bourne has been freed, Mr Danielson might be more forthcoming.'

CHAPTER FOURTEEN

Shortly after Bourne achieved his freedom, Mr and Mrs Young hosted an afternoon tea at their home in Waltham Abbey. Mr Young, who was still recuperating from his distress at recent events, had accepted that Bourne was an innocent dupe of Gorrie's scheme. I thought he wanted an assembly of persons to finally clear the air and help him understand what had occurred.

On our arrival at Waltham Cross station, Holmes and I took the opportunity to visit Mr Newman and Miss O'Hara at the Queen Eleanor Inn. I was delighted to see that the patient, who had been carefully tended under the direction of Dr Evans, was sufficiently healed that the two Pinkerton agents planned to return to America very soon. Miss O'Hara promised to write if there were any interesting developments relevant to our recent enquiries. As we said our farewells, I was a little nervous in case Miss O'Hara should kiss me again, but she merely winked her eye. I hoped Holmes did not notice. If he did, he was good enough not to mention it.

Aside from Holmes and myself, the gathering at Sun Street included the Bournes, Professor Novak, and Inspectors Lestrade and Tubb. Mr Bourne had arrived in disguise requiring a wig and a change of posture, which added twenty years to his true age. He was quite relieved to resume his normal appearance once inside.

Mr Young looked a little better than he had done the last time we saw him. 'I would very much like to return to the mill, soon,' he said. 'Idleness can be so tiring.'

Mrs Young smiled and patted his hand. 'In a few days,' she said. 'Remember what Dr Henderson said.'

I asked how Miss Jenkins was faring.

'She is much better,' said Mr Young. 'She will soon be well enough to travel and will go to live with her niece in Cheshunt.'

Holmes nodded approvingly.

The maid came and served drinks and a tray of savouries. 'I must admit, you had me completely fooled, Mr Bourne,' said Young. 'I never once suspected you were any other than Dr Baumann, a Swiss scientist.'

'Ah, well,' said Bourne with a smile, 'that is down to what we in the profession call acting. But I was fooled too — I had no idea what Gorrie was really up to until all was revealed.'

'You believed that he had devised the entire project himself?' asked Mrs Young. 'He had no academic qualifications, as far as we know.'

'He told me it was all his idea, though I think he was inspired by the work of Keely. These clever men can sometimes be a bit eccentric. I was glad when he introduced me to Professor Novak, it was good to have a wise head to advise me on the finer points.'

'But Gorrie engaged you through Mr Danielson and arranged everything?' asked Holmes.

'He did, yes.'

'I believe he was a far more intelligent fellow than he was ever given credit for,' said Novak. 'Appearances can be deceptive.'

'But we still do not know all the circumstances of his death,' said Mrs Young. 'Inspector, is it true that he was killed for the bag he carried? There are so many stories going about, one hardly knows what to believe.'

'As to that, I have the answer for you,' said Holmes.

'You do?' exclaimed Lestrade.

'Yes, you see a great many falsehoods have abounded, and misled us, but in the end it all comes down to something Professor Novak said to me quite recently, which I found extremely helpful to my deliberations.'

'Oh?' said Novak. 'Whatever could that be?'

'You said that a scheme like the Baumann motor required three minds; the scientist who understands the theory, the mechanic who builds the machine, and the promotor who attracts investors.'

'Yes, that is true.'

'And try as I might I could not picture Mr Gorrie formulating the entire scheme from the beginning, even with the example of Mr Keely to follow.'

'But that is what happened,' said Bourne.

'My main question, the one to which I have been seeking an answer, was how Mr Gorrie was able to convince Mr Danielson that he was a suitable person to engage the services of Mr Bourne.'

'That was what Danielson told me,' said Bourne. 'They met at his office.'

'But you did not meet him then?'

'No, I didn't meet Gorrie until we were about to board ship.'

'And how were you to know Mr Gorrie when you met him?'

'He was carrying a carpetbag, which bore a label with his initials.'

'I have here,' said Holmes, taking a paper from his pocket, 'a reply to my enquiry of Mr Danielson. I asked him to supply me with a description of the man calling himself Gorrie who met with him and arranged to engage Mr Bourne. Shall I read it?'

At this, Professor Novak chuckled. 'Ah, Mr Holmes, what a clever young man you are. I do not deny it; it was I who met with Mr Danielson calling myself Gorrie. I was hardly about to go by my real name, of course. As you know, I have from the start made every effort not to attach my name to the project.'

'But I thought you didn't meet Gorrie until you were on the voyage,' said Mr Young. 'Or am I missing something?'

'Only what I have not yet revealed,' said Novak. 'I would have done so in time, of course, once the motor was completed and patented but —' he sighed and opened his hands in a brief gesture of regret — 'it was not to be. At least, not yet. I still believe a viable motor will emerge one day. I suppose I had better tell you the story from the start. It can do no harm now. But this is only for this very select circle. Reputations in the academic world are still at stake.'

'Please proceed,' said Holmes.

'I was in the last few weeks of my lectureship. I had already determined to use my new leisure time to visit my family and booked my passage. I received an unexpected visit from Mr Gorrie. I had never met him before, but his story engaged my interest. He told me he had been to Philadelphia to view the Keely motor with the object of offering his services to the inventor. Mr Keely refused to engage him, he said he worked alone. But Gorrie was permitted to see a demonstration. What he saw changed his intentions. The other persons who saw the motor were businessmen, financiers, scientists, but Gorrie, being a mechanic, was able to see past the theory, and he came to understand how the motor worked.'

Holmes leaned back in his chair and steepled his fingers together. The expression on his face was quite extraordinary, as if a clear thought had blossomed in his mind, and he knew everything. He said nothing, however, and Novak continued his story.

'As a result of this observation, Gorrie felt sure that he would be able to make something similar himself. On his return to New York, he assembled a small model motor and thought I might like to see it. Naturally I did so, and I was confident that he had solved the mystery which Mr Keely had been so reluctant to share. Gorrie proposed to rent a workshop and wanted me to join him in his enterprise and be the public face of the project. He thought that my name would bring in investors. Of course, I was obliged to inform him that I would not be able to play any part in his endeavour, for reasons he did not then appreciate.'

Mr Young shook his head. 'Erna and I knew nothing of this,' he said.

'No, of course not,' said Novak. 'So many things had to be kept private. But when Gorrie mentioned a workshop, it did occur to me that, having been told about the spacious premises of Abbey Mill, there might be a portion which could be used to develop the motor. I knew John would be very interested.'

Mr Young made no comment.

'I suggested to Gorrie that he accompany me, and we would try our enterprise in England. He had no commitments in America and agreed. But we needed a man to be the public face.' He glanced at Bourne as he said this. 'I hope you don't mind, Mr Bourne, but I must go on.'

'Oh, feel free,' said Bourne.

'At that time the newspapers, those which deliver scandal and the more shocking the better, often with no foundation in truth, had been announcing that Jackson Bourne, a popular figure on the stage, had become embroiled in some personal difficulties. It was claimed that his career was over, and he was facing financial ruin. I said, humorously to Mr Gorrie, that if Mr Bourne was free for an engagement, he would be just the man for our purpose. Gorrie took my suggestion seriously, and so I arranged a meeting with Mr Danielson, under the pseudonym Gorrie. I offered Mr Bourne a role. The script to be written by me. The inventor of a new device who needed to raise funds from investors. When I said that he would be obliged to leave New York for some time, this, far from being an obstacle, appeared to be of interest. Thus, it was settled. Mr Bourne was anxious that it was not generally known he had gone away. He travelled under the name Howard McGuckin, posing as an invalid. His ability to transform himself by art alone into quite another individual astonished me. I travelled as a simple physician, and Gorrie was his valet. During the voyage we discussed and perfected our plans. The rest you know.'

Mr Young was understandably upset. 'You introduced me to Mr Bourne as Dr Baumann, a man of science with important business,' he said accusingly. 'You said he was a coming man and should be encouraged. You told me you were not involved in his work, just an interested observer.'

'I did,' Novak admitted. 'John, I am sorry I had to deceive you, but I truly believed the motor was genuine, and the endeavour should be protected. Naturally I wished to maintain an eye on the operation and add a voice which would encourage investment. I therefore attended the demonstrations under the name of Professor Novak of Prague, and provided information where Dr Baumann appeared to hesitate.'

'And that was all you did?' asked Lestrade. 'You didn't study the motor yourself?'

'No, I only saw what everyone else did.'

'You don't have a key to the workshop?'

'No. My admission to that room was on the same terms as everyone else.'

'Did you ever meet with Bourne and Gorrie to discuss the project?' asked Holmes.

Novak smiled. 'No, neither did we exchange correspondence on the matter. It was essential that I did not attract any suspicion of my involvement. Mr Gorrie insisted that when the work was being carried out, the only other person he would admit to the workshop was Bourne. Not being a mechanic, Bourne would never have questioned anything Gorrie did.'

'I left it to Gorrie alone most of the time,' added Bourne. 'He just told me what to say and do at the demonstrations.'

'Do you really believe, Professor, that the Baumann motor or another like it will have a future?' asked Lestrade.

'I believe another man will eventually succeed, and change our world for the better,' said Novak. 'But I will play no more part in such endeavours. I am seeking a position as a tutor in chemistry and am writing a book on the subject, suitable for students.'

'And you, Mr Bourne? What will you do now?'

'Much as I would like to return to America and continue my career, that is not possible. Emily and I will remain here until various outstanding difficulties are resolved.'

'I have asked my father to help us,' said Mrs Bourne, 'and I think he will. I have not given up hope.' She gazed at her husband fondly.

Holmes and I returned to the New Inn. The weather remained fine, and Holmes sat outside in the beer garden, puffing away at his briar. He had that thoughtful expression which I knew meant he wasn't to be disturbed. I sat at a distance, sipping a pleasant locally-brewed ale, until at last he knocked out the pipe, and put it away.

'Have you come to any conclusion, Holmes?' I asked.

'I came to a conclusion some while ago,' he said with a smile. 'It was only a matter of arranging the facts in the correct order.'

'I would like to return to London soon,' I said. 'I — er — have some business to attend to. And I am not sure we have much more to do here. But before I go, I would like to pay a visit to Miss Jenkins and see how she is doing.'

'That was also my intention. And I would like a word with Mr Norris, too. Let us both go,' said Holmes.

We hired a little trap to convey us to Abbey Mill.

Mr Norris, ever efficient, was manning the office and keeping the business arrangements going in the absence of Mr Young. He looked busy but not hard-pressed. 'How may I help you, gentlemen?' he asked.

'I noticed that when the Baumann motor demonstrations were being held, and you admitted the observers, you confirmed their names from a list,' said Holmes.

Norris looked unhappy at the memory. 'That is very much something we wish to forget,' he said.

'Do you still have the lists?' asked Holmes.

'They are a part of the company records, so yes. Do you wish to see them?'

'There was a meeting arranged which had to be cancelled due to the unexpected absence of Mr Gorrie,' said Holmes. 'Gorrie had seen the names of the gentlemen who wished to attend, because Mr Young showed him the list a few days before he disappeared. That is the one I wish to see.'

Norris opened his record book and glanced through it. 'Yes,' he said. 'This is the one.'

Holmes studied the list. 'Ah yes, a stockbroker, an accountant, a chemist, and —' he tapped his fingertip on the page — 'three names which appear familiar.'

'They are the gentlemen recommended by Reverend Woodley,' said Norris.

'Mr Hodgkins, general manager of Hodgkins Furnishings Ltd; Mr Ross, master brewer of the Old Hertford Brewery; and Mr Feather, builder and surveyor, Associate of the School of Engineering, Norwood,' said Holmes.

'But they never attended, of course,' said Norris.

'No, they did not. Thank you, Mr Norris.'

Holmes looked satisfied, although he was not prepared to tell me why, and we went to see Miss Jenkins.

We were pleased to see Miss Jenkins out of bed and fully dressed. She was sitting at the table with a towel draped over her head, which was bent over a fragrant basin.

'She is much better, sirs,' said Mrs Cooper with a fond smile. 'But once she is able to travel, I will take her up to live with me.' She spoke to Miss Jenkins. 'Aunt Maggie, here is the doctor to see you.'

Miss Jenkins looked up, her face shining with condensation from the hot water. She wiped it away with the towel.

'How are you faring today?' I asked her.

'Oh, thank you kindly, sir, I am doing well.'

I conducted a brief examination and reassured her that with warmth and good feeding she would soon be well again.

Mrs Cooper carried the basin away and went to make tea.

'I am only sorry I was not well enough to see Solomon buried,' said Miss Jenkins. 'The doctor as good as said if I got out of bed and went to the graveside, it would not be worth my while going home again. But I shall go when I am better and lay some flowers.'

'The last time I spoke to your brother he told me a very interesting story,' I said. 'It was the morning after the day that Mr Gorrie died, and he woke up early to look after you. He looked out of the window and saw a man passing by. A stranger. Did he ever tell you about what he had seen? Did he describe the man? I was hoping to learn more from him, but it wasn't to be.'

Miss Jenkins nodded. 'Yes, he did say something about that — a man he saw walk past. He thought he might have been a pedlar. Most of them are honest folk making what they can, but not all.'

'And there was another man who passed by a little later on that same morning,' said Holmes. 'I believe you saw him?'

'Yes, I saw him. When Solomon went to get me a drink to help my cough, I had to get out of bed, for the usual purpose, and I heard someone on the path and looked out of the window. There was a man walking past.'

'Another pedlar?'

'No, I didn't think he was.'

'Why not?' asked Holmes.

'Well, they always carry their wares with them — a basket or a pack, and this man didn't have anything like that.'

'I don't suppose you could describe him?'

She hesitated. 'He had a horrid look, sir. I was quite afraid of him. Being so ill, I put it down to a bad dream. I didn't even tell Solomon about it until later. The last time I saw my brother, he told me about the man he had seen, and how the police might be interested in finding him. That was when I told him about the other man.'

'What do you mean by "a horrid look"?' asked Holmes.

'He had these staring eyes.' She shook her head. 'I've not seen him since and I wouldn't want to, either. He looked like some sort of demon. That's why I thought it was a bad dream at first.'

'And now,' said Holmes, as he and I returned to the waiting trap, 'my case is complete.'

'You have solved the mystery?' I exclaimed.

'The observations of Mr Jenkins and his sister appear to provide us with very little information,' said Holmes, 'but small points may speak loudly.'

'Jenkins only saw the back of the man,' I said.

'A man he thought might be a pedlar, walking south in the direction of Waltham Cross and Waltham Abbey.'

'Yes. And then there was the man Miss Jenkins saw.'

'Miss Jenkins saw a man a few minutes later, who she did not think to be a pedlar, but had staring eyes. What can we deduce from this?'

I opened my mouth to speak, but nothing of any value occurred to me. I remained silent. Sometimes, with Holmes, I know better than to offer any suggestions.

'A pedlar will walk from place to place carrying his wares,' continued Holmes. 'Jenkins thought the unknown figure he saw might be a pedlar because he was carrying something. Miss Jenkins, on the other hand, did not think the man she saw was a pedlar because he was not carrying anything.'

I nodded agreement.

'She remarked upon his eyes,' Holmes continued. 'Therefore, she saw his face. He was not walking south towards the bridge, but the opposite way, towards Cheshunt.'

'They must have passed each other!' I exclaimed.

Holmes uttered a weary sigh of disappointment. 'I suggest to you that they were one and the same man. A man walks south carrying something, disposes of it, then turns to walk back the way he came.'

'Oh,' I said.

'All I need to be certain of now is where he walked from and where he walked to,' said Holmes. 'But I think I know the answer.'

'And what he disposed of?'

He gave a small smile. 'That, at least, is clear to me.'

'You think he had something to do with Gorrie's death?' I asked. 'But we know that Gorrie was killed the night before. Or do you dispute that?'

'No, the evidence is clear. Gorrie died soon after eating his supper. The man on the path was there several hours later.'

'And all the possible suspects might have had the opportunity of slipping away for an hour or so during the night unobserved.'

'But only one of them was seen by Mr and Miss Jenkins,' said Holmes.

'What will you do now?'

'I will see Inspector Tubb and unfold all that I know. The rest is up to him.'

We arrived at Waltham Abbey police station just in time to see Inspector Lestrade making his departure. Holmes at once accosted hm.

'If it is convenient, Inspector, you might wish to remain and hear what I have to say to Inspector Tubb,' he said.

'Oh yes?' said Lestrade, with a chuckle. 'Am I to make an arrest?'

'You may very well decide to do so,' said Holmes.

Lestrade glanced at me, but I had to admit that I had not been made privy to Holmes's deliberations.

Inspector Tubb was intrigued by our arrival, and we gathered in his office. 'I confess I am no further forward in discovering the culprit in the death of Mr Gorrie, but you have been very thorough in your work, Mr Holmes, and if Scotland Yard values your observations, then I will do so, too,' he said.

'We can all agree, from personal observation, that the Baumann motor was a humbug from the very beginning,' said Holmes. 'Neither of Gorrie's two associates was aware of this. Mr Bourne, because he had not the technical knowledge, and Novak because he passionately believed in the principle and was overjoyed to see it vindicated. There is no suggestion that Gorrie ever tried to build a genuine motor.

'Crucially, Gorrie, like Mr Keely, is a mechanic, not a theoretician. I think that when he visited Keely, he noticed something that the other investors, primarily businessmen, or academics, would not have seen. Although Keely never permitted visitors to make a detailed study of his device, Gorrie suspected that the Keely motor is a fraud and thought that he could replicate what it did. He saw greedy men, idealistic men, opening their pocketbooks, and money flowing in. The temptation was too great.'

'So, for Gorrie it was a money-making scheme from the start?' said Tubb.

'It was,' said Holmes. 'But he knew he could not do it alone. That was why he approached Dr Nachtnebel, hoping for his support, but matters took a different turn.'

'It was a considerable risk,' said Lestrade.

'It was, but Keely also took a risk and has been living well from it for six years,' Holmes pointed out. 'Once established at the mill, Gorrie imagined he had a good position which would pay well if he kept delivering results, and he expected to be able to continue it for some time. But he reckoned without Bourne making an extravagant promise he could not keep. That the motor would be ready in six months. He started to fear exposure, and a criminal charge. He tried to impose some caution, by speaking to Mr Young, but this didn't help. And crucially in this conversation with Young, he learned of a future visit from Mr Feather, a qualified engineer. I saw Mr Norris today and he showed me the list of visitors, the same list Young would have shown Gorrie. Now Gorrie was afraid. Would this man do what he did when he saw the Keely motor — spot the flaw in the machine? If he did, would he expose everything?'

'Do you think this was the subject of the secret meeting?' I asked.

'That is a strong possibility. Gorrie would have wanted to end the scheme before it was exposed. The only way he could ensure that it ended was to reveal to his associate that it was a fraud. If he had simply fled, he would have risked arrest.'

'Then it was Baumann he met?' ventured Lestrade.

'Mr Jackson Bourne, stage actor, would never have been an advisor. No, Gorrie must have arranged to meet secretly with Professor Novak. They needed to converse somewhere where they would not be seen together. They decided to meet at around seven o'clock, near the signpost, five minutes' walk from the mill.'

'But how was that arranged?' I asked. 'They were careful never to be seen speaking to each other or exchanging notes.'

'When you told me that Gorrie had met someone on the night he died, I interviewed everyone at the mill, and all the investors and directors,' said Lestrade. 'No-one had seen him talk to anyone, no-one had seen a note pass or delivered a message for him.'

'They did it in plain sight,' said Holmes. 'We saw them do it. Gorrie's notebook, the one he kept in his apron, which he showed to Novak with the results of the demonstrations. Novak came to the demonstrations often. I am sure there were many opportunities to exchange messages. And both Young and Bourne would have talked about the arrangements at the mill in Novak's presence. He knew what was taking place, he knew where Bourne was staying, and which cottage was Gorrie's.'

I frowned. 'But doesn't he have an alibi for that night? He dined at the Devonshire Hotel.'

Holmes took the hotel menu from his pocket. 'Russian salad with beef,' he said. 'He ordered a cold supper. The dish is also available for luncheon. We can't be sure precisely when he ate it, but a hotel can prepare and supply cold meals to the residents' rooms at times before the restaurant service begins. The hotel is near Liverpool Street station. Novak ordered his supper, then took a fast train to Cheshunt, which is a short walk from the signpost. A route which would not take him past the mill. Gorrie, carrying a lantern, met him there.'

'We can never know what they discussed,' I said.

'Not precisely,' said Holmes. 'But I think Gorrie wanted to call a halt to the scheme and he could only do this by admitting that the motor was a fraud. He feared that Baumann's promises were already putting them in danger, and a visit from an engineer might be the final straw. He had already spoken to Young expressing his concerns, but without effect. The only safe course to avoid prosecution was probably to admit failure and dismantle the machine, and to do this as soon as possible. Novak was appalled. The consequences of this abrupt failure to Mr Young and the family business, and to him both personally and professionally, hardly bore thinking about.'

'So Novak decided to kill Gorrie?' said Tubb.

'I don't think he is a violent man,' said Holmes. 'Perhaps the altercation turned into a struggle. The lantern fell, there was an angry push, and Gorrie fell back against the sluice gate, striking his head on the turning handle. He then plunged into the head race, passing under the sluice and through the by-wash into the stream.'

'Novak never invested any money in the motor,' I said, 'but then, I suppose for him it was never about profit.'

'Precisely,' said Holmes. 'But now, imagine him standing by the waterside wondering what to do. He knows that Gorrie has already discussed his concerns with Young, and it would not be a great surprise if he should abruptly decide to leave. Novak formed a plan to make it seem that Gorrie had left. He picked up the lantern, not noticing the candle had fallen out, and walked back to Gorrie's cottage. He was fortunate, as many of the men were having supper indoors and he was not seen. The door to Gorrie's cottage was open. He lit a candle — the candle seen by Phillips, who thought it was Gorrie. Novak searched the cottage, found the carpetbag, gathered Gorrie's few possessions, and put them in the bag. Knowing the little notebook was in the apron pocket, he removed it. Did he see the packet of newspapers inside the carpetbag? Maybe not, and the light would have been poor for reading in any case. All this took time, and it was now dark. The sun had set, and clouds covered the moon. Novak's poor eyesight made him nervous about trying to find his way back to Cheshunt along country paths, especially as he did not want to take a lantern to light the way. The only place he was safe from being seen was inside the cottage. He decided to wait until first light. After all, no-one would know that he had not slept in his hotel room.'

'Then it is he who Jenkins and his sister saw?'

'Yes, as soon as there was enough light to see his way he left the cottage, walked down to the bridge and threw the carpetbag and its key into the stream. He then walked back to Cheshunt station and took the first train to Liverpool Street. I assume he burned the notebook. He appeared at the breakfast table as usual that morning.'

'Miss Jenkins said the man she saw had staring eyes, like a demon,' I said.

'She saw the rays of the rising sun reflected from the heavy lenses of his spectacles,' said Holmes.

'And what about Jenkins?' I asked.

'Jenkins was intending to report to the police about the sighting on the path. He even told the directors when he took them on the tour, at a time when the sunlight was very bright through the open doors. Turning to address the visitors, he saw the demon's eyes his sister had described. Did he realise at that moment this Miss Jenkins must have seen Novak? We shall never know. But he was not tripped or pushed. I think that Dr Henderson was right and Jenkins's heart stopped, and he died from shock.'

'Then he was not murdered,' I said. 'But what about Gorrie?'

'Novak was certainly involved in Gorrie's death,' said Holmes.

'He might claim it was an accident, or have the charge reduced to manslaughter,' said Lestrade. 'Well, I think we had better return to Mr Young's house and have a quiet word with his father-in-law.'

We were met at the front door by the maid, and Mrs Young came to greet us. 'I have had a long conversation with my father,' she said. 'I have urged him to hide nothing from us. He is ready to speak to you now.'

She conducted us to the drawing room, where Professor Novak sat comfortably, with a glass of whisky and a contented smile.

We listened as Novak freely confessed to having held a secret meeting with Mr Gorrie. The mechanic had urged him to end the scheme as he feared that the real operation of his motor would be exposed. Gorrie admitted that it had been a fraud. Until that moment, Novak had sincerely believed that the Baumann motor was genuine, and able to harness the etheric force. The shock of being told it was a fraud had caused a temporary breakdown in his mind. There had been a confused tussle in the dark. Novak said he could not recall having pushed the man and had never intended to injure him. When he was able to reflect on the position, he had decided to dispose of Gorrie's belongings to make it appear that he had gone away. He had not told anyone about the quarrel or revealed his prior knowledge of the fraud, as he wished to protect his son-in-law from any hint of suspicion.

Novak was arrested and charged with the manslaughter of Edward Gorrie. Lodged in one of the cells at Waltham Abbey police station, he asked only for his books, some paper, pen and ink. While waiting to appear before the magistrates he began to compose an impassioned treatise advocating the brilliance of the much-criticised man of science, Baron Carl von Reichenbach.

CHAPTER FIFTEEN

Two weeks later we received a letter from Miss O'Hara.

Dear Mr Holmes and Mr Stamford,

I am sure you will be pleased to know that Frank and I have arrived safely in New York. Frank's injuries are healing, but his doctor thinks he may never have full use of his gun hand. He has been offered a new post instructing young detectives, which will suit him very well.

I don't know if you have heard the news from New York, which may not have been covered by the English newspapers. Eddie Delaney has been murdered. He was in a barber's shop, one where the owner paid him for protection, and was in the chair, about to have a shave. It seems that someone entered the shop, picked up a razor and gave him a closer shave than he had been expecting. Strange to report, no-one in the shop at the time saw a thing. Eddie had a great many enemies in all walks of life, so the number of suspects will make finding the killer a hard task.

The funeral was very expensive and well-attended. Eddie's younger brother, Jimmy, was chief mourner and has taken over the family business. He is as ruthless as Eddie but without the same streak of uncontrolled violence. He was accompanied by a young lady, who wore a veil but who onlookers thought was Ruby Chavez. It is thought that he had been hiding her to protect her from Eddie.

I did hear a rumour that Miss Chavez was one of Jackson Bourne's mistresses, and when he fled the country, she stole money from Eddie to fund her lover's escape. If that is true, I can't wonder that Eddie sent Cassidy and Jones after Bourne to murder him. But it looks like Jimmy has no issues with Mr Bourne, and he is now safe from the Delaney gang as long as he doesn't cross them again.

In friendship, Kitty O'Hara

If Eddie Delaney's surviving gunman, Jones, was hoping that younger brother Jimmy would somehow free him from the charge of attempted murder, he was to be disappointed. Firing a hailstorm of bullets in the peaceful and historic town of Waltham Cross was not regarded lightly by British courts, and he was sentenced to twenty years' imprisonment.

Mr Ineson, despite all the recent difficulties, was content to continue to act for his difficult client. 'Mrs Beauregard's anger knows no bounds,' he observed. 'She is determined to sue everyone she can think of, and a good many others she has yet to think of. The only person she does not blame is Mr Bourne, who she regards as a victim of Mr Gorrie's criminality. I think if Bourne went to her and confessed to murdering Gorrie she would think it a task well done. I am thankful that Ineson and Randall did not at any time support the Baumann motor investment. Our hands are clean, and we will be receiving our reward for many years to come.'

On hearing that there was no further threat from the Delaney gang, Mr and Mrs Bourne started to make plans for their return to America. They had agreed to appear in public as a devoted couple and be photographed as a family group with their children, but live discreetly in separate households. Mrs Bourne had prevailed upon her father to agree to her wishes and provide the funds required to meet them. The divorce proceedings would be quietly forgotten. Mr Danielson wrote to the newspapers to announce that his client was recovered from his indisposition and would soon return to the stage as Davy Crockett.

*

'I do not think Mr Bourne should return to America,' said Holmes, 'and I have told him so, but he has not heeded my warning.'

'I suppose there are still the paternity suits against him,' I said.

'The law can prove nothing,' said Holmes. 'He will make a good showing in court, and his wife will stand by him. If money is involved, her father will pay the cost. He will win and become notorious.'

'Then what does he have to fear?'

'His greatest enemy,' said Holmes.

Jackson Bourne arrived in New York to the wild acclaim of an enormous welcoming crowd. Two weeks later he was back in the buckskins and received an unprecedented ovation from an adoring audience. Both men and women were gathered at the stage door clamouring for his signature on the *carte de visites* they had purchased. Someone, and it was never seen who, used the cover of the excited gathering to shoot him dead.

'You knew that would happen, Holmes!' I said as I read the story in *The Times*.

'I was afraid it might,' said Holmes. 'It was something Mrs Bourne said — that her father would do anything to keep them apart. When he agreed so easily to abandon the divorce proceedings, accommodate his daughter's wishes, and meet all the expenses, I scented danger.'

Professor Novak was eventually tried for the manslaughter of Mr Gorrie, the main evidence being the distance between the bank of the stream and the mark on the sluice handle showing he must have been pushed. His disposal of the carpetbag, and retrieval of the notebook from the apron pocket, were seen as evidence of a cool head, refuting his barrister's suggestion that the defendant had acted out of panic. In those days the accused was not permitted to give evidence in criminal trials, but Novak's long rambling paper about the existence of the etheric force was read out in court by the defence, to suggest that he might not be entirely in his right mind. He was admitted to a private asylum where he was very well treated, spending his days in a little office with his books and papers, where he contentedly continued his work to demonstrate the existence of the force.

I was happy to learn that Miss Jenkins' health improved under the care of her niece, and I believe she lived for many more years. Reverend Woodley met the usual fate of clergymen who have overstepped the mark and was obliged to leave Waltham Cross and take up a less generously rewarded living. The Young family returned to Canada rather earlier than they had intended. They were last heard of building a new factory in Australia. The Abbey Mill waterwheel is now merely a curiosity, the business having been purchased and entirely converted to steam.

While I waited for the Novak trial to take place, I had my own business to attend to. I was about to leave my old lodgings and take up residence at Barts, as a junior surgeon. Packing my books and clothes into a box, I reflected on how few my personal possessions were. I had thanked my dear parents profusely for the support they had given me during my studies, and to my shame I had never really thought about how they had been able to afford it. It was my father who had let slip that they had depleted to almost nothing the savings they had accumulated for their old age. I confess I wept at the thought, humbled by the faith they had shown in me, trusting me to do my utmost to prepare myself for a career in medicine, and knowing that I would never disappoint them.

I formed the fiercest determination that I would labour relentlessly to make a success of my life and work to repay my parents in full for all they had done. My mother had once advised me that I must avoid romantic entanglements with young ladies until such time as my income was sufficient to establish a home, marry and support a growing family. Over the years that followed I saw many men driven to poverty and desperation as the numbers in their household grew, outdistancing the funds available for their upkeep. Since no lady has ever engaged my affections to any degree, I remain to this day contentedly a single man, as has my dear friend George Luckhurst with whom I live a carefree bachelor existence.

In that late summer of 1878, I still had one more obstacle to face. I had to tell Sherlock Holmes that he could no longer call upon my time and lodgings when conducting an enquiry. While I pondered on how to do this, I received a note from him asking me to come to his rooms in Montague Street, where he needed my assistance, and promising a pleasant supper and a glass of sherry for my trouble. My packing was almost done, and I went to him.

Holmes's rooms in those days were dreadfully cramped and cluttered with a variety of materials he considered essential for his enquiries. It was to my great surprise that when I arrived, I saw he had been working at clearing some space to accommodate visitors, or at least, suitable additional seating. Not that the rooms could be described as tidy, but the heaps of newspapers were less substantial than they had been.

'Whatever have you been up to, Holmes?' I asked.

'I will show you before the evening is out,' he said enigmatically. We set to with scissors and paste, extracting and saving articles from the newspapers, in an order dictated by

Holmes. The subjects covered all aspects of society, scientific innovations, matters of law, and the deadliest and most curious crimes. Our supper was roast fish and potatoes, and a pudding, sent from a nearby café, since his landlady was not known for her expertise in the kitchen.

He poured us each a glass of sherry. 'A toast,' he said, 'to your future career, in which I am sure you will make your mark, Stamford. You will miss your old lodgings as will I, but that is the price a young surgeon has to pay, and I will not begrudge the loss of such a charming little office.'

'Oh,' I said, relieved at his words and the ease with which he spoke them. 'I was intending to tell you, but of course it is hard to hide anything from you, Holmes. Will you continue to study at Barts?'

'I will, since there is no space here to set up a chemistry laboratory, and I fear my landlady would object to my establishing a dissection room. I still have much to learn and advances to make in the field of science. In the next few years, the world will come to know me far better than it does at present.'

'I have no doubt of it,' I said.

'To that end,' he continued, 'I have had some new cards made. Let me know what you think of the design. It is simple but concise.'

He handed me a card. It was printed with the address of his lodgings, and below it, just four words:

SHERLOCK HOLMES
CONSULTING DETECTIVE

HISTORICAL NOTES

Locations

Watermills on the River Lea are known to have existed since medieval times. Those unable to make use of tidal waters built up waterpower using weirs, locks or reservoirs. Originally used to grind corn, they were later employed in industries such as grinding chemicals and driving sawmills. The expansion of the railways from the 1840s linking Essex towns and villages with London, encouraged industrial growth in the county. Cornmills adapted for industry did augment waterpower with a steam engine, although by the last quarter of the nineteenth century the more efficient and reliable steam power was replacing the waterwheel. Abbey Mill is fictional.

Waltham Abbey is a historic market town in Essex. The police station in Sun Street was opened in 1876 and closed down in 2011. A description of its extensive amenities can be found in the *Waltham Abbey and Cheshunt Weekly Telegraph* dated 8 January 1876, page 2. The station included lodgings for married police officers and their families. The 1881 census (Essex, Waltham Holy Cross, district 2) for the police station lists Inspector Charles Tubb, age 45, his wife and five daughters, and Constable Joseph West, age 37, his wife and five children.

Waltham Cross railway station (originally named Waltham) which serves both Waltham Cross and Waltham Abbey opened in 1840. It was then located north of the road between Waltham Cross and Waltham Abbey. It moved to its current location in 1885.

Mr Young's house in Sun Street is not based on a specific building. The New Inn at 58 Sun Street was closed in 2010 and is now a restaurant. The White Lion was at 11 Sun Street. It was closed in 2012 and is now a café.

The Queen Eleanor Inn once stood near Waltham Cross station but has been demolished.

The Royal Polytechnic Institution was founded in 1837 to provide instruction (as stated in the prospectus) on 'branches of science connected with manufacturers, mining operations and rural economy.' Education on the practical application of science was not then thought to be appropriate to the universities.

Mr Feather the builder may have attended the School of Engineering and Practical Surveying, Stoneley House, Howard Road, South Norwood. There is an advertisement for this school in the *Cardiff Times* dated 6 January 1877. Perhaps this was where Mr Jonas Oldacre (*The Adventure of the Norwood Builder*) studied?

Communication
The electrical telegraph was in use by UK railways companies from the 1840s. The first successful transatlantic cable was laid in 1866, enabling messages to be sent between the UK and USA in a matter of minutes. The word 'cablegram' soon came into use to mean a telegram sent by submarine cable, and despite early objections to the word, it caught on.

People

John Ernst Worrell Keely (1837–1898) first demonstrated his motor in 1872, claiming to have discovered a new force. He attracted numerous investors and formed the Keely Motor Company. As time wore on without a patentable device, the investors became impatient, especially since Keely remained secretive about how his motor worked. In 1878, after an investigation by an engineer, the Keely motor was declared to be debunked, and the company worthless.

Despite this, Keely continued to promote his motor. In 1881 he attracted the attention of wealthy widow Clara Jessup Bloomfield-Moore, who passionately believed in his work. She donated $100,000 and paid Keely a monthly salary of $250. Her book, *Keely and His Discoveries* can be read here: https://archive.org/details/keelyhisdiscover00moorrich/page/n5/mode/2up

The stockholders remained frustrated by Keely's secrecy and his repeated promises of success in a few weeks, followed by delays. But their attempts to use legal means to force him to reveal his secrets failed. Following Keely's death in November 1898 the shareholders remained optimistic; however, an investigation of his workshop carried out by *The Philadelphia Press* in the following year found concealed compressed-air machines which Keely had used to power his motor. The Keely motor, it was announced on 19 January, was a fraud. Mrs Bloomfield-Moore had died two weeks previously.

Thomas Alva Edison (1847–1931) was an American inventor who, like many of his contemporaries, was interested in the possibilities of the force believed to pervade the ether of space. In 1875 he announced that he had discovered what he called the 'etheric force' but other scientists were sceptical, and he abandoned the study for some years. He later showed it could be used as a means of wireless transmission and took out a patent, but did not develop it further.

John Langley King (1838–1891) was a popular lecturer at the Royal Polytechnic Institution.

John Brodie Henderson MD (1843–1905) was born in Scotland. In the 1870s he lived in Sewardstone Street, Waltham Abbey.

The 1881 census lists 47-year-old Inspector James Moore at Cheshunt police station and Dr Nicholl Evans, aged 43, at Walnut Tree House, Turner's Hill, Cheshunt.

Dr William Palmer of Rugeley (1824–1856) was a notorious multiple murderer. It was believed that it was impossible to find an unbiased jury in Staffordshire, where he was well-known, and an Act of Parliament was passed (The Central Criminal Court Act 1856) so the trial could be transferred to the Old Bailey. This is sometimes referred to as 'The Palmer Act.' Palmer was found guilty and hanged. Holmes was well acquainted with the case which he mentions in *The Adventure of the Speckled Band*.

Karl Ludwig Freiherr von Reichenbach, (1788–1869) was a German scientist who made a number of important discoveries. In his last years he devoted his work to a study of a new form of energy, which he called the 'Odic force'. The force, which had both a light and dark side, could only be seen in total darkness by sensitive individuals, who could also emanate it.

An English translation of his work can be read here: https://archive.org/details/physicophysiolo02ashbgoog/page/n6/mode/2up

The Pinkerton detective agency was founded in the United States in the 1850s. Agents were hired to track outlaws, conduct espionage, and transport money and valuables. They were usually armed. As early as 1856 the agency employed female detectives.

In 1878, Charles Samuel Block was the stationmaster at Waltham Cross.

Holmes

Professor Novak's quote from Goethe is later quoted by Holmes in Chapter Six of *The Sign of Four*. Until well into the twentieth century a knowledge of the German language was a requirement for the study of chemistry.

Holmes's lock-picking tools in this adventure must have been his first such purchase in these early days. By the 1890s he had acquired a state-of-the-art burglary kit, as described in *The Adventure of Charles Augustus Milverton* in *The Return of Sherlock Holmes*.

Other

Davy Crockett, or Be Sure You're Right, Then Go Ahead by Frank Murdoch was a popular drama first produced in 1872.

A NOTE TO THE READER

Reviews are so important to authors, and if you enjoyed this novel I would be grateful if you could spare a few minutes to post a review on **Amazon** and **Goodreads**. I love hearing from readers, and you can connect with me online, **on Facebook**, **Twitter**, and **Instagram**.

You can also stay up to date with all my news via **my website** and by signing up to **my newsletter**.

Linda Stratmann

2025

lindastratmann.com

Sapere Books is an exciting new publisher of brilliant fiction and popular history.

To find out more about our latest releases and our monthly bargain books visit our website:
saperebooks.com